To Kim,

The Budgerigar

wishing you all the best
and thankyou for following
'The Budgerigar'. I hope you
enjoy!
Anita x

Anita Philpott

Contents

Dedication

To all my grandchildren who have so much to discover and so much to teach us. Go explore!

Acknowledgments

Firstly, my thanks go to Helga Green, who told me about her budgerigar. She grew up in Leipzig, her father was a Nazi policeman and she had a little budgie. She had to move away from the town in 1942. She ignited an interest in this period and so this became the beginning of my research. Helga died a few years ago but gave me permission to use her story.

I would like to thank all those people who lived through these times who left a legacy of writings and testimonies that told the stories of what happened to the people of Germany. Reading so many personal accounts has educated and informed me. The excellent resources available to the public in various museums and online archives was invaluable. Thank you to Yad Vashen in Jeruselem, United States Holocaust Memorial Museum, and The Imperial War Museum. A special thanks to Pawel Sawicki and the staff at Auschwitz Memorial Museum who helped me understand some of the realities of life in a concentration camp. The seminars and library there added to my knowledge and walking the vast expanse of Birkenau camp put the enormity of the crimes into perspective. My time there brought home with chilling clarity how cruel man can be to man and despite history teaching us lessons, sadly nothing has changed.

Thank you Gemma Taylor of Oak Leaf Editing my ever patient literary editor who checked and amended my manuscript and kept me in line with encouragement and good humour. You were invaluable.

About the Author

Anita has written poetry and short stories all her life. She lives with her husband in a beautiful 17th century Essex cottage with dogs and chickens, the perfect setting to encourage creativity. She is the mother of four remarkable sons and grandmother to their expanding tribe of curious children. She works as a therapist and when she isn't working or writing she spends her spare time reading, researching, sculpting and going to the theatre. She loves to cook and she will make you a great cocktail!

Contact: Info@anitaphilpott.co.uk

This novel's story and characters are fictitious. Certain historical events and settings are real, and the experiences based in truth. However, the characters involved are wholly imaginary.

The Sudetenland

10 May 1945

Eight years after it began

HILDE

I remembered it was the night the maid and the housekeeper left.

My mother came running into my room wearing her white nightgown. She had her hair tied in rags, her nightly beauty regime to ensure that she would have curls the next day. People noticed her. I liked that she was often given extra rations when we shopped.

For the past week, though, neither Mama nor I had left the house. Papa told us that there were gangs of locals attacking Germans and that we had to stay inside with doors and windows bolted and curtains closed. Our gardener, Tony, had not come to do the garden this week, which was unusual.

'Quickly,' Mama said, 'put some clothes in here. We are going home to Leipzig.' She tried to sound jolly and although the prospect of going home was exciting, it was sudden and unplanned and made me feel uneasy. She reached up on top of the wardrobe and dragged down a small brown leather suitcase. As she did so, she dislodged a jar of pickles which had been stored next to the case. The jar fell onto the wooden floor and smashed, sending shards of glass, vegetables, and vinegar in all directions. An oozing mass of wet pickles surrounded our feet.

Papa appeared in the doorway and barked, 'Elsa, what happened?' Seeing the mess, he made a growling sound and said, 'Get ready now.' I had never seen him as serious or animated. I knew from the sound of his boots on the polished floor that he had gone to his office. His movements seemed erratic, and I could hear him rustling paper, dropping it into the waste bin, or tearing it up. There was intermittent crashing as he opened and closed the drawers in his desk and the metallic clunk of the filing cabinet. He was clearly trying to find something important that he needed to take with him.

My mother had disappeared but returned with a mop and bucket and proceeded to clean the floor. She dropped the sodden head of the mop into the cradle and twisted. I could hear the trickle of liquid draining into the metal bucket and the crunch of the fragments of glass as she pressed down on the mop.

'Fit whatever clothes you can into your case,' she said. 'And you'll need a coat, too.'

'But Mama, it's really warm. It's nearly summertime.'

'Hilde, please, just do as I say—' but she didn't finish her sentence; Papa came into the room. 'Get ready this instant, we leave in five minutes,' he said to both of us, looking at the mop and then his watch. He grabbed my mother by the arm and pulled her into the hallway, hissing words under his breath that I could not make out. The mop clattered to the floor.

I did not cry but felt miserable. My parents rarely argued, and it felt uncomfortable to hear. Papa had an important job, and Mama said he worked hard, and she liked to keep everywhere clean and stress-free. She wanted our home to be a harmonious contrast to the harsh reality of his work.

What could be that urgent, I thought, that we would leave broken glass and the full contents of a pickle jar on my bedroom floor without clearing it up? Where was Anna, the maid who often played with me between chores when Frau Obermeyer, the housekeeper, was out? Anna would have heard all the commotion, but she didn't come to help us. None of this made any sense. Last night at dinner, everything seemed normal. We lived in a beautiful old house on the side of a hill surrounded by trees. We had a large garden to relax in, and Papa was just a few minutes from his work.

There were announcements on the radio about the war, and, of course, I realised this was what the panic was about. But my parents listened at night and I think, shielded me to a great extent from the true nature of the war.

I put on my shoes, my school ones, which were the most comfortable and easy to slip on. I put on my best dress, made of soft brown wool with an embroidered collar and cuffs that had been made for my thirteenth birthday, and a lilac cardigan with pearl buttons knitted by my Oma Ostler. I found stockings and tights, two blouses, my girl's league dress and navy shirt, a sundress, and a hat with a bobble, plus some underwear. This just about fits into my case. I managed to add my toothbrush, a flannel and a comb, some pencils, and a little notepad and squashed everything down with my book of famous ballerinas. Last of all, I put my pink and white barrette, my tin with the alpine scene, and my precious marble into a silk pocket in the lid. The suitcase closed shut.

I realised from the shaft of light coming through the curtains that it was no longer night. I dragged my grey winter coat off the hanger and tiptoed back to my bed so as not to splash any more of the vinegar over myself.

My mother appeared in the doorway, now dressed, and motioned for me to follow her. I heaved my suitcase to take to Papa, who was loading the car. As we got to the living room, I saw Froh-Froh's cage, still with a cover over it from the night before.

'Mama, I must take Froh-Froh!' I implored, suddenly overcome with panic. She had been with me for the past five years now. She was my constant companion and friend. She was the prettiest, most clever budgerigar, and she was my connection to my old life. She was more than just a little bird.

'Mama, who will look after her if I can't?'

'I'm not sure if we have room in the car, *Liebchen*,' Mama said hesitantly and kissed me on the head.

I heard the engine running in the street and the sound of Papa's boots coming up the stone steps from the road. He stopped in the entranceway and looked to the bend in the road up the hill, about a quarter of a mile away. He was looking for someone or something and seemed jittery.

'Right, the luggage is all in,' he said.

'Papa,' I said, 'what about Froh-Froh? I am not going without Froh-Froh!' I thought I might be pushing my luck, and he would be angry, but he ran his hand through his hair, gave a deep sigh, and said, 'Listen, Hilde, we have to go. I'll bring the bird, but you have to move; get down those stairs now, please. Wait! Take her cover.' He stepped towards the birdcage, removed the cotton cover, and threw it to me. Unhooking the birdcage from its stand he motioned us to leave as he held the cage aloft.

My mother hesitated and picked up a magazine that had fallen on the floor.

'Elsa, no! We must go this minute. There is no time for that. Please come,' he said.

'I feel bad leaving the house untidy,' she said and gave a quick backwards glance as we left as if knowing that she would not be coming back here.

I saw the hall clock said 5.10 am. It was going to be a glorious May day; though the night chill was still there, the sun had risen and was beginning to shine down on us. As I came down the steps, I saw flowers, their pastel-coloured petals so delicate, almost translucent, with little tributaries carrying food to nourish them and traces of deep orange stamens showing through their silken fabric. These plants had survived the cold night and the winds that come down off the hills. Coated with glistening dew, they were prepared to open up, to share their delicate beauty for another day. I thought they were lucky because I must leave, and they could stay.

I did not know then that, like those flowers, we were stronger than we seemed, even though what surrounded us could so easily destroy us.

The driver saluted Papa and opened the door for me. I got in the back of the big black staff car. Papa perched Froh-Froh's cage on top of the cases, packed tightly onto the seat next to me.

'Hilde, you must do as I say. There are gangs hiding along the road, and we must try to avoid them. Keep as quiet as you can when I warn you to. The Russian army is nearly here, so that is why we must get back to Germany as soon as we can.'

'Yes, Papa,' I said.

I poked my finger into the cage, and my little bird flew onto it. 'Good morning, Froh-Froh,' I said, and she replied, 'Good morning, Froh-Froh.'

I giggled.

'Shush now, Hilde! We need to be careful!' said Papa.

I was suddenly a little scared by this journey. I thought about the town we were heading back to, Leipzig, and wondered what and who would greet us there. I had always felt that by keeping Froh-Froh safe, I was protecting those people back home that I cared about, and I hoped I was right.

As we moved off down the empty street, I realised that the bell for the start of the day at the factory hadn't rung at 5 am. I wondered if the workers knew about the Russians. I also wondered about Anna and Frau Obermeyer and if they were safe. And I hoped this smell of vinegar on my clothes would disappear soon.

Part 1
Hilde and Morrie 1937-1939

Chapter 1

The Beginning – Leipzig

1937

HILDE

It took four men all morning to carry the piano up the four flights of stairs. Morrie and I were lying on our tummies playing our special game of marbles. The hallway floor was black and white and, on a hot day like today, it was smooth and cold on our skin. We tried to see who could get their marble onto the middle of the big diamond shape in the centre of the hall floor.

Frau Silbermann was rushing back and forth, looking down the stairs, clip-clopping in her high heeled shoes, running down to the next level to see how the men were getting on, only to return onto our landing flustered and worried.

'Please be careful, the piano is so precious!' she called down the stairs and then to us she said, 'Children, you must move, the piano is nearly here.'

As the men got to our floor we jumped up and pinned ourselves against the wall to let them pass.

The piano was deposited in the Silbermann's apartment. It took the men some time to unwrap each part that had been carefully bound and protected in heavy blankets for the transportation. They assembled it piece by piece, the biggest item first was the case containing the internal action and the keyboard, then the legs and pedals and finally the lid. We watched in fascination.

It was made of shiny brown wood, called mahogany, that reflected the lights in their living room. When the workmen left, Frau Silbermann went over to the grand piano and lifted the big butterfly lid, exposing the strings and hammers inside. She stroked the ornate brass music desk that was used to display sheet music and then, from one of the large leather chests in the living room, she selected two pieces of paper with musical notes on them and placed them on the stand. She pulled up the stool in front of the piano, smoothed her skirt and gently swept her hands across the polished wood that covered the keys, as though remembering a happy memory from another time.

She opened the lid over the keyboard, and with the lightness of a feather, she began to touch the black and white keys and to play a tune. I recognised that music. It was a sweet melodic tune that I believed was an old folk song. I realised that she was silently crying but did not understand why. I watched her and could tell playing this piano was important to her. She played for a few minutes and neither Morrie nor I moved. We were just tall enough to peer over the side so we could see the internal parts moving inside the piano. This was a special moment for us all.

After a few minutes she stopped and looked at us.

'Children, come,' she beckoned.

We stood on either side of her, and she put her arms around us and pulled us close to her.

'My little *leibchens* I want you two to be safe, always look after each other,' she said still crying softly.

Morrie said reassuringly, 'We will, Mama.'

I smiled at them both.

***

I discovered that Frau Silbermann had been a ballet dancer in Berlin before Morrie was born. She could play a wide range of pieces on the piano too. After the arrival of the piano at her apartment, Frau Silbermann began teaching Morrie who immediately understood the instrument and made it sound sweet and rhythmic. He practiced for many hours a day, so he no longer had as much time to play with me. But he always wanted me there, so I spent long hours with Frau Silbermann, looking through her many books about opera and ballet while Morrie practiced. She showed me pictures of great paintings too, and explained what they were about and who the artists were.

'One day I want to paint like that,' I said.

'That is good, Hilde. We must all have dreams of what we want to do,' she smiled.

She had saved programmes from performances that she had given, which she kept in a bulky scrapbook. She had travelled to London and Paris and had worked her way up from the corps de ballet to becoming a principal ballerina. She showed me newspaper cuttings of her as the character *Giselle*, who she told me was a peasant girl who fell in love with a prince but who dies of a broken heart.

My favourite times were when Frau Silbermann would tell me about how she and Herr Silbermann had met. She was a good storyteller, and I enjoyed listening to her voice. Ben Silbermann was from a Jewish family who had lived in Leipzig for at least four generations. He had met the beautiful dancer, known as Clara Schwan, when he was in Berlin. A friend had tickets to go to the opera house. It was to watch Tchaikovsky's Opera, Eugene Onegin, a passionate and rousing event with memorable tunes.

Afterwards there was a reception in an elaborate long ballroom with chandeliers and mirrors on every wall. It was here that Morrie's parents had met. She had been dancing in the opera. He had been struck by her beauty. She told me she had worn a dove grey satin dress and a single strand of pearls around her neck. He had asked to be introduced to her and was immediately captivated by her smile.

They spoke only a few words together. She said she was from a small village in Saxony, and he said he lived close by in Leipzig and was in Berlin for just the night and he would be going home tomorrow. That was it, the sum of their conversation, but it was enough!

She told me, when I was looking at some photographs of them, that when she first met Herr Silbermann, she was struck by his handsome face with his dark expressive eyes, and she was a little embarrassed to look him in the eye with her face still bearing traces of greasepaint.

She was travelling around Europe performing at theatres and concert halls and Herr Silbermann was running a busy shop in Leipzig. Yet, somehow, they arranged a meeting, then another. They both knew they had found their lifelong partner.

'I love you, Clara, but you cannot spend so much time travelling and we so little time together,' he said, and he asked Clara to marry him. Clara had been known as 'little swan' as a child because she was so graceful and had the distinctive white-blonde hair she became known for. The world knew her as Clara Schwan, but her real name was Clara Freidman. She said yes to Ben's proposal and had already moved in with her father in Leipzig. They married in 1929 and she continued performing as a dancer until Morrie was born in 1931. When he was born, he had the same silvery blond hair as his mother and, as he grew, became engaging and clever like his father.

Frau Silbermann began giving piano lessons to other people too. I tried to learn but got muddled and found it too difficult; instead, I would dance around in time to the music when Morrie played the piano. Frau Silbermann asked Mama if I could learn ballet with her. She did not want any money to teach me, but I did need to buy some ballet shoes. My mother thought about it.

Mama had to find the money for the shoes herself because she knew Papa would not want me to have lessons with Frau Silbermann. He had said that I was spending too much time with Morrie and my mother often didn't tell him that I'd spent as much time in their apartment as I had. I learnt my ballet positions with Frau Silbermann but practised in my bare feet as I had no shoes.

My sixth birthday was on 9th November 1937 and I had two celebrations. First of all, my parents got a car – they had never had one before! It was for Papa's work but nobody I knew had a car which made this very special and unusual for us. Papa took Mama and me for a drive into the countryside for my birthday. We had a wicker hamper full of food and we felt very grand. Papa said that we would have a picnic on the grassy slope that led to nearby woodland a short drive from town, but we ended up staying in the car because it was such a cold day even though it was dry and sunny. Some donkeys came through the bushes and we could see their breath in the air. Food was expensive and some things were unavailable, but Papa knew someone who was able to get a delicious pie for my birthday from a bakery in the centre of Leipzig. We weren't at the picnic long, just long enough to eat, as we had to come back home because Papa had to work. I gave the donkeys some crumbs left over from the picnic. I had hoped that we would play games, chasing each other or playing hide and seek like at a real birthday party, but Papa said we couldn't do it today.

The second celebration started when Papa had gone to work. My grandmother came to visit. My Oma sat me down and began to brush my long blond hair. She pulled it and scraped it into a ponytail at the top of my head. Eventually she twisted it into a small tight knot. She said something to Mama who gave her a tin box. Oma rummaged around in the box until she found a pink and white enamelled barrette that she slid into the side of my hair.

'How beautiful you are, my *leibchen*. Your Mama used to wear this when she was little,' she said.

Mama, Oma and I went to see Frau Silbermann, who was so excited to help us celebrate my birthday and to have visitors, she fussed around giving us drinks and making sure we were comfortable. I sat on a big sofa and opened my presents. Mama had bought me a pair of peach coloured ballet shoes and a leotard. Oma had knitted me a pale pink cross-over angora cardigan and Frau Silbermann gave me a book with glossy pictures of famous ballerinas. Straightaway, I looked for her in the pages, but she told me that she wasn't famous enough to be in the book. Morrie gave me his favourite marble, a pink and gold cats-eye. I knew it was his favourite.

I put on my new dancing clothes and began pirouetting around the apartment. I looked in the long gold mirror in the hall.

'Now you are a real ballerina, little maus!' said Frau Silbermann.

Everyone laughed and clapped along as I leapt in the air. Frau Silbermann then played something called 'The Grand Gallop' and Morrie and I twirled and ran around the apartment in our own made-up ballet. We eventually fell in a heap on the floor exhausted and, according to my Oma, we were over-excited!

Oma had made an apple cake to celebrate, and we all stood around the piano eating the sticky confection while Frau Silbermann played Happy Birthday and some of our favourite nursery songs. We kept calling out different titles and she played whatever we asked for. It was the most wonderful birthday.

***

After kindergarten I used to play with Morrie or go straight to their apartment where Frau Silbermann taught me ballet now that I had the correct shoes. I loved to dance but things had changed. Frau Silbermann no longer picked me up from school and Mama did not take Morrie in the mornings. Mama and Frau Silbermann were still friends but only saw one another when nobody knew, and I could only go to her apartment when Papa was not around.

Papa's job was to find new homes for people to move to because that was what the government wanted. I didn't understand why they couldn't stay in the place they already lived if they didn't want to move. Frau Silbermann told Mama that some of her friends had been relocated and had no say in it. They had been escorted from their houses and had to leave their possessions behind. The Silbermanns did not want to go anywhere else and so kept themselves to themselves in the hope that they would not get asked to move. I didn't want them to go. Morrie was my best friend, and I could not imagine life without him or without the music, books and dancing I had discovered in that apartment.

Chapter 2

Leipzig

1938

CLARA

I sat at the piano. I was troubled and could not play. Too many laws were being introduced.

A new decree had been passed to say that all Jewish businesses must be registered. There was only one reason for this, I knew, as did everyone. They wanted us out and they wanted to seize anything of worth, all for the benefit of the glorious Third Reich.

I was, after all, German as well as Jewish but there was an attitude towards us that had been simmering for some time. It was often subtle, but lately had been troubling me. We tried not to parade our Jewishness in case it provoked comment. I was careful what clothes I wore; I didn't dress in expensive fashionable outfits as I once did and nor did I wear anything to connect me with my faith. I wore smart everyday clothes as would any middle-class German housewife who had social engagements and who might be married to a professional man. I walked with my eyes straight ahead and always at a fast pace to show I was busy and had somewhere to be. Since last year, so many of our friends had left the city; they were frightened of what might be coming. It could be that we were being oversensitive but it seemed anything Jewish was viewed with disgust. I feared for Morrie and Ben as well as my friends. I had no family left, just my son and husband.

Every day in Jewish businesses, contracts were frozen, or money was not handed over for goods sold. There was intimidation and stories of violence all over our city and robberies from Jewish properties that were not investigated by the police. No one reported these incidents anymore. Similar events had happened before at other times in other countries, other centuries. This was our history, and the stories passed down to us tell us that, as Jews, we must be careful.

The image of 'the wandering Jew' has appeared in literature and music for hundreds of years. He was some kind of evil miscreant, a moneylender who was scapegoated for all manner of disasters that had befallen societies world-wide, not least that he was said to have rejected Christ and been forced to wander the earth. There seemed to be an innate distrust that went hand in glove with the establishment of any Jewish settlement and, though we were aware of this, we could do nothing to stop that belief. We were ordinary citizens who wanted to lead a good life, work hard and pay our taxes. I was sure there were Jews who were not to be trusted, just as there were in every group of people. I was proud there have been so many remarkable Jewish people in history who had changed the world to make it a far better place for us all to live, great people of science and the arts. But all Jews, even great historical figures, at this time in Nazi Germany, were seen as undesirable and a scourge on society. Hitler was happy to steal our wealth and blame us for economic disaster and conflict and we had no way of stopping that.

My father told me to work hard and enjoy our success but never get complacent because when we have built a future for ourselves, we may be moved on because other people would be envious. We Jews have a sense of survival, perhaps because of centuries of persecution. We have been knocked down so often, but have the tenacity and drive to rise again, which antagonises our critics. Whenever a regime seeks to restrict us, we know we must be prepared to fight it: it was a way to feel more powerful and gain back control and it came from deep within our psyche. My father sensed that bad things would be coming. He had attended political rallies in recent times, where Nazi fervour infected the crowds and he found himself amongst a chanting fevered mob. He discussed with friends and fellow academics long into the night – behind closed doors – what this meant for the Jewish community here in Leipzig and across the whole of Germany. They formed help groups for people who needed advice away from the synagogue, which was always threatened, and so meetings took place in private houses and in storerooms behind shops. They feared that it may be difficult to earn a living if new laws created even greater restrictions for our community. It seemed this new decree may be the beginning of this clamping down.

'You can always start a business again,' he said to me, 'but remember, Clara, your family is your home. If you have nothing else, that is all that matters, protect it at all costs.'

My family have lived in this city since 1890. Before that they had lived in Vienna where my grandfather was the assistant director of the glorious *Musikvereine* concert hall. This opulent structure was famous for its Golden Hall surrounded by viewing boxes and furnished with plush red velvet seats. It was a place to be seen, and somewhere visited by the grandest orchestras and soloists from around the world. Every New Year's Day there was a concert held there and it was the event of the year. Ladies from wealthy families swept in wearing the finest silks and taffetas, draped in sumptuous fur stoles with decollates adorned with glittering jewels. My father remembered as a young teenager being dressed in his brown woollen loden jacket, trimmed with grey velvet with shiny brass buttons, feeling he was elegant enough to mingle with the rich and cultured of Vienna. Those were glorious days; there was no political upheaval, Vienna was expanding, people flooded in from the countryside, hospitals and schools were built and my grandfather helped establish the music school. That Austria had faded, now Hitler had declared the Anschluss, the union of Germany and

Austria. I feared this would not help us. It felt like change was happening too often and too fast.

Music had formed my life and that of my family. Now I wanted Morrie to learn to love music too. I was grateful for the education I have had, the music I have played, and the dance productions I have danced in. My father worked in the music department of Leipzig University and was Professor of Composition.

Morrie had only been learning the piano for a few months, but he had a gift and that really pleased me. He would carry on the family tradition, I was sure. There were few activities in this world that gave so much pleasure to everyone, both to the person practicing their art and to those watching or listening. Making music was both a privilege and an honour. Morrie was too young to understand any of this, but I wanted him to know that music lived deep within our souls and could be a place to escape to that was full of love and peace. It would always give him strength.

I told him, 'Fill your head with as much music as you can. Whatever else is taken away from you, no-one can take away the music in your head.'

One day I hoped he would play music that brought joy to audiences across the world.

My piano was my father's. He died, a year ago, I think of a broken heart. He was forced to leave the university and all his music collected over a lifetime was locked away. A day before he was taken away, two of his ex-students managed to remove his precious Blüthner piano from his rooms at his college, load it on a trailer and hide it in a barn belonging to a friend on the outskirts of the town. He was escorted to a resettlement house the next day, along with other Jewish academics. He was not allowed to leave and was there for two months. He sent a message to me to tell me not to try to visit him because he feared for my safety. I went to the university a few weeks later and there was a huge bonfire outside in the platz. I asked someone what was being burned and was told, 'It is Jewish writings, filth they have removed from the university, and it contaminates the purity of Germany.'

Could my father's own compositions, arrangements, transpositions for instruments in the college orchestras, the seminal works of both Aryan and Jewish students whom he taught, manuscripts with music that had been practised repeatedly, sweated over, revised and annotated with flair and ambition, be these papers? Could this be his work?

Did my father hear about this?

Was this the final straw?

I did not like to wait around and show any interest in the contents of the fire. I came home and wept.

Two weeks later I had a message that he had died. He was found dead in his bed by his roommate, but there was no medical enquiry that established the cause of death. He was an honourable man, a man of great talent and knowledge who believed in promoting the talent of budding musicians, whatever their religion. But, above all, he was my father. He was my family and I had not protected him.

I looked down at the keys and began to play a Beethoven sonata. I had so much pain and emotion bubbling inside. I could do nothing about all the hatred that was welling up against us. I played this because it was all I knew to do.

Soon I had to collect Morrie from kindergarten. It had become difficult; I didn't want to go out as people knew we were Jewish. The kindergarten teachers smiled and were pleasant to Morrie, he told me that he did many interesting activities.

But I did not trust the caretaker.

He always saluted and said, 'Heil Hitler,' when each adult arrived at the gate, and I knew too that his wife was one of the teachers.

I'd say, 'Heil Hitler,' in return to him and felt ashamed because I knew I was being treacherous. I told myself that this was survival.

As I approached the kindergarten, I saw Hilde and Elsa leave. But we just nodded, and we did not walk home together. I deliberately went round the park perimeter, as I knew Elsa would walk Hilde through it. I did not want to make life difficult for her.

Chapter 3

Leipzig

1938

MORRIE

I felt sad. I couldn't go to kindergarten anymore; it was not allowed.

We, Hilde and I, had been going to the same kindergarten for two years. We had many friends there and were both good students. In August we were going to start elementary school together, except now we would not be doing that.

We were so looking forward to our first day of school. On the night before, we were supposed to be taken out for a meal because that was the tradition. As I didn't have any grandparents still living, I was going to celebrate with Hilde's grandparents, who were very kind and liked me. Hilde said that although I couldn't go to school we would still go to Oma and Opi's house, called Arkadien. There would be spaetzle and snitzel, potato pancakes and bratwurst, strudel and baked apple. That was what I hoped for, anyway. We have not had much variety in our food lately and we were so excited to be going to our own party.

In our class, we had been making our *schultutes*. These were very big cones, almost as tall as some of us children. They were made of card that we decorated ourselves with paint or crayons, pretty pictures cut out of magazines, motifs from greetings cards, coloured paper, cellophane, ribbons and sequins, if we had them, and lots of writing. These were for each of us to carry on the first day of school. Parents filled these with sweetmeats and candy as well as small toys, balloons and cakes. Everyone was proud of their *schultutes,* and parents attended a ceremony at school and took photographs to put in the albums of their children holding them. I painted mine a dark blue with lighter blue beams like the sky when the moon was shining. I stuck on bright yellow stars and circles of different colours to represent the planets, red for Mars and mauve for Neptune. This week we were meant to make the tops to fit on, but I was not there, and this worried me.

I had been at home with my Mama. She too thinks it was wrong that I could not go to school.

I spent many hours today playing the piano because I knew it made Mama happy when I practised, but I loved the music too and I knew that the more I played, the better I would become, and the more I would enjoy it.

Mama began giving piano lessons last year and there were a few children as well as two ladies who came to our apartment for lessons each week, but they have all stopped coming. Mama was only small, she was pretty, gentle, and smiled a lot, though I didn't hear her laugh as she once did, so I didn't understand why the people didn't come for lessons anymore. She was just as nice as she always was even if she didn't laugh. When I asked her, she said, '*Leibchen*, it is sometimes dangerous for people to go out now, besides it means we can have the piano all to ourselves!'

I did not understand.

Outside kindergarten, three people started shouting 'Juden, Juden Juden!' and they spat at us. This was the last time I went there. When this happened, Mama picked me up and ran towards home. I was big enough to walk and complained but I think she wanted me to get away from there. When we got round to the other side of the park, where Hilde and I used to chase the birds, she put me on a bench next to the big willow tree where we used to hide, and she sat beside me. She held my hand and cuddled me close. At first, she was panting and crying. I could feel her heart beating through her flowery cotton dress that was damp from sweating and that smelled of Mama.

She told me the story of 'The Ugly Ducking.' He was grey and small, and nobody took much notice of him. On the water, surrounding the reeds where his family nested, there were many big strong birds with luxurious feathers that looked beautiful. These birds paraded around and believed they were better than any other bird, and when they looked at the little duckling, they laughed at him and his scruffy feathers. The little duckling was good and kind, but he was very young. At first, he tried to make friends, but the big birds scared him. For many weeks he hid in the reeds away from the taunts of the pack of birds that snapped at him. He fed and rested and hoped they wouldn't return to attack him. One day, he realised he had grown much bigger and had magnificent feathers too and was no longer a tiny grey bird; in fact, he was a swan. So he swam across the water, gliding like a serene galleon upon a silvery lake. Back and forth he went. Other swans watched him and admired him. He realised that he was now as good as any of them.

Majestically, he raised himself up, and with his big feet running on the surface of the lake he started to take off. He splashed and flapped his huge wings, sweeping air behind him until ripples of water flowed outwards to lap up the sides of the bank. Up into the blue sky he soared. He flew higher and higher, marvelling at how brave and magnificent he had become. He had learnt how to be what he wanted to be.

Mama said, 'I like to think that the swan will remember how it felt when people laughed at him just because he was small and insignificant. One day, Morrie, you will be a swan; strong enough to say and do what you feel is right. Those people back there, who called us names, are wrong but we live in difficult times. I must tell you, Morrie, that because we are Jewish some people do not like us.'

'What did we do wrong, Mama? Did we upset them?' I said.

'*Leibchen*, I did nothing wrong nor did Papa, nor you. We must be careful though. Like the duckling hiding away in the reeds we must stay safe and not go near angry people. I hope when you are grown you realise that being cruel hurts and is always wrong. One day you will fly like the swan, magnificent and strong.'

'Will I really be able to fly, Mama?'

'No, *leibchen*!' she laughed out loud, 'No, but I meant you will be able to follow your dreams – though perhaps you will fly in an aeroplane some day, if that's what you want to do!'

'Oh yes! I would like that, Mama,' I said, smiling up at her.

Now Mama was playing *Liebestraum* by Franz Liszt on the piano. This was her favourite piece of music, and she played it most days. I looked at the musical notes, but I did not understand them and couldn't play any of it, though I knew exactly how the tune went. I sat on the piano stool next to her and watched her long fingers going back and forth across the keys. She said that when she was playing *Liebestraum* she forgot about everything else, and she imagined she was in another world. It was a world of familiarity and calm, re-visiting in her head the same places that relaxed and soothed her yesterday and the day before that. One day I hoped that I could play *Liebestraum* and go to the same places as my Mama.

The doorbell rang.

'Morrie, look, I have got your *schultute*!' Hilde said, beaming her big smile and jumping up and down with excitement. Her mother was next to her, holding both of our *schultutes*. Mine was the blue one and Hilde's was pink and yellow with stitches round the top. 'Look, Morrie, Frau Brunn put the top on and painted it the same blue you like, and I stuck on a red felt letter M. M for Morrie! Do you like it?'

Hilde's Mama bent down and gave it to me.

'I know you can't come to school with me, but we can fill your *schultute* with sweets and fruit and pretend,' Hilde said.

Here I was, me and Hilde and the *schultute* that I could never use.

Chapter 4

Leipzig

Kristallnacht, 9 November 1938

HILDE

Yesterday was my seventh birthday. It was not like last year. To begin with, I'd had chickenpox and had nasty dried spots all over my face, so I hadn't been to school. Papa had to work. Morrie was really unwell, as he caught the chickenpox from me but was about a week behind me so he was still itching but without a fever now. Mama made me a Streusel Cake because she managed to get some sugar and nuts. Papa sent some chocolate that we all shared. We went into Frau Silbermann's and she played some music for us, but she seemed unwell lately and it was not like last year. Mama said she was suffering with her nerves and this made her cry a lot.

Herr Silbermann was attacked coming home from work last month and had only just gone back to work again. He needed a stick to walk as he now had a damaged leg.

As I sat beside Morrie, keeping him company while he rested, I overheard Frau Silbermann telling Mama about something else that had happened to Morrie's father earlier today. In the early hours of this morning, Herr Silbermann was woken by a good deal of noise outside in the street and when he looked outside, he could see a red glow over the Bruhl district of the town.

'Clara, there is fire near the shop, I must go and see what is happening,' he said.

'No, Ben, it is too dark and too dangerous, I don't want you to go alone, let me come too,' Clara said, throwing back the bedding. 'I can ask Elsa to look after Morrie,' she said, thinking aloud.

'No, let me go, it'll be easier alone. I can dodge into doorways and move faster, I need you to look after things here.' He pulled on his work trousers, jumper, overcoat, and hat and leaned over to kiss her on her cheek, she grabbed his arm.

'I will be fine, *leibchen* - just let me go,' he said taking hold of his stick for support. He pulled away from her and he was gone.

Now Herr Silbermann was missing.

That was hours ago, and he should have returned by now. There had been fires all over the city and Frau Silbermann got up shortly after her husband and brought Morrie into us. She had been out on the street trying to find her husband in the dark of the early morning. Papa had not come home for the past week as he was staying at staff headquarters where he worked. Mama hadn't been to work because she didn't want to leave me alone and was frightened of the crowds of angry people wandering the streets, destroying buildings and threatening people. Morrie would stay with us for the moment, which I was happy about. 'We must not tell Papa about this,' Mama said.

Frau Silbermann came back to our apartment later this morning and told us what she'd seen. The Bruhl was the fur district of Leipzig, where Herr Silbermann's jewellery shop was, and the shop was badly damaged. The glass in the windows was smashed, the doors broken and hanging from their hinges and the yellow Star of David had been painted on the wall next to them. I didn't know why this yellow star was a bad thing.

Inside, the glass and wooden counters were broken, and in the workshop, the door was beaten down and trampled on; Herr Silbermann's paraphernalia, trays of instruments, forceps, clamps, moulds and magnifying glasses were scattered everywhere, smashed and ground underfoot. There was still the strong smell of turpentine, methylated spirit and oil that always filled the workshop. There was no jewellery or watches to be found, the safe had been blasted open. Someone had taken it all. Maybe it was Herr Silbermann, I hoped so.

The building next door to the shop had completely burnt down, as had many others. Despite the bottles of spirit in Herr Silbermann's shop, it had somehow survived the fire. There were buildings that hadn't been touched by the fire because the firemen had water hoses on them to stop them catching alight. This was strange. Just the Jewish buildings were on fire, the non-Jewish German ones were not. Frau Silbermann said there were police and firemen standing around, but no one was putting out flames nor stopping the people who were lighting the fires, they just watched them as they lit more. She told us that most of the shops in the Bruhl were damaged. These were mainly small furriers as well as large department stores, some of which were owned by people who were not German or who were German but Jews, which was the reason they were attacked. The furs had all been looted, stolen away as they were valuable and there would be plenty of people who would make a great deal of money on these.

There was glass everywhere and fires all around. There was a system of alleyways and, at night, the dark corners were somewhere you would be scared to go alone, but now everywhere had a red glow and there was choking smoke. Earlier, Frau Silbermann was told there were groups of people gathering in the street, chanting 'Jews Out!' and brandishing pieces of wood as weapons, knocking on doors, shouting for the residents to come out and when they didn't answer, ramming doors until they broke open and the mob had gained entry. They pulled people out of their beds and began abusing them, slapping, punching and spitting at them. It must have been a terrible sight.

After Frau Silbermann recounted all this, she fell asleep on the couch but as soon as she woke up, she got ready to go searching again.

'Elsa, it is my fault: I should never have let Ben go alone, he already has an injured leg! What sort of wife am I?' she said.

'Don't fret, Clara, you have done nothing wrong. All this anger on the street is not your fault, but go now if it makes you feel better. Please be careful. If you can't find him, leave it for today, it'll get dark early,' Mama said.

Mama and Frau Silbermann hugged each other.

Frau Silbermann kissed Morrie on his forehead and squeezed his face between her hands.

'I love you so much, Morrie, my little scabby baby, I will be back.'

She blew me a kiss, gave a wan smile and went out of the door.

***

We heard that they were calling the previous evening, 'The Night of Broken Glass' - *Kristallnacht* - because so many windows were smashed and there was glass strewn across pavements in the city.

Out on the street, now in daylight, Frau Silbermann would have to try to blend in and hope that she wouldn't be recognised as Herr Silbermann's wife. I hoped that the smoke was helping her stay in the shadows. Mama said she would be alright as long as nobody recognised her as a Jew. Mama was worried about her, as she was in an anxious state even before *Kristallnacht.*

When Morrie had first moved into Friedrichstrasse, we became inseparable. People who didn't know us thought we were twins. We had the same hair colouring and eyes, were the same size and were just two months apart in age, we laughed at all the same things and played and fought – I supposed like real twins might. This was good for Morrie, as he didn't get picked on as much as some of the other Jewish children. I had begun to think I was protecting him. Now, though, he couldn't go outside except at night with his Mama and Papa. Neither of us was allowed out today under any circumstances because it was dangerous.

There was a pale winter sun shining into the apartment painting everything a dull orange. It would be sunset in a few minutes. Morrie had been pressing his nose against the window for the past two hours, creating white misted glass streaked with dripping condensation while waiting for his Mama to return. He hadn't spoken to me once since she'd left. I knew Morrie, and that he was scared that neither she nor his Papa would come back. We could only just see the street from the apartment, and he couldn't possibly identify an individual figure from here in the half light. I knew his mother would be trying to be inconspicuous and would be creeping along, trying not to draw attention to herself or get stopped by an official. He wouldn't find her by looking from our window on the second floor, I knew that.

'Morrie, shall we go to your apartment? You could play 'Fur Elise' to me, I love that piece,' I said, trying to distract him and stop him worrying about his Mama and Papa. But he simply ignored me.

Chapter 5

Leipzig

11 November 1938

ELSA

Clara hadn't returned, nor had Ben Silbermann. It was 6 am and still dark. All night I had been listening for the lobby door to open. I couldn't have Morrie here much longer, but I couldn't leave him, he was just seven years old. It was time to make a decision.

With no time to waste, I hurriedly got myself dressed. The children were still asleep.

Raoul hadn't returned from work for the past week, I knew that he had many people to organise and paperwork to deal with. Morrie couldn't be in our apartment when Raoul returned. There were rules to follow. Jews were being removed from the city. We were told not to speak to them. There were announcements on the radio, in newspapers and on posters that had appeared on the side of buildings and on pamphlets handed out on street corners.

When he was a simple policeman, life was calmer, but since the party took over the police, the demands on Raoul had increased. Everything had been restructured and his responsibilities constantly changed. He felt that he must always try to impress his senior officers. He was expected to promote the Führer and the ideals of the Nazi party. Already he'd had a small promotion this year. He wanted to see Germany great again, as we all did, but there were food shortages and an atmosphere of unrest and distrust everywhere. He said he must work to protect and support his family. He had always been a kind man, but his work must come first. I could only guess that the party had confidential information that I didn't have, which meant there were good reasons for the things that happened. The newspapers said that not only were the Jews making life difficult for ordinary Germans here in Germany, but they were also trying to turn other countries against us. It was said that ordinary Germans were outnumbered by Jews in this city, and that they used underhand methods and trickery to control the finances in this town. I did not argue with Raoul on any of this. It was hard to know what was true, but I did know that the Jews I knew were my friends and they were good people. I had to help the Silbermanns, if I could, before it was too difficult for me to do that.

Using the key Clara had left with me, I entered the Silbermann's apartment. I put a note on the hall mat so Clara would see it when she returned. She had been gone for almost a day now.

The note said,

'*Clara, do not worry. I have Morrie with Hilde and me. It is Friday morning. We will be back later.*'

I closed the apartment door and went to wake the children so we could get ready. The sleeping pair had a blanket pulled up to their chins and their breath formed plumes of vapour. Morrie was a little weak from the chickenpox, but I couldn't leave him here and we had to find his parents. They roused slowly; it was warm in the bed and they were reluctant to get up. I poured some warmed water from a pan into the sink and quickly washed the children's faces and hands. They were both shivering so I quickly got them dried and into warm clothes.

I left the children eating a piece of black bread and a slice of sausage each for their breakfast while I slipped back into the Silbermann's apartment – I'd realised Morrie needed outdoor clothes. It was so long since he'd been outside.

I hunted in his cupboard until I found the blue hat and scarf I was looking for. I eventually found his warm coat and boots. Returning to the children, I fetched Hilde's coat and blue hat and scarf. I hoped the idea I had might help us, it was risky for us to go outside but the streets seemed quiet. Last Christmas my mother, Oma Osler, made the two children a hat and scarf each. They were identical and made from the wool she had unravelled from two old cardigans. Sky blue with white stripes. Each hat had a big blue and white pompom on it.

'Look, my little babies, now you really do look like twins!' Oma had chuckled but they had never been able to go out together to wear them. Morrie had not left the house for months; Clara was too scared he would be attacked.

I knew going out was a risk, and I didn't want to put the children in danger, but I didn't know what to do with Morrie. I had to find his parents. He was Jewish and may be harmed if he was found alone. I couldn't leave the children alone. Herr Müller downstairs was a party member and Clara was wary of him; I didn't want to involve him in any of this. He was the only neighbour I knew. Some of the apartments in our building had been taken over temporarily by army personnel, who came and then went again, but I was unsure which apartments were occupied and by whom. Clara had become more worried each day that as the only Jewish family here there may be reprisals and possible violence. It was not long since Ben was attacked on the street.

'Listen, children, there have been people on the streets fighting and causing damage. It seems much quieter today, so try not to be scared, but we must look for your Mama, so we are going to visit some of the places that I think she may be. She will be looking for your Papa, Morrie. You two look like twins now with your bobble hats on, I need you to hold hands at all times and never leave my side and we will be safe.'

I wasn't sure this was the right thing to do but I had no other ideas. Morrie dropped his head and cried quietly.

'Don't worry, Morrie, we will help you,' said Hilde with her arm around Morrie's shoulder. She was a brave little girl full of innocence and hope, not yet tarnished by the events going on in this city. I was pleased they could support one another.

The children clip-clopped down the marble staircase from the second floor, chasing each other, but before they reached Herr Müller's apartment, I motioned for them to slow down.

'Be really quiet, children – on tippy toes!' I whispered. I didn't want anyone to know what we were doing, particularly not Herr Müller.

It was raining outside and very cold on the street. Sticking close together we walked down the wide pavement of Friedrichstrasse. There were people rushing to work, cars and buses on the road on what looked like a normal sort of day, the sort of day when I would be going to the factory for my shift.

This was a road of tall grey buildings, mainly apartment houses like ours but some office buildings too. There was a doctor's surgery, a café and a few shops selling groceries, confectionery, and tobacco – though many of the normal things we would expect to see were not available now. A few shops were boarded up, glass fragments still glinted from the kerb, and discarded, disintegrating anti-Jewish pamphlets peeled from the walls. Our road was not too badly damaged in the riots because it was not a Jewish area and had few Jewish businesses here.

There was a man lying on the pavement, up against a wall. He was slumped over, and I was unsure if he was still alive. Nobody took any notice of him, except the children.

'What's the matter with that man, Mama?' Hilde asked loudly.

'I don't know, *leibchen,* I think he is asleep,' I replied, ushering the children past him as quickly as I could. 'Do you think you are alright to walk, Morrie? I know it is cold, do you feel unwell?'

'I like to be outside with you and Hilde. It's like an adventure. A hunting Mama adventure!' he said.

I loved the enthusiasm and innocence of this little boy, but feared for what might happen to him if I couldn't find his parents.

I heard the sound of footsteps on the road. A group of men appeared, perhaps fifty or sixty of them. They were being marched up the middle of the road, approaching us. The children stopped to watch as the men attempted to march but, in effect, shuffled past us. If they were an army, they were a very dishevelled one. But I realised that they were not soldiers. They were carrying bundles of clothes or suitcases. One of them carried a stack of books that looked very heavy, and he looked as though he might drop them.

I could see that some of the men were injured, they were bloodied with torn clothing. Some were limping or dragging their legs. Soldiers marched behind and beside them, urging them to speed up, poking their rifles into the men's backs. One man fell to his knees. The soldier closest to him shouted at him to get up. The man staggered to his feet, but it was a great effort and he was slow, so he was harangued again by the soldier. I saw dried blood in his hair and mud on his face. Slowly, he followed the rest of the men, though he looked as though he might fall again.

Morrie, fascinated by the scene, had turned around to watch as the men trooped away from us. He stood, open-mouthed. 'Why did that man fall over? Should we help him? he asked.

I looked too, and though I didn't know where they were going, it was in the direction of the railway station so I suspected they were Jews being sent out of the city. I wanted the children to move on. We could not attract attention, especially from the soldiers, by making comments or showing too much interest.

'Stop gawping, that's rude. That man is alright now, he just fell over. Keep walking, we need to look for your Mama, Morrie,' I admonished, trying to distract him. Morrie jerked his chin to his chest.

I was not sure what I had just witnessed. Did one of the men in the front group look back over his shoulder at me as they were forced on?

'Where are those men going?' asked Morrie, breaking into a trot to keep up with my faster pace.

'I think that they may be going to live somewhere else, Morrie. Some new home out of this city,' I said, suddenly feeling a heavy cloud of realisation descend on me as the sound of the marching feet faded. Sick with dread, I steered the children towards the Jewish cemetery.

Chapter 6

Leipzig

11 November 1938

HILDE

I held Morrie's hand tightly. He was sad that both his Mama and Papa were missing. Today we came outside. Mama and I would find them, I was sure. I thought that the Night of Broken glass had stopped because everywhere seemed normal but there were many more soldiers and policemen on the street than usual. I should be at school, but Mama thought it was closed for the rest of this week.

The Jewish cemetery was close to where we lived and I knew that Morrie and his father, Ben, sometimes visited the graves of his family there. We decided to visit here in case either Clara or Ben was there. It was not likely, but Mama decided we must go to all the places she could think of. She said we must tick off, one-by-one, all the places they might have gone to. We walked alongside the stone wall then through the gates of the cemetery and Morrie was keen to show us the way to the Silbermann's plot. He rushed off, but Mama called him back.

'You must stay with me all the time,' she told him.

We only took a few steps when Mama stopped.

'Oh my goodness!' she half whispered. She was looking towards the small chapel to the right of the cemetery. It was made of stone and brown bricks, with a tall pointed roof in the centre and a magnificent wooden door within an ornate frame of stone. Somebody had broken all the glass where the windowpanes should have been. The wide wooden doors and the walls surrounding them had been hacked to pieces with an axe or something similar. Bricks, dust and splintered wood lay in a heap on the driveway, paint had been daubed on the walls and grass.

I thought that this must be part of the *Kristallnacht* damage from yesterday, though nobody had yet started to clear it up.

'Oh no!' Mama cried out. 'Look away children, *now*!'

On the ground in front of us were bodies, wrapped in cloth shrouds and laying in a random and careless fashion on the ground. There were holes and piles of soil near them. Many of the newer graves had been dug up and the bodies cruelly and disrespectfully tossed to the ground, their limbs contorted. Some of the wet, dirtied shrouds had been slashed and the emaciated remains of people were just visible.

This was a place of great reverence. There were lines of cherished headstones and graves that families tended so carefully. It was always peaceful and orderly here. Such disarray was shocking and the nature of it was a truly dreadful sight.

It was too late to tell us to look away because we had both seen it.

We grabbed hold of Mama and began to cry.

Just then, two policemen appeared.

'What are you doing here?' the taller one asked sternly.

Mama was holding both Morrie's hand and mine and I felt her squeeze very hard. She didn't want Morrie to say that he was looking for his parents, his Jewish parents.

'This is a short cut to Lenostrasse isn't it? We need to get to Lenostrasse,' Mama said.

'No, it isn't. There is no way through here,' the policeman said. 'Papers,' he demanded, holding out his hand.

Mama pulled her papers from her coat pocket and handed them over. We waited in frightened silence while he read them. He thrust them back at Mama.

'So, these two?' he said nodding towards Morrie and me.

'My twins.'

He looked us up and down, taking in everything including our matching hats and scarves, 'What are those marks on their faces?'

'They have both had chicken pox but the doctor says they need some good fresh air in their lungs and they aren't infectious anymore. They do have rosy cheeks though now because it is a really cold day!' she said, beaming at us.

'*Schone kinder*, good to be healthy!' he said, smiling approvingly.

'Thank you,' Mama said politely.

'OK, so turn right out of here, then right again and the second right is Lenostrasse and don't come into here again, it is not a good place. This is no place for children.'

'Thank you,' Mama repeated and ushered us out of the cemetery in the direction of Lenostrasse.

The shorter policeman, who had remained silent and watchful, crossed his arms and kept his gaze on us as we walked away. I wanted to keep moving, I wasn't sure what he was thinking.

After a few steps and out of earshot of the policemen, Morrie said, 'Papa says the cemetery is a good place, a place of peace where we should come to pray quietly or just to think, why did that policeman say it was not a good place?'

'I think it is only special if you are Jewish, Morrie, and you saw what people have done to it. It is not a good place at the moment, is it?' said Mama. 'I'm so sorry you saw that just now, children, it was horrible and I hope that those poor people will soon be reburied. Nobody should ever be disrespected like that.'

I couldn't understand why those policemen were not dealing with what had happened in the cemetery. How was it that we were outside on the road, just a few yards away, where the cars and people were going by enjoying their day and yet no-one cared about the dead bodies behind the wall? Perhaps they didn't know what had happened? But whoever did it must know? Maybe they weren't all people in those sacks. Would someone bury them? Why would anyone do that to those graves? What for?

'Mama and Papa were not there. Where will we look next?' asked Morrie, hoping Mama had a plan.

'I don't know. Many people don't like Jews, Morrie. I was worried the policeman may ask your name and I hope he didn't hear me call you Morrie.' Mama said. 'I think we should play a little game while we are out on the streets. If anyone asks, say your name is Max, Max Franck, the same surname as Hilde and me. Let's pretend that you are real twins until we find your Mama. It will protect you. Hilde, you must call him Max too, can you do that?'

'Yes Mama,' I said and understood that we had to be careful.

'So, Max, where shall we go next?'

We had to keep walking in the direction of Lenostrasse in case either of the policemen were watching, but this was not where Mama wanted to go. Once we were a safe distance from the cemetery, we began going to the areas that Mama thought Morrie's Mama or Papa might be.

We walked a long way, visiting parks and buildings that Ben and Clara spoke of, but without seeing them or finding anyone who'd had contact with them in the last two days. Eventually, we got to Rosenthal Park. This was a very large park with hundreds of trees and benches dotted around. It was an area that many Jewish families visited on social occasions or walked to on the Sabbath when they were not allowed to work.

When we'd left home earlier, Mama had given each of us a hot potato to put in our pockets to warm our hands. They had been partly cooked yesterday and then left cooking in a very low oven overnight. They were just warm. We found a wooden bench by a small clearing and sat down in a row. Someone had painted 'Jews not wanted here' on the bench. We hoped whoever wrote this was not still here. There were hardly any people around, just one man with his dog in the distance. We bit into our potatoes. Even though they were rather uninteresting and were brown, dry and crinkly on the outside they were fluffy and satisfying inside. We ate every last piece.

A few yards away, on the edge of the clearing, was a grand drinking fountain with a magnificent dolphin rising from its centre and sea serpents twisting around the base towards the top. It was made of a dark metal with bright turquoise-green streaks running down it. The four serpent's heads each had a spout that you could drink from.

'Don't go wandering off, children, get a drink and come straight back,' Mama called to us.

Morrie and I climbed the steps that surrounded the drinking fountain and, on tip toes, leaned over the trough, bent out heads to the side, pressed the buttons and thirstily gulped down the sweet cold water. We drank and drank until we were not catching it properly and were gagging. The water went all over our chins and we started splashing each other. This was so much fun after not being able to play like this for so long. We were laughing and screaming with excitement and were getting very wet, but that was half the fun. We began chasing each other round the huge dolphin throwing handfuls of water at one another.

'Stop! Come here,' said Mama, realising what we were doing. 'You're all wet, I can't have you getting chills.' She mopped the water with her handkerchief while we squirmed but we were still dripping wet. Her handkerchief was soaked through, too. We began to giggle and be silly, but our laughs soon turned to shivers. It wasn't raining anymore but it was November, and it was less than two hours till sunset.

Mama suddenly realised that as it was Friday, it would be the Jewish Sabbath. Surely, if Ben and Clara could, they would make sure they were indoors by sunset? They always celebrated this family time. Usually, Clara would have been cooking in her kitchen, preparing the special meal when prayers were said and traditional dishes eaten. She had learnt to cook from her Mama and her aunt as a small child, and from the women of the synagogue. Once she was married, she learnt the rituals that she should follow, though they were not an orthodox Jewish family. There was a strong sense of community and a great emphasis on observing the different Jewish festivals and feast days. Ben and Clara were not strict about their religion and did not always attend the synagogue, but the Jewish New Year 'Rosh Hashanah' and the winter festival of lights 'Hanukkah' were always celebrated, as well as the Friday night dinner, Shabbat.

'Children you are both so wet and you have only just got over chickenpox, I must get you warm and dry or you will become ill again and your Mama will never forgive me, Morrie! Oops! Max! So what do you think about going to see Oma and Opi for a while?'

'Yes, can we Mama?' I said smiling at the prospect of being spoiled for a few hours by my kind, attentive grandparents.

Morrie squealed, 'Please, please, please!' as he jumped up and down, clapping his hands together while his teeth chattered with cold.

I knew that tonight Papa would be coming home for the weekend, so I didn't think we would stay long at Arkadien.

Chapter 7

Leipzig

11 November 1938

MARTIN

Martin Müller was a member of the HJ (*Hitlerjugend*). He was eighteen, and during the four years in the organisation, he had moved up the ranks and was now section leader. Soon he would be moving into an army corp. He was encouraged by his father, an ex-serving officer himself, to use this as a stepping-stone to his career, as well as by Martin's doting mother who liked the idea of her strong athletic son being singled out to fight for the honour of Germany.

Martin had been an event steward two years before at the Olympic Games in Berlin and, on one occasion, stood only a few yards from the Führer himself. He was a good athlete, who excelled at callisthenics and was part of the local display team. He was precise in his demeanour and outward appearance, though looked sour most of the time. He had won awards in his section for his vigilance and initiative and had been awarded a medal for service from the city coordinator last year. Martin had few friends. He distrusted people and his only interest was in the organisations doing the Führer's work.

On the 11th of November, he had been preparing to leave his apartment for the day. It was not yet 7 am, there was no school, but an extra meeting had been arranged. The disturbances caused by the Jews meant that the HJ were needed to help clear up the mess on the streets and restore everything to its normal status. Glancing out of the window, he saw Frau Franck with Hilde and another child leaving the building. He watched spitting rain falling steadily in the glow of the streetlight.

Where were they going at this hour? Shops were not yet open, and school was closed. He was not certain, but he thought the other child was the blond Jewish boy who lived next to the Francks. He was the only other small child in the apartments. Elsa Franck was married to Raoul Franck, a police official and well-respected party man who Martin tried hard to impress in the hope might put in a good word for him. Franck would not be happy that his wife was so friendly with a Jew. Martin's father, the landlord, didn't want these Jews here anymore. Every day, the newspapers and the radio spoke about the bad business deals of Jews and how they were ruining Germany. People were encouraged to distance themselves from them.

So, why was Frau Franck going out with the children? Should he tell Herr Franck? Would that be a good thing to do? Perhaps he would look upstairs, see if there were any clues.

ELSA

'Can you remember where you are dear?' the nurse asked gently.

'Hospital I think?' I replied.

'And can you tell me your name and date of birth?'

'Elsa Franck, Frau, 8th January 1906.'

'That's good. You are doing very well but no more talking, just relax and get some rest. The operation went well but the anaesthetic will make you feel groggy for some time.'

She left my bed, and her footsteps faded.

I didn't know exactly how long I'd been here. I was still disorientated and in pain. I'd broken some ribs and had to have an operation on my face as I'd broken my cheekbone when I hit my head. I couldn't see properly out of my right eye and the doctors couldn't say if I had lost some sight in that eye. They were kind here. It was very clean but surprisingly noisy. The floors were made of tiles and the high ceiling had large windows which could be opened. Everything seemed so white and bright.

The noises came from the trolleys grinding along the ward, the clicking of the nurses' shoes and their voices echoing in the cavernous space. Even the starched linen on the bed made a crunching noise whenever I moved. It was as if the sounds of everyday were being amplified and I could not make sense of my thoughts or where I was. Slowly, I began to put together what happened before I got here. The drugs confused me, my head felt muzzy and strange, I kept seeing flashes in my eyes and I was so sleepy.

Next thing, Raoul was sitting beside me on a wooden chair, holding my hand. He looked very concerned. I was unable to speak to him, but I thought I remembered him trying to hold onto me at the top of some stairs.

I drifted in and out of sleep. In my dream I took Hilde and Morrie to my parent's house, Arkadien. It was a warm brown brick, rambling house with pretty windows and three sets of chimneys and ivy growing all along the side wall. My father had removed the ivy several times but it always came back, so he said it was meant to be there.

My parents were very happy to have the children there, although my father said Morrie must not leave their house for his own safety and, though my father didn't say it, for the safety of Oma and Opi too. Did this happen? Did I get the children to safety or was this some sort of hallucinatory state?

I could see the children disappearing into Opi's workshop, a true Aladdin's cave for little children, full of the smell of sawn wood, with sawdust on the floor that coated their shoes. The workshop was crammed with boxes and tins full of nails, screws, nuts and bolts and a workbench littered with sandpaper, tins of black and yellow grease and all manner of garden products that Opi used to take cuttings or kill aphids on plants. There were rows of specialised metal tools, strangely shaped, each with a unique purpose, hanging on the wall, and pots full of paintbrushes squashed together with their bristles pointing upwards creating a family of hedgehogs on the end of the bench. There was a small mountain of paint pots, all nearly empty, the dregs from the many projects undertaken around the house over the years but, despite having only a little left, the remains were precious because paint was scarce now. Today, Opi said he had a new project the children would love. They were in safe hands, I knew. I remembered being grateful and sensing a great love for my father at that moment. Morrie loved the workshop, it had many of the elements he was familiar with at his father's jewellery business, and he wanted to help Opi. Hilde loved watching whatever project her grandfather was working on.

I tried to piece together exactly what happened after I left my parents and the children. I'd stopped at a few places on my way back to our apartment but found nothing that would help me find Clara or Ben. Ben did have some distant relatives, but I didn't know where to look.

My ability to think disappeared and suddenly, with no warning, I was fighting for breath, red darting lights filling my head. There was a whooshing sound like a great wall of water crashing down on me, the muzziness had gone, replaced now by a searing pain. I was overwhelmed by images. Hilde and Morrie, Oma and Opi, leaning over like spectres, all screaming at me. Nurses, doctors and Raoul moving me, shouting my name, forcing my head to the side, a curtain being dragged across a metal rod, more trolleys speeding towards me, a crescendo of panic and then black silence.

Sometime later, was it a day or a week or a month later, I could not say because I was not part of this world at that time, I was inhabiting some strange place where thoughts were disjointed and incomplete. Repeated visions of the past plagued my mind and events happened in the wrong order, though in time, my brain slowly began to make sense of it.

I kept returning to a flashing image, again and again. It was of the men walking down the road, the work party of Jews being taken to the station when I was walking to the cemetery with Hilde and Morrie. There had been something familiar about the man who'd looked back at me. I saw his eyes and couldn't forget what I saw. Those eyes flashed before me again. He was a hunched figure in filthy clothes, but I was horribly afraid it had been Ben. Those eyes were calling out, appealing to me. He was limping. Was I imagining that? Ben had a limp caused by the beating he had received. He couldn't acknowledge me or little Morrie by my side. Maybe he knew to keep quiet. But his eyes had bored into me. Ben adored his son and would have wanted him to stay safe even if Ben himself was not. His eyes were his best feature and this was what I thought I recognised in that grimy, fearful face. They were always expressive and kind. Was he looking at me, imploring me to look after his son? I couldn't be sure it was him because the Ben I knew looked so different; he was always dressed in a smart suit with an immaculate shirt with a crisp white collar. He was a jeweller and so wore jewellery to advertise his wares, just a little and he always looked elegant, he'd wear maybe one or two rings, a wristwatch and always a lapel badge of gold with a single diamond.

But then, those eyes, looking at me, was it him?

I could not make my brain work properly, memories of my childhood came tumbling out and became muddled with Oma and Opi as they were now. But, gradually, more and more did come back to me about that day.

I thought I remembered being tucked up in bed by Oma because I had a fever, but I realised it wasn't me, it was Morrie who had a fever and Oma persuaded me to let him stay with her. I needed to protect him. I should not have brought him out in the rain.

I remembered that I got back to our apartment at 4pm. It was nearing sunset and I hoped that everything was alright, that I was wrong about Ben being in the work party, that Clara was nowhere to be found outside because she'd been busy preparing for the

Shabbat and that she would now be back in her apartment making soup and bread.

I'd left Clara's apartment unlocked. I hadn't known what to do because I'd had her only key. I was worried what Clara would say about me taking Morrie to my parents, but he'd stayed overnight with them before so I didn't think – with her husband missing – she would mind. At least the little boy was safe.

When I got to Clara's apartment that evening there was no light showing under the door. Stepping inside, I switched on the light but sensed immediately that nobody was there. I walked into the large living room and could see the music stand on the piano glinting from the light in the hallway. Clara was not home. As I left, I went to turn off the light in the hall and realised the note I'd left on the door mat had gone. I looked around, thinking a gust of wind may have blown it into a corner but it wasn't there. Somebody must have taken it.

As I came out of the Silbermann's apartment I heard a tread on the stairs. Raoul opened the swing doors onto our landing. I knew he'd prearranged to have a day's leave and that he was coming home tonight. Taking the children was not ideal but I'd done what I felt was right.

He looked so impressive and handsome in his uniform, but he also looked serious. Tall and slim with wavy thick brown hair now greying at the sides, he had just the hint of a middle age spread about his waist. He came into the hall and said to me, 'Elsa where is Hilde, is she in the apartment?'

'No Raoul, I have taken her to my parents – for a treat!'

'Why would you do that? You knew I was coming home tonight and I didn't get to see her on her birthday! You know I had to work. It's been so difficult this week and I've had so much to sort out. Well, what possible reason, eh?' he spat. 'And why were you coming out of that Jew's apartment? I have told you; we aren't supposed to mix, and it is not fitting that an officer of the Third Reich has a wife who flouts all the rules. Do you want me to lose my job?'

I didn't want a confrontation with Raoul. When he felt I'd done something wrong, he expected me to obey him and to apologise. He was the man of the house; that was the expected norm, but sometimes I did express my own opinion, which made him angry. He'd never hit me, but at times he'd grip my arms so tightly I had bruises up my arms for days.

'Please don't shout at me, Raoul, I've been on my own here this week and I thought that Hilde may enjoy some time with her Opi and Oma. We haven't been able to go out, there's been so much violence on the streets, and you've not been here. Today seemed a good opportunity.'

Raoul grabbed hold of both of my shoulders and pushed me against the swing doors.

'Tch! OK, so where is the Jewish boy? Is he with Hilde? What are you playing at, Elsa? Whatever you are up to, tell me!' he demanded.

'He is not well, Raoul. He's had chickenpox, and Oma is taking care of him.'

I struggled to get away from him, but his powerful frame made me lose my balance I stumbled backwards against the door. It swung open and I knew that I was falling. I remember jarring my neck as I twisted, hitting my head once, and then again, as I fell backwards down the marble steps. I remember Raoul's hands reaching out, him calling, 'Elsa!'

I heard my body thud, my neck cracked, and then I just remember blackness, no pain, just blackness.

Chapter 8

Arkadien

12 November 1938

HILDE

Last night, Morrie and I watched as my grandfather hammered pieces of wire. He formed them into a shape we didn't recognise, but it was in fact the start of a birdcage. It was about twenty inches tall but curved at the top, made with two strong pieces of wire that were attached to the metal floor and then bent into an arch to slot into holes drilled into the other side.

Next, he told us to sit away from his workbench. He then used small pieces of pale grey solder and a fierce jet of flame from a blow torch to secure the wires. The flame roared, splayed out and spat pieces of metal onto his old wooden bench. Opi wore goggles to protect his eyes and elbow length gauntlets to shield his hands and we watched, agog, at this hellish spectacle. Once the basic shape of the cage was obvious, and Opi was happy that the two arches ran parallel, he turned the knob on the blowtorch. The flame changed from white to gold and red, then diminished eventually into a sharp lapping blue tongue, it made a *phut* sound and finally fell silent.

'That is enough for tonight *kinder*,' he said. 'I shall work on this so that tomorrow you will see a big difference, but I still have a lot to do.'

We sat with Oma and had a glass of warm milk. 'Shall I tell you story children?' she asked.

Both Morrie and I squealed with delight. Oma was a good storyteller because she made the stories extra special, always using different voices for each character and sometimes jumping around, acting out the most dramatic parts to bring the story to life.

She got down her book of fairy tales, which we both loved. She had just one book which had been hers as a child, then handed down to my mother and nowadays was here to be read to me. It was made of cardboard with a rough grass-green cloth binding along the spine and a dark khaki cover. On the front was a painting of the Pied Piper of Hamelin wearing a colourful outfit like Columbine, with a red pixie hat and red curled slippers. He was dancing down the street playing a flute, followed by an army of rats. The picture was rather rubbed away by so many little fingers over the years but still brought the promise of excitement for what was to come. Each of the stories, and there were many, had one full-plate glossy picture to go with it. We would stare at that one image fixedly while the story was being told, always expecting it to come to life. These were fairy stories after all, and anything might happen if you really longed for it.

'So, what would you like? The Princess and the Pea, Pied Piper, or maybe Hansel and Gretel?'

'Pied Piper!' we yelled in unison, and both laughed.

There was good reason for this. It wasn't my favourite story, but it was the best bedtime story. If we were staying the night, we knew that at the end of the story when all the children were lured out of the town, Oma would say, 'Here comes the Piper!' and chase us up to bed. Our bedroom was in the eaves bedroom right at the top of the house and Oma never caught us, we were too quick, and she was getting older. We loved this and because we knew it was only a story it didn't scare us nor stop us from sleeping.

Morrie and I were soon tucked into the truckle bed. We fitted in top-to-toe with the crowns of our heads poking out the end of our quilt. The mattress was very old fashioned and made of straw, giving the room a musty smell. The light through the window, from the stars and from a sliver of moon, shone across our coverlet. Before long, we were fast asleep.

That was last night, but today we woke to the sound of a cockerel crowing. He belonged to Gunther, the farmer next door, and was called Oswald after a cheeky cartoon rabbit, because he often got into mischief and was also mainly black and white.

Opi was true to his word. While we were asleep he had completed the birdcage. It had many wires threaded around the uprights to form a cage. The floor was made of metal from one of Oma's baking trays. There was a wooden platform inside and two round perches cut from the handle of an old garden broom. Opi had secured inside a drinking bowl made from a small glass food jar. He'd even crafted a small door which rose and fell like a portcullis, so that we could get our hands inside. Some heavy sandpaper, scavenged from a prior building project, had been placed on the floor of the cage, and there was a half inch gap to slide paper in and out when it required cleaning. On the outside, at the very top of the cage, he'd designed a pretty flower shape, resembling a rose, made of metal wires with a ring at the centre so the cage could be suspended.

'Now, *kinder*, I must paint this. But first, do you want to know what will go into the cage?' he asked.

'A bird?' I said, thinking this was obvious, though I hadn't considered where we might get one.

'Come with me, I have a surprise for you. Get your coats,' Opi motioned to our coats on the peg. He climbed down from his high stool at the bench and went towards the door.

'But we can't go out,' I said, immediately worried. I knew Morrie must be careful. We weren't allowed out, but we trusted Opi. I knew he would always look after us, and it was the back entrance we were going to, anyway.

'Don't worry, Hilde, you'll be fine. We're only going from our garden into Gunther's.'

Crossing the lawn outside Opi's workshop, I noticed it was covered in toadstool fairy rings and was a luxuriant green from the rain. We went past 'old Holstein', Opi's oldest apple tree, which cropped sacks full of golden apples every autumn. It had been in the garden when my grandparents moved into the house and had never failed to produce apples. Once, when Mama was small, it had been struck by lightning and split in half but, miraculously, both sides still grew fruit. Opi had great respect for the tree and said to us, 'As long as Old Holstein is producing fruit, we will all be safe in Arkadien.'

We followed him down towards the stream where the water was very high and moving fast. Pushing through some bushes and a small copse of trees, we found ourselves at the back of Gunther's farmyard with its array of barns and tumbled-down walls and sheds. I had never been here before, though I knew Gunther. Everything smelled strongly of pigs. I could hear them squealing and snuffling in the nearest barn to us. The farmyard was splattered with animal waste and straw, everything was wet and muddy. There were abandoned buckets and rusted farm machinery, a wheel barrow with a pile of rotten potatoes, and a small tractor that I knew still worked because I'd seen it driven in the field, across the stream, behind our garden. There were chickens gathering to watch us, but they clucked and moved away as we climbed the slight hill towards the biggest barn and the farmhouse. Oswald, the cockerel, was there to greet us. He was standing on top of a wheelless, rusted maroon car perched on piles of bricks that were almost hidden under a curtain of ivy. He raised his neck, lifted his head high, the feathers around his neck parted ready for him to declare his majestic crow.

Gunther appeared. He was of similar age to my grandfather, dressed in many layers of woollen clothes in various shades of brown and grey. He had a wide tan leather belt over his knitted jumper, a battered green alpine hat with a badge on the front, and rubber boots up to his knees.

'Greetings, *kinder*, are you excited?' he asked enquiringly with a huge grin.

'I haven't told them,' Opi said.

'You'll need a cage though, Opi? Gunther looked concerned.

'Don't worry, I'm making it and it's nearly finished – they've seen that part of the surprise.'

'Come,' Gunther said, marching over to a wooden building with a painting of a peacock on the door. 'Come into my special place, *kinder*. You are very honoured, you know!'

As he opened the door, we were amazed at what we saw. Behind a mesh wall running the length of the shed was a world inhabited by birds, beautiful birds of every conceivable colour. A tree grew up into the room and there were perches and poles coming out of the walls. There were windows high up along the back wall, wood shavings covered the floor except for one area where there was a small artificial pond of water. The birds were yellow, orange, red, green, blue, white, pink and black, brown and gold and many combinations of these. They were mainly small birds though some were larger with long tail feathers. I spotted two cockatiels and a brightly coloured parrot. The noise was overwhelming. We stood watching, not believing what we were seeing. This kaleidoscope seemed unreal and did not fit into our world. It was like something from one of Oma's fairy stories or a page from one of Clara Silbermann's glossy natural history books. The birds flew back and forth, settling for just a moment before flying off again. They pecked at seed and squabbled with each other. It was a city of birds, I decided. Like a city of people all going about their daily life, energetic or sleepy or argumentative or playful or industrious or lazy or stupid or quiet or just plain grumpy. I decided the biggest birds were in charge. The colourful parrot was probably the king, and the white and yellow cockatiels were his beautiful queen and princess daughter, and all the other birds were his subjects and had to do as he asked.

Morrie and I pressed our faces to the wire mesh with the wire digging into our noses. This was the most exciting event I thought I'd ever seen. When a pink and black bird dive-bombed the wire, almost hitting our faces, Morrie and I jumped back, yelping. The birds scattered and made loud squawking noises.

'No! Please be calm, *kinder*,' Gunther said firmly, 'screaming upsets the birds.'

Both Morrie and I knew we had been reprimanded. We instinctively held hands because that had always made us feel safe and united. I felt I might cry.

'Follow me,' Gunther said, not unkindly. Opi looked a little sternly at me but then smiled reassuringly, which made me feel better.

At the far end of the shed a small area had been sectioned off. It still had mesh; this was finer though, and we could see through, but this area had less light coming in and had a heat lamp hanging down low from the roof to keep the birds warm. Inside were about twelve bright blue birds and maybe five tiny baby birds.

'These are budgerigars,' Gunther explained, 'and the little ones are their babies, baby budgerigars. These budgerigars are extra special because they are blue. Wild budgerigars are yellow and green, and it has taken me many years to produce these little masterpieces. A few years ago, they cost a lot of money if you wanted to buy one. Opi and I were talking, and we both think now is a very good time for you to have a pet while you are staying at

Arkadien. So, I want you to pick out the one you like best, Hilde, and when that baby is big enough you can put him in your Opi's birdcage.'

Morrie and I squatted down to get a closer look through the mesh. One of the tiny birds seemed to be as curious as we were, it hopped closer to look at our faces.

'Hello, baby bird,' I said. 'Would you like to come and live with us?'

The little bird cocked its head to one side when I spoke. We all laughed at that.

'This one, Onkle Gunther, this one, he likes us I think,' I said.

'I think he has chosen you, *leibchen*!' said Gunther, laughing.

'Will he really be mine – and Morrie's too? Will he be ours forever, to keep?' I asked. 'Can I take him home to show our Mamas and Papas?'

Gunther laughed, 'Yes, he will be yours and you can show him to whoever you want. You will have to learn how to look after him though. It will be a big responsibility to look after a living creature. Would you like to do that?'

Morrie and I squealed in unison and then realised we were being noisy so clamped our hands to our mouths and giggled behind them.

'Yes please, I shall call him Froh because he makes me so happy. Yes, Froh!' I said. 'Is it a him or a her?'

'We don't know yet,' said Gunther. 'Give it time, little one. There'll be lots to learn.'

I couldn't wait to go and tell Oma.

***

It was nearing year's end, and little did we children know but war was soon to be upon us. The adults surrounding us were constantly debating daily events, listening to the radio, arguing the rationale behind the harsh dictates of the Nazi party and worrying about how this affected shortages of certain food and restrictions in our daily lives. Herr Hitler encouraged us to believe that to be German at this time was to be superior to any other nationality, and a great future was predicted for us Germans. We were told that Jews had to be removed from our society and this was accepted by the majority of the population. I didn't know what my family's thoughts were on this, but I did know we had Jewish friends which was against the law. My parents, grandparents and Gunther could see the mounting tensions within our country, and the rise in conflicts with countries surrounding us.

Morrie and I stayed at Arkadien and didn't venture outside at any time because Opi and Oma feared for our safety, particularly

Morrie's. They were acting as guardians to us both and would do so for many months to come.

Jewish or not, Morrie was a little boy who needed to be looked after and whose parents were missing. My grandparents were always kind and dependable.

On September 3rd 1939 Great Britain and France declared war on Germany, and I gave Froh-Froh a new sprig of millet.

Part 2

Friedrichstrasse 1940 -1942

Chapter 1

Arkadien

Early Spring 1940

MORRIE

Hilde and I stayed at Oma and Opi's for a very long time. I hoped and prayed that Mama and Papa would come and find me. They would have known that I was with Hilde. They would also have known where this house was because I'd stayed here before and they had come here for a summer party in the garden. That seemed years ago, though, and it made me unhappy to think about those times when we were a family of three, always together, every day. I remember my Mama looking beautiful in a white summer dress with embroidered flowers, her hair long and curled, and my Papa standing on the lawn with people all around listening and laughing at his funny stories.

Sometimes at Arkadien I would slip into bed with Oma because I had a nightmare in the dark and could not get back to sleep. Wondering if I'd ever see my parents again made my heart hurt, and although Oma and Opi were kind, I missed Mama and Papa and being at our apartment, my home.

One consolation was an upright piano in the reception room, which I was allowed to use. It was old, made of walnut and had not been tuned for a long time. I got used to two of the keys feeling spongy and one that made no sound – I learned to play the extra note in my head. There were various pieces of sheet music stored in the piano stool, but nothing I knew. Under the haphazard pile was a book of Beethoven sonatas, which I had never seen nor attempted before, but I enjoyed trying to play them and decided to learn one of them perfectly for Mama, to show her that I had kept up playing. Mama played some Beethoven pieces, I remembered that, but I didn't know which ones. When I sat at the piano and played I thought of Mama, and I felt a little happier.

Hilde was unhappy too because her Mama was in hospital. She'd had a bad fall down the marble stairs at our apartment block, but when she got to hospital something else happened to her and she had a stroke which meant she couldn't walk or talk and was sent to a convalescent hospital to get better. She'd now been there for well over a year and nobody knew if she would come home again. This meant that there were no parents to look after Hilde and me, so we stayed at Oma's house for her to take care of us. She and Opi were teaching us our lessons. Between them they knew so much. Hilde read and drew of an afternoon, and I played the piano.

Last year, for Hilde's eighth birthday, 9th November 1939, we went to visit Hilde's Mama. The war had just started, and we were frightened to be away from Arkadien. The hospital was in the countryside. We went by car and travelled for two hours up into some hills. The building was on one level, it was large, white and airy with many glass windows and doors. It stood in the middle of an expansive lawn with flower beds and many benches sheltered under ancient trees. Some trees were the weeping sort whose branches leaned over to touch the grass, like the one in the park by our apartment that Hilde and I used to hide in when we were little. The building and grounds were surrounded by a forest of pine trees that covered the hills as far as I could see. Aeroplanes flying above us broke the silence as we stood in the tranquil garden.

A nurse wearing a tall white starched headdress, a long white dress and blue belt led us briskly through the building. Hilde's Mama was sitting inside in a brown winged chair. Glass doors opened into a small courtyard with a view of the grounds and her bed had been pushed outside. Elsa was thinner than she used to be, I noticed grey streaks in her hair that someone had tied back into a knot. Slowly, using a walking aid, she stood to greet us and smiled. Hilde and I both ran to her because we were so happy to see her, it had been so long. Wrapping our arms around her legs, we buried our heads in the folds of her dressing gown.

'Be careful, kinder,' the nurse said. 'Your Mama has only just mastered standing up.'

We let go. Elsa slowly sat back down in the soft chair with a little sigh.

'Ah, leibchens, you have grown so big,' she whispered so faintly it was hard to hear her.

It was so difficult talking with her. She put her hand to her throat and pushed on the outside of her voice-box. This somehow supported her neck and meant she could project her voice with greater volume, and we could hear her voice a little better, though her speech was a little slurred. Oma tried to speak to her about me and what we should do as nobody knew where my Mama and Papa were, but it took Elsa so long to answer that Oma did not pursue this.

A doctor in a white coat, with slicked down black hair, came into the room holding some papers. Oma explained that she was Elsa's mother and asked when she could come home. The doctor explained that as soon as Elsa could walk again, and he was convinced she would, she would be discharged from hospital. She had been unconscious after the stroke for some time and the body takes time to get back to normal. Her speech was getting better each day, she was making huge progress and her eyesight had recovered but she was still very tired and needed to sleep once or twice in the daytime.

'In fact, now is the time for her nap,' he said kindly, looking at a chart on the wall. 'Let us get you settled, Elsa, then you can all say goodbye for today.'

He pulled over a wheelchair and helped Elsa into it. After wheeling her into the garden, he and the nurse held her steady while she eased herself into bed. They covered her up with many blankets, including one like a hood over her head, and the nurse put a long pottery hot water bottle wrapped in a towel under the covers by her feet. It was very cold outside but there was a blue sky, and the strong smell of the pine trees made the air feel clean.

'She is getting the very best treatment here, lots of fresh air, sitz baths, mud treatments, herbal enemas, hydrotherapy, infusions and massages and nourishing food to encourage her body to fight back after the stroke, as well as medication and physiotherapy of course. She has done very well and improved so much. I am sure she will be back with you all soon. '

He left. We all kissed Hilde's Mama goodbye. Hilde didn't want to leave her.

We passed a convoy of tanks, ten of them I counted. Oma said they had just come from a nearby factory where they were made and would be going into battle soon. Hilde was tearful as she had expected her Mama to be as she used to be and not as unwell as she still seemed. She couldn't bear another Christmas without her Mama. Pushing down my own sadness, I held her hands and tried to soothe her. Eventually, we both fell into a restless sleep until we returned to Leipzig.

Hilde's Papa had visited Oma and Opi's to see Hilde most weeks since we had been there. The first time, we sat and had a meal together. Raoul still lived in the apartment on Friedrichstrasse, so when we began eating, I asked him if he could check to see if Mama and Papa had come back to our apartment.

'No, Morrie, I can't do that. I don't know where your parents are,' he said. He did not look at me.

The next week I asked him again, 'Please could you just look inside our apartment?'

'No, no, no!' he barked as he got up from the table, scraping his chair on the stone floor before it tumbled to the ground. He quickly picked it up and roughly pushed it under the table. He walked around in a circle pushing his hand through his hair.

'This is impossible!' he said. 'What am I to do? I should have him removed from here immediately. If anyone finds out about this...?'

Then he stood still, looked at me and said, 'Get him out!' He then said something about 'this situation being dangerous' for us all.

Opi said, 'Go to your room, Morrie.'

I crept upstairs but I could hear Opi and Hilde's Papa talking loudly and they sounded angry.

Then I heard Raoul shout, 'Hilde!' That was because Hilde had left the table and followed me upstairs to the bedroom.

After that, I always stayed out of the living room when he came, but Hilde would sit at the table with her father, Oma and Opi, because he only came to see her, and she knew he loved her and that he was a little lost and missed his wife. I seemed to make him angry.

Oma would always come up to the bedroom after he'd gone. She would sit on the bed with her arms around us both and read a poem or tell us a story before tucking us into bed.

It wasn't too bad being on my own when Hilde's Papa came. We knew which days he would be coming so Opi would organise an activity for me to do in his workshop, sorting out his nails or cleaning brushes and then I would have something to look forward to. Sometimes I would just do more practice on the piano.

Shortly after we came here with Hilde's Mama more than a year ago, farmer Gunther, who lives next door, gave Hilde and me a baby budgerigar. Opi had made a cage that was to be the budgerigar's home. He had painted the cage a pretty bright blue with a yellow nest box and a yellow wire rose with a hook on top. He didn't have many paint colours to choose from, but we liked that they matched the little bird. We spent a lot of time watching her. We decided she was a girl and, anyway, as Hilde had chosen the name Froh, which means joyful, it sounded like a girl's name. Hilde called her Froh-Froh.

One day, Oma had been gone all day and we didn't see her even at bedtime, which was very unusual, and Opi had to put us to bed. He told us a story about how he had grown up on a farm not far from here and how every August he would help gather in the hay. He got to ride on top of a wooden wagon pulled by two horses and, on the last day of cutting, they would all sit around a fire in a circle, in a field of stubble, eating, drinking and singing traditional songs, to celebrate getting the harvest in.

The next day we heard Oma talking with Opi. She was crying and he was raising his voice, but we didn't know what was happening. Later, Hilde's Papa arrived but not on the day we expected. We were sent to our room. We sat on the top stair of the second floor where we couldn't be seen but we couldn't hear much either. After a while we heard the front door close, and we knew we'd hear no more. This was a conversation we were not meant to be privy to.

The next day, both Hilde and I were cleaning out Froh-Froh's cage. We had spread lots of newspapers across the table to empty the droppings onto before replacing the paper at the bottom of the cage. We did this every week. Gunther had told us it was a big responsibility looking after a living creature, so we took the job seriously. We both loved Froh-Froh and cared for her has best we could.

'Sit down, kinder,' said Opi, who had been listening to the man on the radio talking about the war, 'I have something that I must tell you.'

Hilde's Papa had told Opi and Oma that they could not keep me at their house. I was a Jew, and it was against the law. I'd lived here for more than a year but I hadn't gone out of the house so they hoped no-one knew I was here. If I was discovered, they would be arrested. Hilde's Papa would lose his job and might also be arrested, and I would be taken away.

Oma had discovered the names of some of my relatives who lived on the other side of the city. Yesterday, she spent the day looking for anyone with the name Silbermann who would be willing to look after me until I could be reunited with Mama and Papa.

She told us how she'd found an old directory in the library listing merchants in the city. She then spoke to a Jewish jeweller who she vaguely knew. He was no longer allowed to work and was secretly staying in a house of his former cleaner, Oma's best friend. The two women had shared secrets all their lives and would never betray each other. She asked him if he knew the whereabouts of my Papa's family. With the little information she gleaned, she eventually found an address believed to be the home of Papa's cousin, Jacob, who I think I met once. She visited Jacob's house but, along with the rest of the street, it was burnt down and there was no one to ask about who lived there or where the inhabitants had gone.

My entire family seemed to have disappeared. There was just me left here now.

Chapter 2

Leipzig

December 1940

ERNST

Ernst Grauman lifted the lid of Clara Silbermann's piano. Although there was a book of musical notation on the upstand, he began playing and did not look at this music. The music he played was Chopin's Nocturne Op 9 No.2. He closed his eyes and was lost in the reverie of the moment. He knew this so well, he played freely with ease and an obvious love for this familiar piece.

He had not intended being a soldier of any kind, but Germany had changed. He'd been taught at home with a governess. His mother had some vague hope that he would be a gentleman like the people that surrounded her when she was growing up. He had been sickly as a child, and the rigours of normal school were deemed too much for him. His mother had inherited the large house they lived in. He loved books and playing the piano. Once his mother had taught him all she knew on the piano, his parents decided to employ a piano teacher. He excelled at academic work, but his passion was music.

He was taught for several years by Frau Mensch who visited daily, but by the time he was twelve it was apparent that he had the ability and dedication to become a professional musician and required greater experiences. He was taught by many visiting masters who each imparted their own knowledge. He listened and learned and was happy to consider different approaches to music. The more he learned, the more he was open to new ideas. He was inventive and imaginative but was fascinated too by the tradition and scholarship employed by the great composers.

When he was eighteen, Ernst enrolled at the University of Leipzig. In the second year, he was placed under the pupillage of Professor Leo Friedman, fondly known by all his students as Prof. Ernst was stretched in ways he had not expected. He was popular and enjoyed collaborating with others in all aspects of college life. He worked with many musicians on innovative compositions and played in ensembles as well as constantly perfecting a repertoire as a solo pianist. Life at university was challenging and novel for this young man who had lived isolated from the company of other young people. His weekly tutorials with the Prof became more and more intense. He keenly wanted to learn, and the Prof singled him out as an exceptionally talented composer and performing musician. They formed a symbiotic relationship born out of a shared passion to perfect whatever music was being studied. It would not be long before Ernst was getting the attention of other prestigious centres of musical excellence.

Over the years, he became stronger and was no longer the sickly boy of his childhood. There had been a family meeting with his father and uncles, and it was decided that a career in the army would be the next experience he should have. Ernst knew he had no say in this decision. His mother had always fought his corner, moulded his future and up until now his father was content with this until matters of state became serious enough that every household in Germany felt an obligation to encourage their young men to become serving soldiers and the Grauman family, who were leaders of the community, intended to play their part to secure the future of the country.

While acknowledging that music was important and that his son, Ernst, had exceptional talent, his father was determined that his son should do his duty, for the honour of the family as well as the country.

'You are a man now, Ernst, and Germany requires people of your calibre to do the work that is needed. One day, when our country doesn't have so many enemies trying to destroy us, and when Germany is victorious, you can resume a career in music. Tomorrow, you must report to the Wehrmacht,' he said.

Ernst had said farewell to Professor Friedman and his fellow students and promised to stay in touch. That was two years ago. He had been lucky, his analytical brain and genteel demeanour meant that he was a valuable staff member who was not only excellent at overseeing logistics and strategical accounting within the war machine, but he was often asked to travel and to represent his department at conferences and important meetings across the country.

He had never been asked to work in the front line or in any sort of combat situation. He felt grateful of his abilities because he was not one of life's natural soldiers, and working hard in his department brought a certain level of success and satisfaction. He had been promoted twice, which unnerved him a little as the more responsibility he was given, and the more men there were under his control, the more likely it was that he might be asked to oversee men on active service. A bright future was predicted for Ernst, but music was never far from his thoughts.

He was deeply saddened when he learned of Prof Friedman's death and, secretly, he made it his business to find out about the Prof's family. He'd heard rumours about his Blüthner piano being rescued. The piano was a wondrous thing, the envy of all the students at the university and it was considered a great honour if you were allowed to play it. The trail went cold, and for many months he heard nothing of Clara and wondered if the family had left the city.

Ernst had met Clara, the Prof's daughter, several times at the university and had played duets with her in her father's study. She was older than him and married, but so beautiful that he'd developed a crush on her which he kept a guarded secret, never mentioning this to anyone, though he'd suspected that Prof was aware of this.

Nine months ago, he had moved into Friedrichstrasse and there it was, the piano, a mahogany Blüthner, made in this city about twenty years before, each key seasoned with a unique wisdom by the fingers of the Prof and by many wonderful visiting pianists, by chosen students at the university, and by him and Clara Freidman too.

The department for the resettlement of people in Leipzig had grown so that there were many police and army personnel attached to it. Jews were being moved into houses that were clustered in the same area of the city. Houses believed to be more suitable for officials and regular Germans of Aryan stock were cleared of Jews to make way for Germans. Herr Müller, who had long wanted the Silbermanns out, was delighted they had gone. He was not allowed, though, to rent the apartment and had to wait for the reassignment of the tenancy.

Ernst still wanted to locate Clara Silbermann but by pure chance – when he wasn't actually looking for her – he encountered Raoul who happened to know both Ben and Clara Silbermann. Ernst was looking for a new apartment, a reward as part of his promotion, and the reason why he was directed to Raoul.

Raoul told Ernst that two years before, just after Kristallnacht, both Silbermanns had disappeared, assumed killed or perhaps sent to work camps. Raoul had looked into lists of deportees after his wife had begged him to but he was busy, there were too many Jews being moved around to know who was who, and he had to be careful not to appear in collaboration with any Jewish faction. Resultantly, Raoul's investigation was not extensive but was just enough to placate his wife that he had looked.

It was nearly Christmas, and despite the war, there was bound to be music of some description playing in Augustusplatz today. Later, people would don hats and coats, brave the cold, and soak up the Christmas spirit. Ernst hoped there would be joy in the air despite the war, and perhaps even some festive stalls outside the Gewandhaus too, though he didn't know what they might sell and knew that sweet treats were unlikely. Tomorrow there would be a concert in Thomaskirke where Bach's Christmas Oratorio would be performed. He had attended this every year since he was a small child. It was both sacred and a profound musical experience which Ernst felt summed up the essence of the season for him and evoked wonderful childhood memories. It was composed by Bach, the choirmaster of the St Thomas Boys Choir in Leipzig for thirty years, who had written it to be performed in this church.

Leipzig boasted a musical heritage that made it the envy of every great city in the world; only a handful of other cities could claim so many associations with the great composers, conductors and performers as this 'city of music' which it was frequently called. There were records of musical performances in Leipzig going back 1300 years. Ernst knew he was blessed to live somewhere that had nurtured so much music over the centuries. Johanne Sebastian Bach, Felix Mendelssohn, Robert and Clara Schuman and Richard Wagner were just a few of the illustrious musicians that gave this town its reputation, though the work of many other great composers were regularly performed in various auditoria by a diverse range of musical groups, such was its appeal and kudos. It was a city to be proud of. Ernst was part of its musical tradition, and it was part of him.

Since the restrictions on Jews in the city in recent years, there had been distinct discouragement of performing the works of Jewish composers. This was followed by a total Nazi ban on the performance of Jewish music, or indeed any acknowledgement that it had ever existed. On the other hand, there was an emphasis and enthusiasm for performing German works. Bach's 'Christmas Oratorio' was truly German, it was venerated and safe.

Ernst heard a noise and looked up from the keys. He smiled and opened one of the books in front of him on the music stand. It read 'Mozart Eine Kleine Nachtmusik, Piano, Four Hands.'

'So, Morrie, sit next to me and we can try this one today, this is a duet I played with your Mama.'

Chapter 3

Leipzig

Christmas 1940

ELSA

'Mama, help me!' wailed Hilde as the bird flapped around the apartment, banging into walls, and eventually settling on top of a tall cupboard.

Hilde had been talking to Froh-Froh non-stop because she wanted her to be able to talk to us. I didn't think Hilde realised that it would never be a real conversation, but it kept her happy and occupied her time. She had succeeded in teaching Froh-Froh to say good morning and night night and because the bird had heard it spoken so often she had learnt to say Mama all by herself.

Hilde was able to put her hand in the cage and retrieve the bird without it panicking. Froh-Froh was almost at the stage of sitting contentedly on Hilde's finger. She was teaching the budgerigar, with some success, to come to her when she whistled. She wanted the bird to be able to fly outside the cage and come back when she called.

They were becoming friends, and Hilde was kind and diligent in her care of the little creature. Today, though, there was loud gunfire and shouting outside in the street just as Hilde opened the cage door and the little bird took fright.

'Don't worry, leibchen, she will come down when she is ready, she won't come to harm, all the windows and doors are closed. Leave the door of the cage open and she will find her way back,' I reassured my daughter, who was becoming upset.

It was Christmas Eve and I had been back home now for six months. We went out today and brought back as much greenery as Hilde and I could carry to decorate the apartment. We had our little wooden Christmas ornaments that we put out each year, and tonight Raoul would bring home a fir tree we'd decorate together with lights and a little tinsel. The tinsel was very old and had only a little of the sparkly strands left, but tinsel was something that hadn't been available for the last few years. Raoul would also bring in fish, I hoped, a carp if he could get one, for our dinner and I'd made traditional stollen for later. I couldn't buy marzipan or nuts anywhere, so made a mock paste with some bread, sugar I'd saved, almond essence and melted lard. I had just a few pieces of candied fruit which I'd cut very small, but I was pleased; it looked as good as any stollen I'd ever seen. I hoped Raoul would not be told he must go to work tomorrow.

I now walked a little slower than I used to before the accident, and I have a slight limp. I spoke a little quieter too, but I now looked like my old self and didn't slur my words anymore. I worked to get stronger each day and was so pleased to be home. I liked to walk in the fresh air and there were no restrictions on me going out and about, but I would not be returning to work. The factory I'd worked at no longer made textiles but armaments, for the war effort, which was heavy work and too much for me.

Everything had changed, though, in my life. My husband was still busy with his work and neither Hilde nor I saw much of him. There'd been upset in our family between Raoul and my parents, who stepped in to look after both Hilde and Morrie when I was away for what ended up being a year and a half. I didn't know any of what happened to begin with, I was too ill. Once a little better, nobody told me, as they didn't want to worry me. I had to fill in the gaps and heard different versions of the story, though the outcome was the same.

The Jewish situation had now worsened further still. Every week there were new rules. Thousands of Jews had been transported out of the city. I heard all the time about people being taken away, but nobody knew where they were sent, and we didn't ask questions. Most Jewish owned businesses were closed down or taken over by government authorities. There was now a curfew where Jews were not allowed out after sunset. There were soldiers on the street all the time, moving in convoys or challenging people on the street, asking for papers or going into houses where they suspected Jews were hiding. The restrictions affected us all because we were not allowed to have contact with Jews. Neither I nor Hilde could contact Morrie, even though he was just next door. Nobody bothered us Aryan Germans, but our children were expected to tell their teachers if they thought their parents had collaborated with Jews or gypsies. So many people loved the Führer and our children were encouraged to take up his ideas for a brave new Germany.

My parents had risked being arrested for harbouring Morrie. Before I came home, Raoul instructed them to hand him over to the local authorities, otherwise they'd be taken away themselves. He hadn't informed the authorities but he would eventually be forced to. He told them there were people in our neighbourhood, like the Müller's downstairs, who knew that Hilde and Morrie were always together, and it wouldn't be long until someone came knocking, and they would also point a finger at Raoul for not doing his duty and reporting collaborators.

However, when Raoul went to collect Morrie from Arkadien, he'd disappeared. Raoul knew how caring they were and that they couldn't have lost the child. He guessed Morrie must have been hidden somewhere, but my parents never admitted to that.

Oma and Opi were distraught because they couldn't risk being arrested because of Hilde, but they wanted to save the boy too. Raoul went berserk and told Hilde she must come back to our apartment to live with him. Hilde had refused, saying he would always be at work and she was happy where she was, and anyway, maybe Morrie would be coming back soon and she must be here when he returned. She had not been told where he was, for her own safety, all she knew was that he was safe.

Raoul went to her bedroom at the top of the house, dragging her behind him up the stairs.

'Come on Hilde, walk please! Stop being difficult, help me get your things together, you are coming home with me!'

He found her clothes and started to pack her suitcase. Opi came up the stairs into the little room to remonstrate with him.

'You cannot take Hilde, you can't look after her if you are working, she won't be safe, she is too young and we promised Elsa we would protect the children.'

Opi said he believed it was the mention of me that made Raoul stop. No-one doubted that Raoul missed me and, although I had regained consciousness, he still worried that I would never recover.

Raoul slammed the suitcase onto the bed in a fit of pique, accidently tipping most of the contents onto the floor, he swung round to face Opi who thought at that moment Raoul may be about to strike him, but Raoul restrained himself. He stood still without speaking, looked at them both, grandfather and granddaughter, the father and daughter of his dearest Elsa, then turned and went down the stairs two at a time and out the front door.

Two hours later, there was a knock on the door. Two policemen from a department seeking out Jews in hiding – not connected to where Raoul worked – barged in, demanding Morrie be brought out. Opi said that he was not there, but one policeman said that he had information that Morrie was being hidden at Arkadien. He pushed Opi aside and began opening doors, looking in cupboards. The second policeman stood in the kitchen, watching Opi and Oma who he motioned to sit while his colleague went up all three floors, slamming doors and pulling down objects so they crashed to the floor. They could hear his rough movements as he rushed around the floorboards above.

Hilde was in bed, and she woke up to find this man in her bedroom. She screamed and came running down the stairs to find her grandmother who she clung to, sobbing. Oma was so angry, but she knew she had to tread carefully.

'We know that he is here,' the first policeman said. 'Bring him now or we will take the girl.' He made a lunge towards Hilde. Opi instantly retaliated by raising his fist to hit the policeman but Oma, who was a strong woman, intuitively guessed his reaction and with a vice-like grip pulled her husband back. The officer dropped his arm to his side, adjusting his tunic he stood motionless, looking at Opi with a combination of malice and hatred. 'You will not make a fool of me, old man'.

My grandparents had to come up with some explanation. Somehow, they had to protect everyone, and it was Oma who answered. She said that Morrie had been with them after his parent's disappearance but that she knew he couldn't stay, and she felt it was important to find some of his own family. She said that after doing some research and asking around she had discovered a Herr Jacob Silbermann in a district north of here and he had happily agreed to take Morrie, who was his nephew. Morrie was now living with that family who she understood were hoping to emigrate to Palestine.

'So, little girl, tell me what did you and Morrie do today? Did you play games or climb trees or maybe you played the piano together? Well!' The policeman spoke in a cajoling, sarcastic way, trying to catch her out.

'I haven't seen Morrie. He had to go away, and I don't play the piano,' Hilde replied, realising the man thought she was a naive child, but my daughter was every inch his match.

'I hear what you say. I do not believe you but give me this address you speak of, and I will see if what you say is true. But I think that I will be back.' He clicked his heels, turned, motioned to the other policeman, who had not said a word, and they left.

Raoul told me what happened next. It was a total chance meeting, but he thought it was a solution to the worsening problem of what to do with Morrie. He was not aware of the visit of the policemen to Arkadien, though once he was told what had happened, he suspected young Müller, from apartment 1 Friedrichstrasse, was trying to make a name for himself to impress the party, by seeking out Jews in hiding and had finally found out the address of Arkadien.

Ernst Grauman, a young Wehrmacht officer looking for accommodation, went to Raoul's department to see what was available. By then, the Silbermann's apartment had been empty for well over a year and there was no sign they would be back. It had been requisitioned and had recently been released to let and was waiting for the right applicant to move in. It was reserved for selected personnel. This young officer fitted the criteria of a potential tenant, and he went to view the apartment with Raoul, as it was next-door. It was fortunate because this gave them the opportunity to talk.

Ernst Grauman was totally overwhelmed when he went into the Silbermann's apartment. It was left exactly as it was when they'd lived there, as if someone had popped out to the shops and would be returning: books open on the table, flowers, now dead, in a vase, underwear strung out on a line to dry in the bathroom and washed dishes left to drain before being put away. This was just what had happened here, of course.

Grauman admitted to Raoul that he knew the Silbermann family and had been looking for them. One by one he picked up photographs, of Clara dressed in a ballet tutu when she was a in her teens; Ben, Clara and Morrie at a funfair; and a picture of Professor Friedman holding a new-born baby, that Ernst assumed was Clara's son.

Ernst revealed how he'd known Clara and her father and was himself a trained pianist and composer. The piano in the apartment was one he'd played before and something he'd always admired and coveted. He opened the lid that covered the keys, found middle C and played that one note. He carefully lowered the lid and stood motionless, seemingly deep in thought, for a minute or so.

He turned to face Raoul. He wanted to know all about the family and where they were now. Raoul told him what he knew, which was not very much. Ben had disappeared on Kristallnacht and Clara the following evening. Then he asked about Morrie. Raoul was evasive. He realised that he was sitting on the fence, trying to protect Morrie, Opi and Oma, but he was also trying to protect his job and reputation. He was cursing his in-laws for putting him in such a difficult situation and Morrie for even existing!

Ernst did remember that Clara had a son and he wanted to know more about the boy. He seemed to be obsessed with the family, Raoul thought, Clara especially. Raoul told him that Morrie was the same age as his little girl and maybe because they were standing there next to the piano, it reminded Raoul of the music played in this apartment in the past and so he mentioned that Morrie's passion was playing the piano and that his Mama had been teaching him.

Ernst smiled broadly.

'Bring him to me,' Ernst said.

'But I am not sure where he is,' said Raoul. 'Why do you want me to get him?' he asked, a little hesitantly, as Ernst out-ranked him and it was not Raoul's job to ask such things. He didn't want to put himself or the boy in danger.

'I shall teach him,' Ernst said. 'Yes, I shall teach him the pianoforte! I shall take the apartment.'

'I shall have it cleaned and cleared of furniture and all the personal items,' Raoul said his heart racing.

'No! Please don't, leave it just as it is.'

When Raoul returned to my parents, he told them Morrie must go to live with Ernst Grauman. They were unhappy and didn't feel it was safe for Morrie, but eventually they agreed that if this officer was really interested in Morrie – bearing in mind that he already knew he was Jewish – that was a safer option than handing him over to the authorities. Perhaps this Ernst Grauman would protect him? Raoul told them that he apparently knew and liked Clara which they all hoped meant he would not hurt Morrie. They could not keep Morrie at Arkadien or keep him safe in hiding much longer. This might be the answer.

Opi and Oma insisted that Raoul come back later in the day; they didn't want him knowing where the boy was and Opi was keen no-one would be implicated in this cover up. Raoul said he would return at 5pm when it would be dark. It was early spring and luckily there would be hardly any moon. All they hoped was that the police did not return before Raoul collected Morrie.

Opi had to explain to Morrie that this may be a good opportunity, and he had to convince old Gunther, who was hiding him, that this was their best option, because sooner or later they would be found out and the repercussions were likely to be severe.

Once Morrie understood that this man was a friend of his mother, that he would be going back to his old apartment, and that Herr Grauman was a pianist who wanted to teach him, Morrie was happy. It was difficult, though, to explain to him that he was also a Nazi, because Morrie didn't really know what this was. Morrie understood the concept of good people; this meant for him: the Jews he knew, his family and friends, us Francks, Opi, Oma and Gunther; and the bad people he believed were all the other Germans out there that his Mama and me spoke of, those who hated Jews, those who might attack him, shoot him or take him away, people like the Pied Piper in story books. Sometimes though, he thought that if he was taken away, he might be taken to a place where he would meet his Mama and Papa again, but it was very confusing.

Giving Morrie into the care of Ernst Grauman seemed the best solution in the circumstances. Gunther was not so happy and believed that he could have hidden Morrie indefinitely. Opi thanked his dear friend for all his help but said the decision was made. Neither Gunther nor Opi agreed with the Nazi's policies, but it was always prudent to keep that information to yourself.

Gunther had said to Opi on several occasions, 'I will fight injustice when I see it, I am a true German!'

To which Opi would remind him, 'But you are an old man, Gunther, an old German, you don't have the strength or the speed, you would just get arrested or shot!'

'Take me, I don't care. I am ashamed of what this Hitler has done to our country, I have had a good life!' Gunther would retort.

Of course, there was no point in fighting the current regime, they were both too old but they had their opinions and objected in small ways when they could. A little boy's life was at stake here, though, and they had to be sensible.

Raoul collected Morrie later that evening when it was dark and there was no moon in the sky and took him to Ernst Grauman in Friedrichstrasse.

Oma and Hilde slept in the same bed that night, cuddled together because they were scared for Morrie's future and missed him already.

Chapter 4

Leipzig

27 December 1940

MORRIE

Two days ago was Christmas Day, but it was also Hanukkah. Hilde lit a candle and placed it in the window of her bedroom where I could see it, she knew I would like it and this year there would be no celebrations.

I had been perfecting Beethoven's Piano sonata no 10. I started teaching myself this at Arkadien but since I'd been back at our old apartment Ernst had been giving me lessons. I now lived with him, and he was my teacher. He went to work in the daytime but came back as often as he could to play the piano and to instruct me. He thought that I was a good pianist. I learned several pieces of music that I could play well, some by heart too. I didn't know him before, but he was a friend of my mother's. He talked about her and he too wished she was here, and so I trusted him.

When he went out, Frau Müller who lived downstairs, had to stay in the apartment with me. She cleaned and cooked food for us but I didn't like her. She smiled and fawned over Ernst when he was around and did whatever he requested but she hated me. I showed her the leather music case that Ernst gave me for a Christmas present. She said, 'Why did you get that! You are a Jew. You don't celebrate Christmas. Christmas is for Christians.'

I was very happy to get the case and put my own copies of music inside it. It made me feel grown up and I was proud of it, which pleased Ernst. I didn't understand all about Jews and Christians and, although I was a Jew and we had our special holidays when we went to the synagogue, we also celebrated at Christmas by having time off and eating special food like everyone does, though we didn't get presents then or go to church. Ernst said I must forget about Jewish festivals because he didn't know anything about them and, from now on, we would only be celebrating Christian ones.

I was told to go to my room from two o'clock until three o'clock each afternoon, to rest. I was supposed to lie on the bed, with a book if I wanted, as Ernst didn't want me practising the piano all day and exhausting myself. I could not go to school, Jews weren't allowed to go anymore, so I played the piano and sometimes Ernst gave me books that he wanted me to read. He gave me some poetry by Goethe, but I struggled to read some of the words and Ernst said it didn't matter, he just wanted me to get used to this sort of thing and said one day I would read great German literature. He was fine with me reading all my children's books off the bookshelves for the moment. I was so pleased to be able to look through the books I'd looked at with Mama as well as my own children's books.

Frau Müller always went back to her apartment for at least a quarter of an hour when I was meant to be resting. She said she must prepare food for the family supper. During these times, if Hilde was not at school, we could meet on the landing and exchange quiet whispers, but we had to be very careful.

Hanakkah, the Jewish festival of lights, should be a joyous time. I knew it had already started and lasted for more than a week. If Mama and Papa were here, we would be celebrating, we would see friends and there would be feasting and gifts. I knew that when Mama and Papa could return, they would come to the apartment and I would be here waiting for them, that was why I was happy to leave Arkadien. Ernst had been kind to me and loved playing the piano as much as I did, but every night I prayed that Mama and Papa would come and find me.

I didn't like it that I could not play with Hilde anymore. Both Ernst and Herr Franck had forbidden it. So we devised a way of communicating with each other. It was our very special secret that nobody knew about, and we had to be careful that it stayed that way.

At the back of our apartment block, where the two wings of the building stood on each side of Herr Müller's garden. My bedroom and Hilde's had windows that faced each other and could be opened. The Müllers owned this building and kept all three apartments on the ground floor, although they lived in the front one away from us. Herr Müller brought items to be stored in these other apartments. I knew this because Hilde watched him carrying suitcases and bundles of clothes or bedding in through the downstairs lobby. He carried in armfuls of fur coats too. She saw him when she was sitting on the stairs in the dark waiting for her Papa to return from work one evening. A light from the storeroom shone on Herr Müller and she could see his lumbering frame and the shine on his greased down hair that was stuck to his balding head.

The apartment above Hilde was occupied by a very old man who kept the shutters of his window closed and probably didn't use that room. The apartment above me was empty because the officer who lived there had gone to fight in the war.

When Hilde was home, she opened her window a few inches to tell me she was there. Only someone in the garden could see us but we always checked that no-one was there. When Frau Müller went downstairs in the afternoon I'd lift up my window too. Sometimes I could see Hilde there and we'd both wave. Hilde was allowed to play with a ball or marbles on our landing, so when we both knew it was safe, she'd leave her apartment, open the front door gently and quickly come into my apartment. She always told her Mama she was playing on the landing, but sometimes I thought Elsa knew she had been speaking to me, though she never commented.

Some days we were really nervous, usually because we weren't sure how long Frau Müller had been downstairs, so then, although Hilde and I could talk, I would stand in my apartment doorway just in case we had to move fast. If we heard the Müller's apartment door click shut, we knew she was coming back.

Today, though, Hilde came across the landing holding something out in front of her, it was cupped in her hands. She said, 'I have a surprise for you, Morrie, for Hanukkah, a Hanukkah present! Get inside quickly!'

She pushed me into my hallway, and I turned the catch so the door locked shut. She opened her fingers and there, nestled in her hands, was Froh-Froh. The bird sat still and calm, its shiny eyes inspecting me. Hilde told me she'd taught her a trick. The bird would come to her when she made a low whistling sound. I knew she had practised this for months and was excited see it had finally worked.

'Watch, Morrie,' she said as she let the bird go.

Froh-Froh flapped her wings, free to fly where she wanted, up onto the chandelier. She flew up and down the hall, around our heads, into the kitchen and back again. Then Hilde made this low whistle which was more of a blowing noise, as she couldn't whistle properly, and Froh-Froh came down and sat on her head. Hilde delved in her pocket and gave her a seed as a reward.

'Good Froh-Froh!' she said.

'That's like a magic trick, Hilde!' I exclaimed. I loved this little bird and had missed not being able to play with her each day or clean her out or give her food. I had only seen Froh-Froh when Hilde held up her cage to show me from her bedroom window and I was a little envious of the time they had together. I had lost that part of my life.

Just then there was a loud bang on the door, 'Silbermann, what are you up to in there? Who is in there with you?'

It was Martin Müller, who was now in the army but was on leave and was staying at the Müller's apartment.

Hilde and I quickly went into my bedroom as quietly as we could.

'Let me in, Silbermann, my mother wants me to look after you for a while, she has to go out. Who are you talking to?'

'No-one, I was singing.'

'Let me in, come on you pathetic little Jew, open up!'

'No, go away!'

'What do you mean, NO? I tell you; you will let me in, or you will be sorry.'

'Go away. I am alright on my own.' I went up to the front door to put the security chain across it.

'Open this door now or I will break it down!'

'I shall tell Herr Grauman that you were going to break down his door and you called me a pathetic Jew.' I didn't know what 'pathetic' meant, but it felt wrong.

'I will be back,' Martin Müller yelled, and I could tell that he was walking away. I could hear him as he went through the swing doors and the sound of his heavy boots on the stone floor.

I rushed back to the bedroom.

'Quick, Hilde you must go!' I said.

But Hilde was not there.

Then I heard her calling Froh-Froh with her strange whistling call. She had gone into my parent's room, now Ernst's room, and was frantically looking for the little budgerigar. She was nowhere to be found, and we realised that she must have flown out of the window in my bedroom.

Chapter 5

Leipzig

1941

MORRIE

'I am going to teach you to be a great pianist, Max,' said Ernst. 'I believe you were born with a remarkable talent, just like your grandfather and your mother, though she did not pursue her career in music. You have just the right attitude, you remind me of myself when I was your age. I think you could have a great future.'

My name was Max now. Ernst said if he kept me close to him, he could protect me but I mustn't draw attention to myself. I saw in the newspaper that I was supposed to wear a yellow star with the word Jew on it, but I didn't think I would have to. Being Jewish was really bad, it was against the true God and against everything the new Germany stood for, Ernst said. He told me I might die if I told people I was a Jew. I told him that I once changed my name to Max for just one day and he said Max was an excellent name and from now onwards I should be called Max Grauman and would say I was his nephew and his apprentice too. I would never say I was Jewish.

I was able to go out everywhere now. No-one stopped me or looked at me as they did when I was with Mama or with Elsa Franck because now I was with Ernst. People commented on my blond hair and blue eyes, which they always have done. People saluted Ernst, opened doors for us and pulled out chairs for us to sit on. There were cafés we sometimes ate in near the platz or at the officer's club. We had good food like meat and potatoes or sauerkraut and sausages. At first, I refused to eat sausages because it was pig meat and pig meat was dirty but Ernst reminded me I must put aside Jewish rules at the moment because I no longer lived as a Jew.

Yesterday, we went to the Blüthner factory and were allowed to go in and watch men working on different processes and making different parts that would eventually be put together to make pianos. This was where our piano had been made many years ago. Ernst knew one of the designers, Josef, who was a friend of my grandfather, Professor Friedman, and this man was happy to let us into the workshops and see how the instruments were made. It was a huge building and there was the smell of wood and shellac in the workshop, and I thought of my father's workshop in the Bruhl and Opi's workshop at Arkadien. I loved being in these places with gifted people who made wonderful creations come to life.

We left the noise of hammering and grinding machinery and were taken to the back of the building, through many corridors, until we reached a door with a series of padlocks opened by Josef. Inside, I was allowed to see the latest grand piano that had just been made. It was ordered by one of the country's leaders for his country retreat. It had an ornate carved music stand, like ours, but it was bigger with more gold on it and the wood on the sides of the piano was so shiny I could see all three of us standing there reflected in its surface like a mirror. It was kept in a windowless room to protect it from sun damage it and it stood on white cotton sheets to prevent grit flying up and scratching it. It was awaiting its final check and last polish before being transported. Just like our piano it would have to be disassembled and wrapped in blankets for the move. Two men would make the long journey with the piano in a padded lorry. At its final destination they would assemble it ready for famous people, including film stars and royalty, to play it – because our leaders mixed with these people.

Josef looked at me and said, 'Listen, young man, I know you are respectful, but I must ask you a question. I want to show you something remarkable, but you must promise me that you will not touch it at all? Can you do that?'

I nodded, not really understanding why he asked this as I hadn't touched this special piano. I wondered what he was going to show me that was so remarkable it was greater than this.

Josef beckoned us over to the piano lift, which was enormous, up onto the top floor of the building. The space had Persian carpets, large vases of fresh flowers on stands, north facing windows draped with elaborate fabric, and four shiny new pianos. It was the salesroom where the public could purchase a brand-new piano, though they entered through a big glass door at the opposite end of the room. As many people were so poor now because of the war, I considered this to be very extravagant and glamorous and I didn't know what sort of people would buy these pianos. There must be people somewhere, I thought, who had a lot of money.

In the middle of the room on a carpeted platform was an unusual grand piano. It had light coloured sides and top. The legs and edging were made of shiny white metal. It was surrounded by glass panels forming a barrier; from what Josef said, it was to stop people touching it. There was room to enter the area inside the screens, which was for select people only, I supposed.

'Is this it?' asked Ernst, marvelling at the piano in wonder.

'If you would like, Ernst, I would be honoured if you played something,' Josef said.

Ernst grinned, 'If you are sure?'

'It was meant to be played, and we hope it will be here for decades to come. Play whatever you want, my dear friend. It was made for hands like yours.'

Josef and I stood and watched as Ernst carefully slid between the glass panels and pulled the piano stool out, sat down and adjusted the seat until he was comfortable. No sheet music was necessary as he knew so many pieces by heart. He began slowly by testing the tone of the keys and playing a scale or two, then, when he was ready, he launched into Franz Liszt's 'Grand Galop', a fast and exciting composition. With a jolt, I was transported back to a time when Mama played this piece for Hilde and me and we danced around the apartment together. I tried not to think of those days, the pain of missing the people I loved was unbearable.

Suddenly it was silent, and Ernst was standing next to me. I couldn't talk to him about the people from my old life, because Ernst said I should have no more to do with them. My mother, though, was different. He spoke about her all the time, which comforted me. I continued to hope she would soon return to the apartment.

Sensing my shift in mood, we exited the factory and Ernst took me to a nearby café for spiced apple-cake. He told me that the piano he'd just played was the most unusual piano Blüthner's had ever made. He told me about an airship, The Hindenburg, which I had heard about. It had travelled all the way from Germany, across the Atlantic Ocean, to North America. During the airship's construction, about six years ago, Herr Hitler and other government members requisitioned the Blüthner factory here in Leipzig to make a very lightweight piano that could go inside the airship for its first flight. This would show the world that travelling on the great German airship was safe and comfortable, with its restaurant and the luxury of live music on board.

It seemed an impossible task: pianos were so heavy and only something virtually weightless would allow the Hindenburg to fly. The designers at the factory came up with all sorts of plans and eventually made a beautiful fully functioning piano out of aluminium – a very lightweight metal. The metal was then covered in pigskin and, amazingly, it played with a rich, melodic sound just like their wooden pianos.

This piano was in pride of place on the airship for its first flight, leaving Germany on 4th March 1936 to cross the Atlantic. A concert was performed mid-flight, the first time ever achieved by man. The pianist on this maiden flight was Franz Wagner from Dresden, close to Leipzig, and was someone Ernst knew well. Ernst revealed he was a little envious that Franz was chosen for this honour. Franz Wagner played pieces he knew the passengers on board would enjoy: Chopin, Liszt, Beethoven and Brahms, as well as popular songs heard on the radio. The singer he accompanied was a lady who sang songs popular in America. From way above the ocean, this music was broadcast live to sixty-three radio stations around the world. As they approached America, Franz Wagner played 'The Blue Danube waltz' by Strauss, and everyone on board cheered, celebrating the successful journey of thousands of miles across the vast ocean. The piano was the star of the day. It was a momentous achievement and Germany was proud she had done it.

'Sadly though, Max, the Hindenburg caught fire and was destroyed in 1937 in America. I don't think they'll build any more airships because they aren't very stable, and I believe aeroplanes will regularly be able to fly that distance before too long.'

'I don't understand. What about the piano, Ernst, was that in the fire?'

'No,' he said. 'It did a few trips and was played by the passengers and the captain of the airship but then, maybe because it is less sturdy than an ordinary piano, they decided to put it on show at the Blüthner factory where it was made before it got damaged. I wished I could have performed on the airship, but I am pleased that – finally – today I got to play the aluminium Hindenburg piano!'

'I loved the Liszt you played today, Ernst,' I said. 'He was my mother's favourite composer, and she played his composition, Leibestraum, nearly every day. She said it took her into a world of familiarity and calm.'

'You and I are lucky to have the piano we have in our apartment. Franz Liszt once said that the Blüthner piano was the best instrument he had ever played on, so your mother chose well by playing his music.'

Chapter 6

Leipzig

1941

ELSA

Hilde hadn't been to school for many weeks now, not since we found out about Morrie. It was an unusually cold winter and we only had a little fuel left, so the apartment was rarely heated. We often wore coats and gloves indoors, and when Hilde was distressed, she and I cuddled under the blankets to warm up for an afternoon nap. I was still supposed to have a rest each day as I hadn't regained my previous strength. My mind was troubled.

I was conflicted. We were constantly told how despicable the Jews were, how they had caused Germany's financial problems and had contributed to the war. There may be truth that there was corruption within banks and big finance, which I knew nothing about, but the Jewish people I knew were just the same as everyone else. Some were friendly and some were off-hand or rude but that was the same for anyone in Leipzig whether they were Jewish or not.

I never verbalised any of these thoughts to Raoul. He toed the party line and quoted all the statements and slogans in the newspapers or on the radio and abided by all the direct orders that landed on his desk. He never let his guard down. On our living room table lay the Illustrieter Beobachter which was the Nazi Party's illustrated newspaper. This issue was called England's Guilt and explained that England started the war and showed how Jews controlled that country.

I didn't believe Raoul was a bad man, that was why I was still with him, but I feared this regime was changing him, pressing him into a homogenous mould, like thousands of other members of the Nazi Party.

My parents were not Party members and never would be, they felt the attitude of our current leaders was too rigid and didn't allow independent thought. My mother fought for the rights of women when she was a military nurse in the Great War. Women had few rights after 1918 and, in her small way, she campaigned, lobbying the authorities, for better maternity care, help for nursing mothers and better working conditions in the factories. My father, too, had been a member of a socialist trades union striving for the rights of workers until 1933, when Herr Hitler abolished all trade unions. He still helped individuals who were distressed and supported causes he could help with, though these days he had to be careful. So many things were against the law and could result in death.

On the day Froh-Froh escaped, Hilde had sat at her bedroom window, opened wide, for most of the night, calling, hoping the budgerigar would return. Both Raoul and I urged her to shut the window. We didn't know how the bird had got out but assumed Hilde had forgotten to close her window.

Winter here meant regular snow flurries. Hilde knew the bird might die in the cold if she didn't find shelter. Hilde had put a little bowl of water on the window ledge to entice the bird back, but she had to keep breaking the ice that formed on the surface as it was so cold.

Eventually, Hilde had fallen asleep on her bed still wearing her day clothes with the winter wind blowing through her open window. She'd told me the following morning how she'd woken, shivering, with stiff icy fingers before realising that Froh-Froh had, by some miracle, returned and was sitting on her head. She was overjoyed. She'd cradled the little bird in her hands and held her gently to warm her up before rushing into our bedroom. This did seem like a miracle to us all. Hilde was convinced it was down to her training sessions and all the attention she had given the budgerigar.

Gunther had told her and Morrie about budgerigars in the wild. They were always green and yellow and only blue or violet budgerigars were bred in captivity. They flew about in huge flocks. They could go many weeks without drinking any water as they had adapted to live in the Australian desert. The Aborigine people believed that nature, the landscape, and the creatures living in it were spiritual entities and that they, the indigenous people of Australia, had a duty to preserve it all by the way they lived and the rituals they performed. The budgerigars were respected by them as they could lead people to water. Gunther always wanted any birds he bred to fly outside of their cage each day, and he liked to help new owners train their little birds.

I knew that Hilde and Morrie waved to each other across the garden but until she later told me about Froh-Froh in Morrie's apartment, I hadn't realised that she had gone in there. I warned her that she must never do that again because she was putting herself in danger.

That had been in the Christmas holidays and a week or so later she returned to school. School had only resumed a few months before, though not for Morrie at all. She would always go to her room as soon as she came home – to wave to Morrie – but he did not appear. She was desperate to tell him that the little budgerigar was safe and had returned to her. Day after day she looked and waited. Morrie still did not appear, and his window was always dropped shut. Since the time the bird escaped in his apartment, Hilde had not seen him. This was uncharacteristic, and I knew she worried he was ill but neither of us thought we should knock to find out. Someone, possibly Morrie, would get into trouble if we attempted to speak with him. If only he would open his window, then she would know he was alright.

When Hilde was at school in February, haulage men appeared and began removing furniture from the Silbermann's apartment. Hilde returned home just as the removal van drove off from outside the apartment block. I was stood in the doorway to greet her, and as she came up the stairs, Herr Müller was descending them carrying two of Clara's ornate table-lamps.

'Why have you got those lamps, they aren't yours!?' Hilde said. Hilde took after me and my mother, always ready to challenge if she believed something was unfair or morally wrong.

'Mind your own business, it has nothing to do with you. You are too forthright for a child. Your parents need to discipline you,' he said. 'Get out of my way, fraulein.'

'But they belong to Herr and Frau Silbermann, you cannot take their things!' she said, her sense of injustice getting the better of her.

'Listen, girl, where they have gone, they won't be coming back. It's my apartment and anything left in it is mine. Now move along or I'll tell your father about you seeing the boy!' he said with a knowing smirk.

I watched her bound up the last flight of stairs and head through the swing doors. I raced after her with the intention of bringing her back to the safety of our own home, but then I saw the open door of the Silbermann's apartment. Hilde had already run through the hall and into the living room and was standing face to face with Martin Müller.

'What d'you want?' he said to her.

'Where's Morrie? What's happened? she said.

As she looked around, I witnessed her dawning realisation that the bookshelf held far fewer books than usual. All the paintings had been removed from the walls and the piano had gone. I followed her into Morrie's bedroom and all the cupboards were open and empty. She went across the room and moved the curtains aside to expose the window. It was closed and she looked across to her own identical window on the other side of the garden. As she let the curtain drop, I saw her catch sight of something wedged into the frame of the window, it looked like a piece of paper. Martin Müller entered the room behind us, and out of the corner of my eye I saw her quickly palm the piece of paper. She held it tight in her fist. I held my breath, hoping he hadn't seen her retrieving it.

'Listen. He's gone now, thank goodness. That's the last Jew out of our building. All Aryans here in the future – Heil Hitler!' he said, standing in the doorway, as he made the Nazi salute.

Hilde turned on her heels, pushed passed him and ran back to our apartment, crying unconsolably.

I'd been home all morning, so I'd had the time to digest the events of today. The piano had taken all morning to be dismantled and carried down the stairs, bit by bit. For Hilde, though, seeing the empty apartment must have been a big shock. I explained to her what had happened that day. I felt a deep sense of sadness and loss.

The Müller family were hovering around. Frau Müller had been employed to clean the apartment, something she had been doing for Ernst Grauman since he moved in. The hauliers took the piano and several boxes of books, and it looked like Herr Müller took anything else he could carry to store in the apartments on the ground floor. He must have had a thriving business selling possessions left in premises vacated by Jewish families.

Morrie, though, was my concern. He had become like a second child to me. My parents felt very protective towards him too and worried that they had delivered him into the hands of some sort of devil. From the little we knew, Ernst Grauman was fair and generous with Morrie, though seemed possessive and discouraged anyone talking to the boy. Frau Müller told me that Ernst and Morrie, who had now adopted the more Germanic name, Max, that I had given him briefly, moved out of the apartment three weeks ago, taking just their clothes.

She also told me that, since the New Year, her son had been looking after Morrie while Ernst Grauman was at work.

'He could handle him better than I could,' she said.

She said Max was difficult and cried a lot and that Martin had to lock him in Ernst's bedroom to control him, and because he caught him with his head out of his window calling for Hilde.

She said, 'We are pleased we've got rid of him, but it is beyond me why that nice Herr Grauman would want to look after him!'

Morrie was the gentlest of boys who I was convinced would become a kind, considerate adult. He was someone who was never difficult and always wanted to please. I wondered what Martin Müller had done to provoke him. This was not the boy we all knew and loved. I hope Martin had not hurt him.

As to where Morrie had gone, Frau Müller could not say, except that Ernst had said he'd been asked to set up an orchestra and that Morrie would be his apprentice.

I decided to question the hauliers to get some answers. When I asked where they were taking the piano, they said, 'Government business. We can't say, but it's going to take us until bedtime to get there at this rate, so do you mind if we get moving!'

I had no idea where Morrie had been taken. Above all, I hoped that he was safe and happy. He would be missing Hilde and everything he had known in his nine short years. Opi had convinced him to return to the apartment to live with Ernst in the hope that Ben and Clara would return there, and I promised Opi that I would keep an eye on him when I returned from hospital. I felt that I had failed in that task, but Hilde, my brave young Hilde, had made sure he was alright, until she was stopped from doing it anymore.

Chapter 7

Leaving Friedrichstrasse

1942

HILDE

Papa had once again been promoted, but this time he needed to move with his job and we would be going with him. Mama told me to organise what I wanted to take with me to the new house. She said we were going to a large house in a place called the Sudetenland and would have servants to help us. It was already furnished, so apart from personal items or family treasures we didn't need to take any of the furniture from Friedrichstrasse.

I felt sad to leave here but it wasn't as it used to be. I would be taking Froh-Froh and her cage of course. Opi had painted a small chest of drawers for me using the same paint as he used for the cage, it was a pretty blue with little yellow ducks walking across the front. Inside it, I found my ballet shoes and leotard, along with my fluffy angora cross-over ballet cardigan. There was no point in taking these with me, they didn't fit anymore and I no longer had ballet lessons.

I pulled off my jacket and put on the cardigan. It was too small. I was ten years old now, but I stretched it so that it covered the tops of my arms and just met in the front. I kicked off my shoes and, in my stockinged feet, pressed my heels together and toes out in first ballet position. I moved my feet apart into position two, then finally placed one foot in front of the other so my heel nearly touched the arch of my back foot. With my head held high in a haughty position, I looked at myself in the mirror, imagining Clara Silbermann standing behind me positioning my arms. The day I received this cardigan had been joyous, but I knew that time had now gone. I packed my ballet things back in the drawer and declared that I would save them and one day give them to my daughter. They must stay here in safety, so they don't get damaged. So many memories would stay here, memories of Morrie, Clara, Oma and Opi, but Papa said it was all temporary and we would be back as soon as this war was over.

From the shelf next to my bed, I picked up a small tin with rounded corners painted with a cheerful alpine scene. Inside I found a piece of paper. In pencil on the outside of the folded paper was my name, Hilde, written by Morrie. This was what I had found wedged into the crack of Morrie's window frame. He'd known I would find it. I opened the tightly folded paper and saw the script; it was written by Gunther in a large heavy hand. He was a gruff man, not prone to sentimentality but always dogged about fairness. He had given this to Morrie when Morrie left his hiding place, behind Gunther's house. This was what he had written.

To Morrie,

Human beings, like birds, should be able to go wherever they choose.

One day I hope you can go wherever you choose without fear.

May peace go with you.

Gunther

Reading this made me realise how dangerous life was for Morrie, and how important he had been to me since we first met. Missing him was unbearable. Now I was leaving Friedrichstrasse. I hoped it wasn't for good but, looking around me, I began thinking about my life here and the memories I was leaving behind.

The Silbermanns had moved into their apartment the day after we moved in. I met Morrie in the hallway outside our apartment as he was rolling marbles along the edge of the wall. The first thing I noticed was his hair was very blond, like mine, and hanging over his eye. I just stood and stared at him to start with, but he straight away said, 'Do you want to play?'

I'd smiled shyly, then sat on the cool marble floor, watching him.

I had never seen marbles before and wasn't allowed out on my own, so having somebody to play with next door would change my life. We became best friends immediately. He was friendly and funny.

Friedrichstrasse had been my home for five and a half years. I had only ever lived in this town. Before we moved to our apartment, we'd lived with my grandparents in their house Arkadien about three kilometres away. If I closed my eyes tightly, I could see myself once again small and standing in my bedroom there.

It was partly in the attic, up a small flight of tiny hand-carved stairs. Inside the room it smelled musty and sweet, but it had different scents as the year moved through the seasons. It was here that Oma hung herbs to dry from the rafters to last her through the winter months; where seed potatoes were spread on trays before planting; and where gladioli corms were kept during the winter in boxes of ash with the lingering smell of burned wood. My bed was an ancient truckle bed below a tiny window. The window opened, but was so small that I couldn't get my head through.

In late autumn, Opi picked the apples from the trees in the garden, standing up a ladder propped against the gnarled trunk of the tree, wearing a long brown leather apron with a big pouch in the front, like a kangaroo. He packed the russet-coloured apples into his apron, then climbed down to fill the apple boxes. He did this all day long for one or two days every autumn, trying to guess accurately when the fruit was ripe enough and at its juiciest before squally winds shook the whole crop onto the ground.

Oma and I used to wash the apples and carefully dry them. Any that were bruised, maggoty or damaged in any way would be put to one side. We smeared each good apple with petroleum jelly to protect it before gently wrapping each one in newspaper. These little round parcels were lined up on racks in a long wooden box that went under my bed. We had apples to eat well into late spring. Because of the racks, my bed was raised up on blocks that made it very high. Oma always told me that I was like the princess in the Princess and the Pea, and it was very special having such a tall bed!

The damaged fruit was never discarded; Oma made apple pies and apple cakes as well as bottled apple sauce and vinegar over the following weeks. Opi made apple wine and with his neighbour and friend farmer, Gunther. They also made schnapps to be drunk at Christmas and at other celebrations where they spent hours discussing politics and planning how to change the world.

Then we moved here. There was nothing in our apartment that I thought interesting, but we did have a cuckoo clock which had been a wedding present to my parents, and also a paisley patterned rug my mother bought in town which was paid for weekly, but we had nothing luxurious. There were no books or anything to do with art or music, and it wasn't until I met Morrie that I was introduced to such things.

I then imagined myself in the Silbermann's apartment, which you wouldn't believe was in the same building because it was nothing like our apartment. This was the imagining exercise I often did in bed to make me feel calm and happy when I couldn't get to sleep. In this magic kingdom, walls were lined with bookshelves containing books of all shapes, sizes and genres. There were children's stories with pictures, big glossy volumes full of photographs of famous film stars, many leather-bound books with gold lettering on the spine, books about the theatre, about dance and great composers, novels, biographies of the great and the good, musical scores and poetry books plus dictionaries and encyclopaedias which fascinated and slightly intimidated me.

The furniture was old like ours, but chosen with great care. It was far more ornate, and I considered it elegant. There were many small tables with sparkling table lights, crystal ashtrays and cigars in pots, leather cases containing unusual objects from around the world and paintings of people with serious faces in gold frames looking down on us from the walls. There was an air of culture and a legacy of knowledge and an appreciation of the finer things in life within that apartment which intrigued me.

I remembered the happy times when my mother and Frau Silbermann became good friends. Morrie played in my apartment sometimes and I played in his. Herr Silbermann was a jeweller and had a tiny shop just three roads away from the apartment. Over the next two years we became very close. My mother got a job at the textile factory working one of the machines, which brought in more money.

Morrie and I were enrolled in the same kindergarten, and we would skip and run across the park together each day with my mother following and trying to keep up. She took us there each morning from Friedrichstrasse, about a fifteen-minute walk. We made up games, seeing who could reach the gate first or who could catch one of the birds that pecked for grubs and worms on the wide areas of grass. Neither of us ever succeeded in doing that.

It was arranged that after kindergarten finished each day, Morrie and I would return to Friedrichstrasse with his mother, as she didn't teach the piano to others at that time. We two children were very happy.

Every night when we went to bed, Morrie and I would wave to each other from our bedrooms across Herr Müller's garden. We felt that we lived in a perfect world.

I looked out of my window now and wished I could go back to that time.

I wished I could see Morrie again.

Part 3

1945 Return to Leipzig

Chapter 1

The Sudetenland

10 May 1945

ELSA

Today we left the big house and the town we had called home since 1942. We were in a staff car driven by Hans, Raoul's driver. It was hard to leave, we had been happy there. We were all in a panic, even Raoul. It seemed unreal that within hours of understanding the situation, we made the decision to return to Leipzig. I was not quite used to the idea. There was a sense of unease, and I was conflicted. It had all been too fast, yet the thought of seeing my parents filled me with joy. I was squeezed into the front seat between Hans and Raoul; Hilde, the budgerigar, and our cases were packed in the back.

After living here for three years, we felt we had integrated well. Raoul and I had been entertained by the mayor and we'd had excellent relations with the local trade's people but that had broken down and none of us felt safe. Each person now must fight for their own survival, and we were unsure who we could trust. Neither the Germans here nor the Czech people could say what the immediate future held, and we were worried about the Red Army and what they might do to us.

There had been so many rumours in town this week. We listened to the radio, German of course, but Czech also and a British broadcast if we could get the signal. Every hour something new was spoken about, there were so many whispers. We hadn't known what to believe and things we thought to be true turned out to be false. It made people twitchy, and I experienced highs and lows in my emotions. We were not in Germany, and we were no longer welcome here.

Raoul had run a factory since being here. He was a Commandant of the local camp workers and had stayed as long as he could, but it was time to leave his post. Hitler was dead. The Third Reich had collapsed, and we had to flee from this place. Raoul had been dedicated to the Party, but the Party did not exist anymore; he owed no allegiance to them, and we were uncertain who was running Germany. There was no chain of command, no-one to take his orders from. For the past day or so, everywhere we went and everyone we encountered was in a state of turmoil. Nobody knew what was expected of them and we, as a family, were suddenly displaced people, desperate to get back to Germany and the life we knew, or at least used to know. We could not say what would be waiting for us. We hoped Opi and Oma were safe but had not heard from them for some months.

Four powers wanted to run Germany: the British, the French, the Americans and the Russians – so what would become of us; would we still be German? We were so nervous, everything had changed. We had to leave today not only because the local people had turned against us, but because the Russians were only a few kilometres from our town, gradually working their way into Germany and, it seemed, killing any Germans they come across. Reports had been sent to Raoul from towns just to the north of us and it seemed that, overnight, the danger had become imminent.

People talked about the atrocities that the Russians had carried out. They said their soldiers were brutish, ill mannered, and ill disciplined. I heard they were not very tall but broad and could break human bones with their bare hands; they were violent and disrespectful of men and women alike. Many women had been attacked and left for dead and spoke of them as being rough, smelling of alcohol or 'stinking like pigs'. Someone said they saw a Russian soldier biting off a dog's head because it was barking. I didn't know what to believe. Some of this was speculation, some panic and some was pure mischief-making, I suspected. I did know from families of soldiers who fought Russians on the Eastern front that they were a tenacious race, fearless and proud and therefore a people to be feared.

For the last few weeks there had been gangs of marauding men attacking Germans here. Local Czech militia had formed units to drive the German population out of Czechoslovakia. Many had been organised by the local authorities, but we were fearful that no-one was controlling their actions. Germans had lived here for many decades, not just since this part of the country was annexed by Germany. But now the local people who used to be friends wanted us all out, even those German families who had been here for generations.

Raoul went to the barrack block next to the factory early today when it was still dark. He gathered his officers and the prison guards together and spoke to them.

'I am no longer your commander, and it is for you to decide what you want to do. I and my family will be returning to Germany. Thank you, and I am sorry that we must abandon this plant. We've done a good job here. I don't know what the Russians will do. I hope you will be reunited with your families soon and advise you to travel back to Germany as soon as you can.'

He did not say Heil Hitler and had not done so for a long time.

Once he had dismissed his men, he called all the prisoners into one of the prison barrack rooms, though they spilled outside into the quadrangle as it was not large enough.

'The camp gates will be left open; it is for you to decide if you go or stay. The Russians will be here within hours and may help you, but they may not. We cannot protect you. I wish you luck. Goodbye.'

He did not get many responses from anyone. One or two of the prisoners shouted obscenities at him. Some were silent and wandered back to their beds in a kind of trance, some stood talking to each other in whispered tones, staring at Raoul. He suddenly feared they might be plotting against him, maybe they wanted to reap revenge for their incarceration? They seemed as unsure about what to do as he did.

Tony, the Italian POW who tended our garden, approached Raoul and said, 'I shall go back to my town in Abruzzo to see my wife and children. I hope that Frau Franck and Fraulein Hilde stay safe. I shall miss my garden here.'

He was the only prisoner allowed out each day and was not involved working on the construction site because he tended the garden in the big house. He took great pride in planting and nurturing the plot and had transformed it into being his garden. There was a weed free sloping lawn, flower beds and a vegetable garden. Tony had grown vegetables within the camp and Raoul utilised his skills in our garden. He also showed Frau Obermayer, our housekeeper, how to cook the vegetables he grew using Italian recipes, when ingredients allowed. We all liked Tony. He was grateful for the job he had and that he didn't have to go on the daily work parties with the other men. The Italians did not have the rights of The Geneva Convention and so some of the guards picked on them and made them do the more unpleasant tasks or tormented them. The guards had bullied him, pushing him around and denying him food but they dared not once he became the Commandant's gardener.

Raoul shook his hand and wished him a safe journey.

Raoul decided not to wear his uniform today. He was wearing civilian clothes in case his uniform made us more of a target. That had been the hardest decision he had to make. His dedication to his country, his pride in his uniform and his consistent hard work, was what has defined him over the past ten years. He fought in the trenches in WWI as one of the lower ranking infantrymen attached to an engineering division, digging and shoring up trenches in Northern France. He hadn't liked the way he was treated then but his bravery and loyalty earned him a commendation. It was at this time he realised he lacked education and he saw the difference between himself and the officers in command whom he so admired. He wanted to gain the same respect and display the same level of self confidence in his own life.

He grew up as a poor country boy with little schooling but after the war was over, he set himself the task of studying the basics so he would enter the workforce with a career path ahead of him. He enrolled at a college in Leipzig. He worked hard and the qualifications he achieved enabled him to get into the police training school. He excelled there to become the Class Captain, leaving the school with honours. He wore that uniform with pride. He felt he had earned it. When he realised he could gain promotion with further examinations he became determined to achieve that, and he did. Furthermore, he liked the kudos that came with the job.

When the police force was taken over by the Nazi Party and changed its name, Raoul was given a different uniform to wear. At first, it was clear he'd felt part of a great movement and that the glory of Germany was worth fighting for. The jobs he was asked to do were not what he had anticipated when he joined the force, and I knew he had a constant fight with his conscience about what was right. He struggled because he always followed the rules. When the war broke out, his role changed again. He paid lip-service to something he didn't really believe in, which gave way to periods of depression. He had to keep this to himself: perceived weakness and any criticism of the methods employed by the Party would not be tolerated. He had been given medication by a friendly doctor, but I did not like him taking these tablets.

The move to the Sudetenland with the factory job seemed a less onerous task, and was a promotion with privileges, like household staff and good food supplies. The workers here were needed to build the fuel plant and the labour force comprised able-bodied men the Gestapo could round up in the towns, along with British and Italian POWs. All were here against their will, but that was what happened in times of war, wasn't it? There were winners and losers, the attackers and the attacked, the imprisoners and the imprisoned, those who controlled and those who were controlled.

My husband controlled all aspects of the camp, and his priority was to get the factory built. There had been some men who escaped from the work parties. The prisoners were fed meagre rations and only provided with a basic wooden bunk bed; sometimes they became sick or were too weak and they died. They did not have a resident doctor. There were often burial parties going up into the forest to bury bodies. He didn't tell me a great deal of what happened in the camp because he felt it better I didn't know the details.

These last six years Germany had been fighting had been so worthless, so many people killed, so many homeless and destitute, so much needless destruction and so much hatred. The high hopes of the German people had not resulted in success and honour, instead Germany had been defeated and our economy collapsed. We were a proud people, and we would be great again, I was sure, but right now we could not feel more lost. The pulse of Germany was barely there.

We were now just two kilometres from the German border. Hans had to travel a circuitous route as there had been gangs of men gathering on the roads ahead of us. They were Czech militia, and we were in a German staff car which was a prime target and easily recognised. We hid for around two hours in a copse of trees. There were the remains of dead bodies that had been buried in shallow graves. It was a gruesome sight. I saw an arm, but it had been chewed by an animal. I tried to keep Hilde looking in a different direction. This was reality, and I might not be able to shield her on the coming journey home.

Hans surveyed the road up ahead until it looked free from danger, and we could once again move. Now, finally, we were about to cross over the border. We were aware that we had delayed our escape and the approaching Russians might soon be here, so we had to move on and could not rest. It was very densely wooded and mountainous here so we couldn't take short cuts and had to stick to main roads.

'Hans, it is time. Please stop the car. Thank you for being my driver. I shall take over, now you must go and find your family. Are we close to the town where your parents live?' Raoul said.

'They are about ten kilometres to the East,' said Hans and smiled. He took a small rucksack from the back of our car.

'Go, we cannot wait any longer,' said Raoul, who had got out and into the driver's side of the car. He waved at Hans.

'Safe journey, I hope your future is good.'

'Safe journey,' returned Hans. He saluted Raoul and then me. Quickly and silently, he slipped under the cover of some trees.

Chapter 2

Journey back to Leipzig

1945

HILDE

We were in Germany. Mama, Papa and I cheered as we came over the border. There were many cars crossing. The countryside looked exactly the same as where we had come from, but we were now in Germany I hoped we would be safe. At least we wouldn't be watching out for the militia groups, but we had to stay ahead of the Russian soldiers.

There was a great swell of people travelling on foot along the road, all going west, carrying bundles of clothes or bedding, some pushing carts or prams, some on bicycles. I hadn't realised so many people would be making the same journey as us. One or two cars went past, sounded their horns and waved at us. We waved back, pleased that we were all travelling home. Children were running alongside their parents and some little ones were sat atop bundles of clothes on whatever transport their parents were pushing along the road. I felt lucky to be in the car.

At the border post, Papa said there was usually a whole troop of border guards who slept there and worked shifts, going on and off duty day and night. They had to check our papers, ask where we had come from and where we were going, and they would usually look at what we were carrying in the car. Today, though, there were just two uniformed Wehrmacht officers who talked to Papa for a moment but checked nothing of ours or of anyone else's. They too were going west, but had just arrived here from further along the border and had stopped to look for food and a change of clothing in the bunk house. They told us that many roads had been bombed, people travelling along them had been killed and that we should lie flat on the ground if we heard aeroplanes overhead. They said sometimes the planes had been American and sometimes British, but it seemed the pilots could not know who was travelling along the roads; they just shot anyway, probably getting rid of their bullets before they flew back to their bases.

Papa said that now the end of the war had been declared there should be no more planes shooting at us. We set off slowly because the road was so full of people, all who came from the Sudetenland or further east, trying to get ahead of the Red Army for fear of what they might do.

We drove for a few miles until we reached a farmyard. There were no animals here, except a horse in the distance eating grass on the side of a hill. Papa went inside the house to speak with the farmer. I climbed into the front seat and cuddled up to Mama, feeling sleepy. It had been a fraught day. We waited for what seemed a long time before Papa came out, followed by the farmer, Jürgen.

'Tonight, we will be sleeping in the barn over there,' Papa said, pointing to a ramshackle black building.

'What will we sleep on?' Mama said in a small voice, sounding exhausted.

'There are bales of straw,' said Jürgen. 'I will give you blankets as well.'

'First we must unload the car and put all our suitcases and bags in the barn,' said Papa.

'Why?' I asked, frowning. 'Why do that, Papa, when we will have to put them all back in the morning?'

Papa said, 'We won't be using the car, we have run out of petrol, Jürgen doesn't have any either, so we must leave the car here. In exchange, he has given us his horse and cart. We will use that to travel back to Leipzig. I'm sure at some point in the future petrol will be available, and the car can be used again. Everything is different to what we know. We must make the best of every opportunity. Please accept things are as they are, at least we are back in Germany, Hilde. The three of us will help each other, yes?'

'Yes Papa,' I said, feeling a little unsure.

I looked up at the horse grazing in the field. He seemed thin and old.

I then had the strangest sensation. I'd always had a home, somewhere to feel comfortable and safe, a place I could just settle and not do – or think about – anything. But now we were forced to live out of a few suitcases. We did have some furniture in Friedrichstrasse, and I was grateful that could still be our home. Suddenly, I was filled with longing to be back there and for our old life. I picked up Froh-Froh's cage and her cover and took her into the barn.

'Froh-Froh,' I said. 'We are going back to our real home. We will start a new adventure there; you will love it!'

It was dark in the barn and my eyes took time to accustom. It was empty apart from piles of straw and a rusted tractor Jürgen said he couldn't use due to the fuel shortage. There were birds flying in and out of the rafters, the blue sky was visible where roof tiles were broken. On the stone floor, empty animal troughs were stacked high. I saw a rat scurry along the far wall.

Jürgen said he'd planted cabbage but these were not yet ready to harvest. He gave us some parsnips and a mouldy onion from a hessian sack hanging on the wall outside. There was a brick fire pit behind the barn with some ancient cast iron pots next to it, used for rendering down fat to make lard sold in the market. That was when he'd been a successful farmer breeding livestock, but now all the animals had gone as he couldn't afford to feed them. The last ones died of starvation. Only his horse had survived with what little Jürgen could scavenge in addition to some straw and grass in his fields.

Papa instructed me to hunt for small pieces of wood to start the fire, and some bigger pieces to add once it was lit. I went into an area of brambles but soon had bloody scratches all over my hands and legs.

'Come out, Hilde,' Mama said. 'You'll be cut to shreds!'

The farmyard was overgrown and there wasn't much wood to be had but I ventured under some trees and found some fallen dried branches. We enjoyed snapping these into pieces until we had a sizeable pile of wood. Papa lit the fire with some straw and twigs and soon we had a blaze of crackling flames. Jürgen brought some broken pieces of old furniture from another barn to add to the pit. The sun had not yet gone down but it was getting cooler, and we were pleased this substantial fire would keep us warm.

Mama had collected water from a pump in the yard and had cut the vegetables into cubes. I washed the dried blood off my hands and legs and asked to help Mama. She noticed there were young nettles growing beside the barn and, knowing they didn't sting if they were still young and tender, I was sent to pick a big bunch. I plucked the leaves off the stems and put these into the pot. Mama, who seemed to charm all people, asked Jürgen if he could spare a little salt for the stew. He returned with both salt and pepper, half a loaf of pumpernickel bread, bowls and spoons. Mama used a fork to mash the vegetables a little, thickening the liquid.

Papa asked Jürgen to join us, which I suspected he had been hoping for. We pushed the barn door wide open to let some light inside, and sat on bales of straw to eat. It was not tasty food, but we were hungry and thankful to Jürgen for sharing his supplies. His wife and child had died in childbirth thirteen years before and he had lived here, first with his parents and then by himself, since then. I got the sense he didn't often have company nor bother to cook for himself, so he enjoyed eating with us.

He and Papa began talking about the last war and about life in the trenches. As they began talking, they realised they'd been in the same infantry division near Loos in France. They had both been engaged in building a duplicate trench system, behind the occupied one, that would enable troops to retreat to it if they had to. Papa said he didn't know if these were ever used, and Jürgen wasn't sure either. Both agreed the job had kept them away from most of the fighting until they were moved onto other duties. Neither of them remembered the other as a young soldier. This was not surprising as there had been so many men in the army, and the number of casualties meant there were always replacement soldiers.

They spoke about the horrific conditions they had to endure, the permanent water they stood in for hours that gave soldiers trench foot; the rats that fed on food scraps; the dead bodies lying just under the surface of the mud; the lice that added to the misery of the whole experience and the fear, always the fear.

Jürgen said he'd been an athlete before the war and was later selected to oversee a wiring party because he was light and fast. They went out into no-man's land at night, hoping not to be shot by snipers or picked out by a flare. Their task was to cut through enemy wiring or install barbed wire in strategic places. The wire would be rolled out still coiled, known as concertina wire, and attached to wooden posts that needed hammering into the ground. This was noisy, with a high risk of alerting the enemy. Jürgen explained how the Germans invented a screw picket which made almost no noise and was used successfully. These wiring parties were constantly depleted, dozens of men killed and left in no-man's land, others dragged back to a trench only to die of infection or dysentery.

Somehow, Jürgen had survived the wiring parties and the war, but he was medically discharged. The work he had done, and his experiences, left him broken mentally and physically until he could no longer function. He did not recall leaving the battlefield, he was sent to a nursing home where he was sedated for many months. He was suffering from shellshock, as we called it now, and was unable to leave there until 1919. He was nursed by a beautiful Dutch girl named Anke.

He married Anke and brought her back to the farm where he had grown up. His father welcomed them and the extra hands to work the farm, but Jürgen said his father was always disappointed in him; he could never be the son the old man wanted. Jürgen's brother, Rolf, had been a captain on a U-boat in the Atlantic Ocean. He'd been awarded a medal for outstanding service, but his submarine was lost at sea, and he never returned. His father somehow resented the fact that Jürgen had returned, and his brother hadn't.

Following the loss of his wife and child, Jürgen said he sank into depression and the awful memories from the war came flooding back to him. He could not work. His father said to him, 'You were a poor soldier, a poor farmer, and a poor husband. Pull yourself together! You are no good to me like this!'

His mother died shortly after Anke. Jürgen tried to be the son his father wanted, and together they ran the farm. It flourished and they even had money in the bank. Just as this war began in 1939, his father died too, leaving Jürgen to run the farm. His health was better, but his demons still haunted him. Farming was difficult, he was working the land on his own, the government brought in some measures to help farmers but everything in Germany was for the war effort and the lack of money to buy animal feed had seen the end to his dairy herd and pigs.

This was an interesting story. Listening to what Papa had done when he was a young man was something I hadn't heard before; but I was sleepy and wanted to go to bed. I hesitated to interrupt their conversation, but Mama said she too needed sleep. She thanked Jürgen for his hospitality and asked to be excused; she was tired because she had missed her afternoon nap, which she still needed sometimes, especially if she was stressed. Jürgen left us and quickly returned with two grey blankets and an earthenware flagon of something.

Papa gently covered us both with the blankets and gave us a straw-filled bolster from Jürgen as a pillow. He deftly placed the cover over Froh-Froh before creaking the door almost closed as he left the barn and went to sit outside with the farmer. We could see the red glow and hear the spitting of the fire. They drank the schnapps or korn or whatever it was Jürgen had in the flagon, which I was sure he had brewed, just as Opi and Gunther used to.

In the barn it smelled of musty sweet straw and my Mama's perfume. I felt cosy and safe, hearing the laughter of Papa and Jürgen as they drank outside while they recounted funny stories of men they'd known and the happy incidents that occurred when men were thrown together as comrades. I was pleased we had stayed here and happy to hear my Papa laugh.

I woke to see Papa stripped to the waist outside the barn doors, washing himself from a big, galvanised bucket. Water poured down his face and over his chest and he was humming a tune. Mama was kneeling on the barn floor, hunting through a suitcase for clean clothes. The sun was shining, and this was a new day.

I clambered off the bale and took the cover from Froh-Froh's cage. 'Good morning,' I said smiling at my little bird.

'Good morning,' Froh-Froh replied as she cocked her head to one side.

Chapter 3

Hermes and the mangold

1945

ELSA

It was three days since we'd left Jürgen's farm. We went with enthusiasm, happy to be going back home to Leipzig, though Raoul worried he didn't have a job and we didn't know if we even had a home anymore but we hoped the familiarity of our old town would be good for us.

The horse was attached to a wooden cart, and he was called Hermes, named after Zeus's messenger, the fastest of all the Gods. Perhaps once this horse had been fleet of foot, but he was old now and underfed. We left with a bag of oats, which we knew would not last long. Raoul was driving us. We had our cases, and the budgerigar in her cage, in the back of the wagon.

There were so many people on the road. Some people had been travelling from other countries, to our east, beyond the Sudetenland and Czechoslovakia, and had been walking for weeks. There was a large group of people who'd been released from an internment camp and been made to march but the soldiers accompanying them hadn't known where they were heading anymore because they'd received no new orders in the last week and so they'd abandoned their prisoners. We were now on the flat plain, which was easier for us to travel along after the hills and forests. For days, the people on the road had tried to keep together for safety, but they'd had no food and no real shelter, save the trees.

When I was at the convalescent clinic, I saw faces like those on these people. They had suffered a trauma which left them empty and frightened. They walked in some kind of oblivion, to where, they did not know and to what, they could not say. For our little family, though, we did have purpose, we were trying to get back to where we came from. There were scuffles along the road between people arguing, usually about food or paltry possessions, but there was nobody to oversee law and order here on this road. People now owned so little, but without a home they needed little anyway. The order of the day was survival. We passed a body on the side of the road. It was a man who had been stabbed, he was grey and bloated. There was dark brown dried blood on his clothes, and he had no shoes; someone had stolen his shoes! I was ashamed that we did not stop to bury him. Later we saw another dead body and then it became quite commonplace. I hated how insensitive this was making me.

I could not bear looking at so much suffering, especially in such a privileged position, with the luxury of transport. Eventually, Raoul agreed that Hilde and I could walk for a while so we could give some people a ride in the cart for a few hours. We offered help to a mother, with two small children, who seemed exhausted, and to an old lady with bandaged legs, as well as two wounded soldiers using sticks to help them walk. No sooner had they got onto the back of the cart they had all fallen asleep. It was so difficult to decide who to take; these few were just a tiny proportion of a big problem. Hermes walked slowly, defying his name, and Hilde and I walked beside him.

People fell because they were too weak to continue, or they sat panting on the grass beside the road. The weather was dry and getting hot. It appeared to be a May heatwave. Along the side of the road possessions were discarded because they could not be carried further. Families had started their journey in a positive frame of mind, carrying items they would need once they had found somewhere to settle, but these soon became a burden, weighing down their exhausted, starved bodies. There were pots and pans, clothing, broken trolleys, furniture, worn out shoes, books with their pages blowing in the wind, and family treasures once thought precious, that represented their heritage, to be saved at all cost. These had now been jettisoned as rubbish, blocking the road or piled in ditches. There was a broken cuckoo clock which reminded me of the one Raoul and I received as a wedding present. I noticed people were examining some of these things, presumably deciding if they could take them, but nobody could carry any more than they had.

Some tried, only to unload the item after a short time. There were bombed-out buildings and the detritus of life everywhere we looked.

There was a certain street-currency as we furthered our journey. Some people had money, many did not, but there was little to buy, and no-one knew if the money would be any good once we got to the big towns. Would the banks be open or honour the bank notes? We saw some men arguing as they gambled with money on the edge of a town, but the currency of the road was mainly blankets, clothes, shoes, jewels, watches and, inevitably, personal favours. The most important commodity that everyone wanted was always the same, food. We were all so very hungry.

We took the people we had transported to a small village with a church that had opened its doors as a shelter. I was reminded of Clara because somebody was playing the organ, Bach, I thought, though I was no expert. This gave such a warm, sumptuous sound that it felt intoxicating next to the stark reality of the day. This music, and perhaps being inside a place of peace and Godliness, seemed to feed my soul. The priest apologised that they had no food to offer, and the church was already full with the overflow of people now gathering outside and sitting on graves. That must have been a strange, unworldly sight as it became dark: those barely living bodies lying down beside the ancient dead within the churchyard. I hoped that, if nothing else, they felt safe.

Although there was no food there was a pump outside the church, so we made sure the horse had water. We refilled Froh-Froh's little bottle and our canvas camping bag.

We moved outside the village and pulled into a field, stopping under some low hanging trees for protection if it rained, though it had been unseasonably dry since we began our journey. Before it got dark, Raoul took Hilde, and they went off across the fields looking for food and something for Froh-Froh as she was down to nipping at the almost spent millet hanging in her cage. There did not appear to be any crops to glean. The first field had been ploughed quite recently and any damaged crops, left on the soil, not collected by the tractor, would have been taken by the people on the road. I lost sight of where Raoul had gone but busied myself making a bed in the back of the cart with cases, coats and dressing gowns and hoping that with the three of us snuggled together we would be cosy and get some sleep.

After a long time, they returned with a huge mangold that was longer than a hand's length and just as broad, it had been partially eaten by a rodent but there was plenty left for us and there were also about ten very small potatoes. Raoul had grown up on a farm and knew the sort of places at the corners of the field that sometimes get missed when the crops were harvested. He recognised both the potato leaves and the mangold leaves from amongst the grasses and wild vegetation that filled the edge of the fields. I didn't know what to do with the mangold, but Raoul quickly peeled it and gave Hilde and me a slice.

'Don't eat this too quickly. Make sure you chew it,' he said. 'It is hard, and you haven't eaten all day. We have to cook the potatoes though or they'll give you belly ache.'

My wonderful husband was so knowledgeable and capable in so many ways, but he could not see this himself, he never believed he was a success. He had not really wanted to talk since we left Jürgen's, and I knew that this was a sign. His inner torment and concerns for our future were making him sink again, back into depression. He had become a little distant, lost in thoughts of his past, memories of the Great War, and too, the events of this war. Being surrounded by so much misery on the road made it so much worse. Despondency and desperation seeped through the pores of every person who walked this path. There were so many disaffected people, all of whom were fearful for what lay ahead. I was determined that we would survive this, and would overcome adversity no matter what it was.

Raoul held out the tuber in the palm of one hand and the potatoes in the other. 'Tonight, we feast,' he said with a smile. Seeing him smile lifted my heart.

Mangold was usually given to animals for fodder. They were a deep orange colour and tasted a bit like a beetroot. We lit a small fire, cut up the remainder of the tuber and, with the potatoes added to the mix, made a soup. It was night-time by the time it was cooked through, but by then Hilde had fallen asleep.

That was last night. We kept the remainder of the soup with us in the back of the cart to keep us warm and this morning, by some sort of symbiosis, exchanging heat with our bodies, it still had warmth to it. We only had a sharp knife and one spoon, that was all, so Hilde ate her fill from the pan with the spoon and we finished the rest.

When we woke, we realised we'd been bitten by mosquitos or spiders, probably as a result of sleeping under the trees. We had nasty red bumps on our bodies and legs, both itchy and painful at the same time, and I didn't feel at all well, but thought maybe that was down to the mangold soup, or the broken night's sleep in the uncomfortable wagon.

We fed the horse the last of the oats and joined the trail of people headed west. Some looked as if they had been walking all night. At no time did this sorry stream of humanity seem to stop. Of course, people needed to rest if they were to have the strength to complete their journey, but someone was always walking along the road, and it was never silent. The huddles of ragged bodies dragged themselves along, zombie-like, trying to distance themselves from their recent experiences. I couldn't walk and had to sit in the cart. As the day went on, I developed a high temperature.

Raoul gave a lift to three more people and Hilde walked alongside the horse but soon became tired. She squeezed in next to her Papa. The horse had slowed and began limping. Thankfully, we spotted a sign that there was a refugee soup kitchen up ahead.

An old warehouse stood before some grassland stretching up the side of a hill, and people were clamouring to get in. We pulled in beyond the crowd and Raoul unhitched the horse, parking the cart in an area strewn with old pieces of rusting metal and other detritus. He let the horse trot off up the hill to indulge in the lush grass. We all watched him go, then Raoul found some rope that he used as a tether.

'I think,' said Raoul, 'that Hermes needs to retire, don't you? He cannot carry us any further. Besides, we have no food for him, perhaps someone else can help him.'

We knew that people were starving, thieving whatever they could to barter with, and so Raoul, Hilde and I had to carry all our possessions from the back of the cart in case they were stolen. Raoul, laden with three suitcases, held Froh-Froh's cage by two fingers.

I gazed at Raoul. He would do whatever was needed to keep us safe and would manage to fetch and carry more than Hilde and I combined. But I considered the three of us now. With no horse, we must carry all our belongings between us. We wouldn't manage that. We'd only just staggered to the queue with our cases. My weak leg meant I was limping and I knew I was burning up. How could we walk another eighty kilometres to Leipzig?

We joined the queue of people entering the building. A man moved along the line up ahead, slowly approaching us. He was squirting everyone in the queue with something from a metal syringe, and even inside the knapsacks they carried on their backs. The line was immediately enveloped in clouds of dust. Raoul realised just in time what was happening, and before the man reached our part of the queue he dropped the cases and quickly hid the budgerigar's cage behind a wheelless abandoned lorry, out of range of the poisonous dust.

'This stuff is lethal, Hilde – it's DDT!' he said as he ran back to us. 'The bird wouldn't survive it.'

Hilde looked worried, 'Thank you, Papa.'

The man with the DDT puffer reached us.

'Do we have to have this poison in our faces, can't we decide for ourselves?' asked Raoul in a rather stern authoritative voice which resulted in him receiving an extra puff.

'Lice! We don't want them, don't care who you are, the lice don't care. Don't get sprayed, friend, you don't come in!' The man laughed and moved on.

I began to cough and could not catch my breath. Raoul held my arm and pulled me into the building. As we entered, we heard further objections raised by people in the queue, and an altercation ensued. There was a scuffle as someone punched the DDT man and others quickly joined in.

It was very basic inside, no chairs or tables except one workbench at the far end of an enormous room where meagre food supplies were being distributed. Suspended metal racks hung off the brick walls, painted in red oxide paint, and metal framed windows had many broken panes of glass. Black and bright blue paint had been sprayed on the walls, and motor industry stickers too, so I assumed this must have been a factory or garage in another lifetime. People were leaning against the walls, sitting, squatting and lying on the floor. There were possessions everywhere, some that looked so ruined they hardly seemed worth keeping. The stench of unkempt nervous humanity pervaded the air. Children cried, though some were laughing; the adults were the same. A mangy dog wandered around, shooed off by most.

I heard people talking about the Russians. It seemed some of them had already reached here but had moved on. They came down this road in the night. It was a terrifying tale. Apparently, one group of travellers, comprising two brothers and their wives, had erected a simple tent, using branches of trees and bedding, at the entrance to a field. This incident took place very close to where we had stopped last night and I wondered if any of the sounds I'd heard in the night, that I had assumed were foxes or owls, were in fact people's cries? The six Russian soldiers had manhandled the couples and stripped them of valuables. They shot both men where they stood at point blank range. They forced the distraught women into a nearby field and, one by one, raped them. One of the women was found alive this morning but nobody knows what became of her. I feared she did not survive for long. People who would normally come to someone's aid were themselves too weak, exhausted and distressed to offer any assistance.

I knew Raoul was listening to all this too, but he was talking quite loudly to Hilde as he didn't want her hearing these details.

There was another queue here inside and Raoul told me and Hilde to sit down while he joined it. He returned after ten minutes with two bowls of a porridge-like broth. He could not get my portion; we could share or I had to queue myself. He had a blue and a red ink mark on his hand to show he had received one adult and one child portion. Adults could get food for their children but for no other adults. We shared what we had. It was tasteless but warm and filling.

Raoul went outside, once the room seemed more peaceful, to retrieve the birdcage. When he returned, he and Hilde cleared a small space and made it into a sleeping area for us, so we could sleep and guard our things while we stayed the night. There were continual arguments as people jostled for floor space. Hilde squatted down and started to sing to Froh-Froh who responded with 'Hello' and 'Papa Papa.'

I didn't say anything to Raoul about feeling unwell, but I did feel quite unsteady as I left them to join the back of the food queue. I could smell the soup which I wanted to get for Hilde and Raoul even if I didn't eat it myself. I didn't feel hungry, but I did feel queasy and hot. Then I felt a familiar dizziness crowding in on me and I wondered why it smelled of hospitals too. All became black and the noises of the room faded into the distance.

Time must have elapsed, as I was laying on a gurney alongside about six other people. I discovered I had fainted and remained unconscious for some time. I was told I was in a temporary infirmary at the back of the soup kitchen. A nurse was taking my temperature and cold wet flannels on my forehead and abdomen were changed for cool ones every few minutes. I was aware of a repetitive sound and realised it was the man next to me. He had a very slow rasping breath, which suddenly stopped. He then let out a deep other-worldly groan that I recognised as the death rattle. Was I in some place that you come to die? I wondered. And if Death doesn't get me right now, would I be laying here, vulnerable, waiting to be attacked by Russians?

Somewhere in the room a man who sounded very young was screaming about being on fire. He was trying to put out the flames, I could see him flailing about, hitting himself in panic but he couldn't stop the non-existent fire from engulfing him. I could hear the nurses and orderly trying to calm him. Then they were restraining him. The poor boy was beyond despair.

I was burning hot; my head was throbbing and I was told I had to stay here until my temperature went down. Leipzig and my old life seemed a fantasy. What I was experiencing now was my own nightmare. I cried myself to sleep.

Chapter 4

Russians and a new cart

1945

HILDE

Do you know how many petals there are on a daisy? I didn't know the answer. I wished there was someone to ask. There were daisies growing all around me now. I picked one and began counting. I couldn't believe I counted thirty. The grass was so green and cool on my feet and daisies with white leaves tinged with pink and sunshine yellow centres were tickling my bare ankles. Papa said we took too many things for granted but I didn't take these beautiful flowers for granted. Despite the war, these flowers still blossomed every spring and the bitter cold winter didn't kill them either, instead it gave them time to rest before they flowered again.

I was glad I could stand in this shady spot when it was so hot, especially after walking along the endless and frightening road. Flowers were nature's optimists, brightening even the most miserable day and I was pleased we had stopped here. Today I had been picking long grass to feed Hermes, but he didn't seem interested. He looked poorly. He was standing up and didn't seem to be hobbling anymore, but he did seem sad and tired.

Earlier, Papa and I went to see Mama. She was awake and a little better than yesterday but must stay in bed. Papa and I moved all our belongings and hid them under the trees near where Hermes was standing. Papa let me stay with the horse and Froh-Froh while he went to look for discarded trolleys or prams along the road. He wanted to make something for us to travel in, some sort of transport for us and all our bags. He said I must be vigilant as I was here alone, but he thought I would be safer out here. I knew he didn't want me feeling anxious, surrounded with the arguing and fighting crowd in the building, and he didn't want me running and bothering Mama either.

I heard a scream nearby, followed by gunfire then more screaming and shouting coming from the building. I dropped to the ground and, half crawling, half running, I left Hermes, desperately trying to get away from the open field where I knew I would be seen. I jumped over the fallen trunk of a tree lying in front of a dense copse; this was where we'd hidden Froh-Froh's cage and all seven suitcases. The commotion continued in the building, but I sensed I must stay where I was and not go to investigate. Staying on all fours, I tentatively raised my head above the tree trunk, but I was at the back of the building, so couldn't see the doorway. Nothing looked any different from where I was.

After a few minutes, I heard voices outside the building and getting closer. There was still a lot of noise coming from inside. I dared not move and feared that my heart, which was pounding in my ears, would be heard. Two men talking in a foreign tongue were approaching Hermes. I placed my head on the ground at the end of the tree trunk and could see with one eye that they were looking at Hermes, checking his hooves, looking in his mouth and ears and they seemed to be discussing him. I hoped my blond hair was not sticking out. Then one of the men left the horse and approached my hiding place. I squeezed my eyes shut in some vain hope this would protect me. Relief flooded me as I heard him step past me to the cart we had unhitched from the horse yesterday. Metal clinked and the man shuffled about. I risked taking a peek to see he'd removed the harness from the cart and was fixing it onto Hermes.

The men led Hermes away. I raised my head after I was sure they'd gone past me and, just as they disappeared in front of the building, I saw one of the men jump onto Hermes' back and dig his heels into the horse's flanks. I wanted to call out, 'No! He is old and cannot carry your weight.' but I knew I mustn't do this. Poor Hermes! They passed along the side of the building and round to the entrance.

I heard the men call out to their comrades inside and, after a few minutes, several of them left the building. I could see them all as they filed down to join the people walking along the road, Hermes once again heading west, but now with two Russian soldiers on his back and others surrounding him.

I waited a few minutes in case there were any more Russians inside. I went to the corner of the building where I could see the doorway. Lots of people had come outside. Many were weeping and leaning on each other for support. These were not Russians. They didn't seem scared, just agitated. One of the nurses appeared outside. I ran up to her, 'What's happened? Is my Mama alright?'

'Don't worry, leibchen, she is just fine, come with me,' she said.

There was a man with blood on his head who she led back to the infirmary by one hand, with me taking the other. It was so noisy in the building. No one was lying down, everyone was animated and talking, crying, or wandering around. I discovered that the Russian soldiers had come in demanding money and jewellery and fired bullets above people heads. They'd taken some bread from the kitchen and pushed people around but after a few minutes they left. A few people had received wounds from ricocheting bullets, but the overriding atmosphere seemed to be relief that the Russians had gone. We had got off lightly.

Mama was sitting on a chair in the infirmary as someone else needed her bed. Life goes on, even in wartime, and a lady had just gone into labour and needed Mama's bed. Mama was happy to be sitting up and not confined to bed, she was still shaky but excited for this young woman, and she was looking forward to helping her get through the next few hours. Since her stroke, she was much more susceptible to illness, which I knew frustrated her and prevented her from doing the things she liked to do.

Then Papa was there, and we told him all the things that had happened. He was just pleased we were both safe and said he should never have left us on our own and wouldn't do it again. I think he was quite proud of me and how I had hidden myself behind the fallen tree trunk when I realised the danger.

During the afternoon, Papa took apart a broken barrow and a pram he had found and, along with some wood from behind the building, he began constructing a cart for us to travel in. The cart was only eight inches off the ground and had three sets of wheels as he had lengthened the base of the pram. It meant Mama could lay on it some of the time as he knew she wasn't strong enough to walk all the way to Leipzig. Papa said it would be a very bumpy experience for Mama.

The orderly, we discovered, was the owner of the building which had once been his repair garage. He loaned Papa some tools, a hammer, tenon saw, pliers, screwdrivers, screws and nails. There was another door at the back of the building, which was padlocked; this door lead into a workshop that still had most of his tools of the trade inside. The orderly was hoping to restart his business eventually, once people had cars again. Papa gave the man money and the orderly agreed he would store some of our suitcases for a few months until we could return once we had some transport.

We asked Mama what clothes she really wanted to keep with her; we could only take two of the seven cases. She went for sensible items and said her best outfit, a pretty blue satin suit, and her flowery summer dresses would have to wait until we could get back to collect then. It was more important that we got back home and, besides, there were still clothes in her bedroom in Friedrichstrasse. Papa and I went through the cases. We put our essentials, underwear, shoes toiletries and personal papers into one case and shirts, blouses, nightwear and jumpers in the other. I couldn't take my case, but Papa let me put my ballerina book in with the essentials. From the little silk pocket inside my case, I retrieved the tin with the alpine scene. It contained Gunther's note and Morrie's marble, that glinted in the sunshine. I hid the tin in my pocket. Sliding my hand into my pocket, I held the precious tin, which fitted perfectly into my hand.

We knew it as best to wear as many clothes as we could, so we planned to wear coats, hats and jumpers – but it was just too hot. Papa said it was OK because we could make these into a kind of mattress to go in the cart and Mama or the cases could sit on top. The orderly took our other suitcases and promised to look after them. Papa was pleased when the man locked the door securely afterwards; this reassured him they would remain safe for the next few months.

Papa had kept back a screwdriver and unscrewed the wheels from the newly finished cart. This confused me. But he explained he was aware it was receiving a great deal of attention and scrutiny from other people staying in the building.

'This will go walkies by morning if I don't keep the wheels with me!' he said.

It was dark by then, and we settled down for one final night in the building. Mama was with Bette, the woman who was having a baby. Thankfully, Mama's temperature had gone down, she was eating again and happy to be helping the young woman and the nurses. Papa and I found a space close to the infirmary and, with our bundle of coats and jumpers as well as three sets of wheels, we settled down for the night.

For the first time in a long time, I dreamed of Morrie. In my dream, we were both about six years old and running and laughing, waving our schultutes at each other. Then we found this little baby in the park all on her own. She was crying and I tried to tell Morrie to pick her up, but he didn't and then I woke up.

I realised that this part was real. Bette had given birth to her baby who was crying in the infirmary. Everyone woke up and cheered.

After lots of happy chatter, people began settling down again. I closed my eyes and felt that this little baby had brought a glimmer of hope to everyone in that place on that night.

Chapter 5

Goodbye dear friends

1945

ELSA

I said goodbye to Bette and her little baby, who was a good weight and looked well. Her Mama was managing to feed the little one, and I prayed that Bette would be strong enough and well-fed enough to continue doing this. There was no milk available anywhere, and we'd already seen two tiny babies dead on the road from lack of nourishment. One woman would not give up her child to be buried and was carrying the newly dead baby. Eventually, the mother was convinced by others to go to the church in the next village where we hoped the priest would help her come to terms with her loss and take the child to be buried.

I started out sitting in the cart that Raoul had made but I really wanted to walk. And so, with the two big suitcases and Froh-Froh's cage secured in the cart, we continued towards home. Nothing had changed on the road, still hundreds of exhausted and starved people walking in groups or alone, many draped with blankets that would be their bedding at nightfall. I was guiltily aware we were refreshed and had been gifted the opportunity to recover from our tiredness over the last two days, though the infection had left me weak.

Raoul was concerned about the budgerigar. We had collected seeds from plants along the road, but she didn't eat them. We travelled through a small town where someone offered us water. We asked if there was anywhere we could buy some seed or corn but it drew a blank and I could tell Raoul felt ridiculous even asking for bird food in the near starvation circumstances we were all in.

At the next village, there were handwritten signs stuck on posts and inside windows saying:

No food here!

and:

Don't stop. Go away. We don't want you here!

It was then that I realised something! We sorry group of travellers, whether we were refugees, returning citizens, internment prisoners, escaped Jews, whatever category we fell into we were, above all competition, competition for food. Germany had no leadership now and the economy, which was floundering by the end of the war, had ground to a halt. Everyone was starving and would eat anything vaguely edible. There was a dead cow in a field, and someone had cut off its udders. People living in the countryside had a little more chance to eat, but the closer we got to the towns, the more critical the lack of food was becoming.

As we walked through the main street of another town, thin ragamuffin children sat on the roof of a shed, pelting the crocodile line of people with stones and bricks. We had to run through this town. Inside the houses on either side of the road we could see faces pressed up against windows, watching us. We ran for fear of being hit. I was struggling to breathe when we reached the edge of the town and Raoul made me get into the cart with one of the cases on my lap. Hilde helped push the cart while Raoul carried the other suitcase and birdcage.

By lunchtime, the day was hot again. We were luckier than most, as we had plenty of water and the real luxury of a small piece of sausage and bread that the orderly had sold Raoul. The orderly had clearly found ways to benefit from this sorry situation, and the black-market food supplies must have been one of them.

In the next small town, there was a park surrounded by tall deciduous trees dressed in their spring finery. Abundant leaves and branches covered in pink blossom swayed and scattered pink confetti in the wind. There was a lawn with flower beds overcrowded with giant rhododendrons putting on a flamboyant display of pinks and red. Someone had just cut the grass. This impressed and shocked me in equal measure: such things seemed of another time and was so strange when surviving this current crisis was most people's priority. It was not the time for gardening, though it did make me smile as I realised it was a good thing to have done because it lifted our spirits. We entered the park and, along with other families, sat on a corner of the lawn. We ate surreptitiously, with our backs to others. It was difficult to eat when you knew others were starving, but everyone here was doing the same. There were good days when you ate and others when you didn't. So we ate quietly, chewing every mouthful thoroughly and savouring the feeling of food in our mouths.

Hilde was talking to Froh-Froh offering her some pumpernickel, but she ignored it. Today the bird was particularly chatty and said Mama, Papa, Hello, Good morning Froh-Froh, and Hildegard which Hilde had taught her recently. Hilde was only ever called Hildegard at school and now by Froh-Froh!

'Hilde,' began Raoul, and I knew what was coming because we'd discussed it last night.

'Hilde, we are going to have to set Froh-Froh free.'

Hilde's lip drooped and her shoulders slumped.

'There's no food available for her. She must be very hungry, and soon she will begin to use up any fat on her body and then she will die. If we set her free she will go and find food for herself. It is warm so she will come to no harm, her natural instincts will kick in and she will find food, better than we can for her,' he said, reassuringly.

'Froh-Froh, I love you but what Papa says is right. I promised Morrie I would look after you,' Hilde said as tears welled in her eyes.

Raoul stood and picked up the cage, he reached out to pull Hilde to her feet.

'Look at those magnificent trees, Hilde. I'm sure your little bird will love to sit amongst all that blossom. She will be so much happier if she is free. Remember what Gunther told you,' he said.

They carried the cage to a shaded piece of ground underneath one of the trees.

'Now, you let her free, Hilde,' he encouraged her.

So, my sweet daughter bent down and, for the final time, opened the door of the blue and yellow cage. Froh-Froh hopped onto her thumb. Hilde kissed her head and then, quick as a flash, the little bird flew off into the trees.

'Bye bye, Froh-Froh,' Hilde said, trembling as she waved her goodbye.

Raoul and Hilde watched the bird fly into the trees and then beyond, until she was no longer visible.

Raoul hugged Hilde to him.

'Let us leave this cage here,' Raoul said. 'It is difficult to carry and perhaps soon someone who finds it will buy a budgerigar and can use the cage.'

We packed up our belongings and silently left the park. None of us wanted to talk; there was nothing to say. Hilde had enjoyed the companionship of this little bird through so many changes. I knew she'd been desperate to get her back to Friedrichstrasse, but she also wanted the best for Froh-Froh. I knew the bird reminded her of Morrie and Opi, but this journey we were now on was more important. We had to concentrate on getting home safely without any more mishaps or illness.

We walked on, with me being pushed for a while, then we swapped, and Hilde had a rest. This was what we did for the next two days. Both nights, we managed to stay in the outbuildings of a farm, though farms were getting less abundant and the owners less willing to take us in.

Inside the cart I had put four jars of pickles, previously stashed in a suitcase as we left the Sudetenland with the hope they wouldn't leak. The smell of vinegar on our clothes had been with us for a few days but had now gone. We hadn't had anything substantial to eat to warrant opening a jar of pickles for our own consumption, and we realised anyway that the pickles were of more value as bargaining tools. They did prove useful, and although Raoul still had a little money this wasn't always what people wanted. We'd exchanged a jar for lodgings and some carrots on the first night, then the second night we were given a bowl of thin soup each and housed in a tiny disused pig shed. Such was the value of any food stuff. I wasn't sure if Hilde was aware the second farm had a silo and outside it was some loose grain. It was a pity we hadn't found this before. Hopefully Froh-Froh had found it for herself.

The next morning, we were back on the road. First, Raoul had to replace the wooden extension on the cart as it had split. The owner of the farm found a sturdy plank of wood, which he sawed to the right size and then helped Raoul screw it all back together. Once again, we were on our way.

That afternoon we heard a commotion and saw a group of six Soviet soldiers exiting a bombed-out building. One of them fired a pistol into the air, over our heads. We all instinctively ducked. They blocked the route of the people walking a few yards ahead of us. They pushed and shoved, demanded food and money off one family and hit them with rifle butts until the mother and father fell to the ground. The soldiers tried to pull the daughter away, but the father held on to her, as did her brother. The crowd started shouting and I had to hold Raoul back. He stopped the cart and said, 'I'm not having this, Elsa.' His old police training and innate sense of justice had kicked in, but it was too dangerous for him to be involved.

'No, don't! You can't fight so many men, and they are armed Raoul, we need you!' I pleaded.

The soldiers hit the boy with a rifle and spat on the father and mother, before running up the road ahead of us, laughing.

I was very concerned about what had just happened and Raoul was frustrated and angry. We realised we had to protect Hilde. The young girl we had just seen was a similar age to her, maybe a year older. Soldiers like these had been starved of female company for so long and had lost their sense of decency and morality.

We began to look for somewhere to stay overnight. Hilde had been calling to Froh-Froh as she walked along. Despite us telling her that the bird was probably miles away by now, Hilde held onto the notion that perhaps the budgerigar would be watching our progress and would follow us back to Friedrichstrasse. It was a vain hope, of course, and I think Hilde did realise that, but she nevertheless thought she would try. Occasionally, I would stop to look at discarded items out of curiosity, but I knew we couldn't carry anything and didn't even know what we would need when we returned home.

There seemed to be another hold up ahead. As we neared, we saw something blocking part of the road. It was a large animal. People were walking around it, looking, but not stopping.

As we approached, we all realised it was Hermes. Hermes who had worked so diligently for us and just needed to rest in his final days had been driven into the ground by the Russian soldiers. We walked around him, and Hilde put her hand on his ribcage. He was so thin, his bones prominent through his skin. He'd been shot through the head.

'He is cold, Papa,' Hilde said quietly.

'He has been dead a few hours. At least those thugs had the decency to put him out of his misery,' said Raoul. 'Keep away from him now, Hilde. Flies are laying eggs and by tomorrow he will be covered in maggots.'

'Goodbye, my dear Hermes. Thank you,' I said.

'I'm sorry I didn't protect you,' said Hilde.

We left the dead beast and continued down the road. For the second time on this journey, we had said a final goodbye to one of our companions.

Once more we were silent, each with our own thoughts.

Chapter 6

Arrival in Leipzig

1945

HILDE

Two days later, we saw the sign that told us we were in the municipal district of Leipzig. We were all a little giddy with excitement, a mixture of anticipation and apprehension. The large cosmopolitan mass sprawled before us. There were so many questions to be asked about what had gone on here; there were places to revisit and friends to locate, but people's biggest concern was how we would live and where to find food.

I knew the city would have changed but I hadn't realised so many buildings would now be rubble. The shape of the skyline was so different before the war. Bricks and dust covered many of the pavements and roads, despite people with barrows clearing it away. The streets were packed with people well before we entered the city; shovelling rubble, carrying all sorts of items to unknown destinations or gathering in small groups to talk. It was three years ago that we left. I was saddened there was nothing left for me to recognise here, nothing that represented home.

If anyone had been watching the long trail of exhausted travellers walking along that day, I do believe they would have thought there was a ghostly air, like a scene from a gothic film. We were a line of dirty individuals wearing mismatched layers of clothing, shuffling and murmuring, pushing a collection of oddities piled high with belongings. But we were, in reality, an army with no leader, united by our shared experiences and by our determination to survive until we achieved our goal. Like battle scarred armies before us, we entered the city in a more or less orderly fashion, the strange shapes of ruined buildings framing us on either side. It was here that we entered the chaos of a decimated city.

On cue it began to rain, great heavy blobs of water that soaked us through within minutes. This was the first rain we had experienced in the two weeks it had taken us to walk here, and it felt that this was the heavens welcoming us back.

Most of the pedestrians on the street were involved in some way with the clearance of debris. There were also American soldiers, some in jeeps and some who were logging the refugees and returners to the city. We were stopped by a tall young soldier who asked if we knew where we were going and if we had accommodation for the night. He told us that a refugee camp had been set up about five miles away if we had nowhere to stay. The soldier told us he was called Chuck. He gave me a bar of chocolate and said he was recording people coming into the city so they could help families reunite. He wrote down our names on a clip-file he was carrying, and Papa gave him Oma and Opi's address as our destination.

Arkadien was only about a mile or so from where we were, and we knew they'd be so happy and relieved to see us. We hoped their home was undamaged and that there was a cosy bed and food waiting for us. I couldn't wait to see them. Mama said once we were rested, maybe tomorrow, we would go to Friedrichstrasse.

As we walked further into the town, we saw that some buildings were intact. Some areas were flattened but some remained untouched. We also saw Russian soldiers marching along in double file. These soldiers looked tidy and organised, not at all like the soldiers we'd seen on the road. We later saw Russian soldiers with clip-files also recording those entering the city. It seemed that both Americans and Russians were now trying to help displaced people find safe refuge in the city, though within weeks the Americans had all left and we only saw Russian soldiers.

There were people going in and out of bombed houses, crawling under fallen beams or into cave-like spaces created by collapsed walls in partially demolished buildings. We saw people sleeping in areas that looked too dangerous to sleep. Perhaps these were their homes and they had nowhere else to go. I saw an old man being led away from a shop with its windows blown out. A man with a red cross on his arm was helping him to walk and I hoped was taking him somewhere safer to sleep. We didn't pass a single shop that wasn't boarded up or demolished and I wondered where we would buy things . I could see it would take a long time for this town to function like it used to.

Finally, I became aware there were features I recognised: the small bridge that went over the river that ran behind Arkadien, my grandparent's house and the enormous magnolia tree with the pink and white flowers that resembled teacups pointing skyward each May when the blossoms came out. This tree was in full bloom today, heralding our return as we approached the road to Oma and Opi's house.

When we got to the other side of the bridge, Papa stopped the cart.

'Elsa, I need to speak to you. I want you to be calm and accept what I am going to say. I have been giving this a lot of thought and, although you won't like what I tell you, I must go through with my decision. I have decided I will not be coming to stay at Arkadien with you and Hilde because…' He didn't finish.

'Raoul, no, please no! We have always been together, fought our battles together and I will always defend you. I won't cope without you!' she almost shouted.

He held up his hand to stop her and went on.

'Listen, it won't be forever. I will not feel comfortable in Opi and Oma's house. Things have changed. They didn't approve of my work and the events that happened when you were in hospital meant we didn't see eye to eye. The war has changed us all. That officer, Lieutenant Schmitt, who was looking for Morrie was nothing to do with me – but they thought he was. We were all members of The Party. Furthermore, I have no work now, Elsa, and I must provide for you and Hilde. If you stay at Arkadien you will both be safe. That's all that matters to me. Tell Opi I will come for you both and repay him for any expenses once I have a job and we can all be together again.'

Mama and Papa hugged. He kissed her and she cried, still begging him not to go.

'Where will you stay?' she said.

'I will go to Friedrichstrasse and get it ready for when you can both come home. Elsa, I need you to be strong for me, for our future. I will be back as soon as I find work. Hilde, it is your job to keep Mama happy. Be a good girl and help around the house and I will see you very soon.'

He gave me a squeeze and kissed the top of my head.

He took one of the suitcases and walked back over the bridge. I realised that yesterday, when he had repacked the cases, he had in fact separated his clothing and paperwork and put these all in one case. Later, we found that he had put our remaining money in the other one for us.

Mama and I stood there and watched until we could see him no more.

I was feeling okay about this because I knew it would only be for a short time and I liked staying with my grandparents.

We reached Arkadien and knocked on the door. I was jumping up and down and was suddenly six years old again! The door opened and Oma was standing there. She stood looking at us, then slowly smiled before holding her arms wide. She seemed smaller than I remembered, and although her hair was now nearly white, it was carefully pinned back in a soft bun, the way she had always worn it. We both fell into her arms, and she embraced us. This was not the joyous laughter-filled reaction I had expected. She held Mama close to her and me so tight that I couldn't breathe, and all the time she sobbed gently.

Her crying was accompanied by a second sound, something so familiar yet almost forgotten so I had to really think what it was. It was piano music, which I recognised was the piece called Leibestraum by Franz Liszt. My grandmother moaned and rocked slowly back and forth still clinging to me. The music stopped, I heard a chair scrape and a door opened, and Clara Silbermann was standing there.

Part 4

Reunions and departures 1945-1948

Chapter 1

Leipzig

1945

OMA

Opi was dead.

There was no way for me to tell them other than to say those words.

'Opi is dead,' I said and then waited for the reaction.

And the reaction came. There had been sobbing and ranting and constant questions. Elsa was consumed by guilt that they'd not seen Opi for the past three years. They couldn't get here, not with the war, he knew that. We both knew that.

I missed my dear husband so much, he was everything I could have wanted in a husband, but I had to learn to accept what had happened. I felt empty. Now I had a new job: I had to provide help for my family. I'd known they would get back here if the war ever ended. I just wished it had been before Opi died.

The day after Raoul collected Morrie from us in 1940, we were once again visited by Lieutenant Schmitt who rifled through our rooms, looking for the boy. He was livid that the place I'd sent him to, in search of Morrie's uncle, was a bombed-out building. He said it wasn't possible that the boy was handed over to his uncle. Of course, he was right. And we weren't sure how we would get round this. Opi argued with Schmitt, who threatened him, but I said it was my fault not Opi's and that I had handed the boy over to someone who knew his uncle, though I was unsure of that person's identity. They said they would take care of him. Schmitt had left then, warning us he'd be return with back up.

We hoped that, without proof of Morrie's presence here, we could not be accused of hiding a Jew.

Turns out we got lucky. Ernst Grauman, whom Morrie went to live with, provided the solution before Schmitt could return. Morrie had told Ernst about the man who had threatened me and Opi and ransacked our house while he was hiding at Gunther's. Morrie, I was sure, hadn't mentioned Gunther. He knew not to involve him in any of this.

Morrie had told Ernst Grauman that he was worried that this man, Schmitt, would return to hurt us. So Grauman intervened. He outranked Schmitt. He called him into his office and told him that the boy was not Jewish but was in fact his nephew and would be living with him. I don't think Schmitt believed him, but he didn't have the authority to override a superior officer, and Grauman had too many good connections to stir up trouble.

Nobody knew the following events, certainly not Raoul Franck or Morrie, but after Schmitt's visit, Ernst Grauman came to see us here and told us about the meeting with Schmitt. He thanked us for looking after Morrie, now called Max, who he said would be in his care. He promised to give the boy the best life possible.

He then said 'I have never met you, nor been to your house and you have never looked after a Jewish boy. Do you understand this? If I see you anywhere, I will never acknowledge you. Neither will Max.'

We both agreed to this and when he left, we hoped that Ernst Grauman's intentions were honourable, though we thought they were probably selfish too. We told each other that now we must stop being concerned for the boy, we had done the best we could considering the rules that we were forced to abide by.

From 1938 both Opi and I had been involved in helping Jews. At first, it was nothing organised. Friends of ours who disliked the ideology of the Nazi Party and wanted to help anyone running from injustice would offer a room, for a day or two, and help with information and contacts. As the years rolled by, it changed. Gunther and Opi became quite involved when Jews were being rounded up and sent away. Occasionally, a Jew slipped the net or escaped, and that was where we came in. I now knew that the Jews were being gathered and sent to camps. At the time, we'd heard rumours but we hadn't known for sure. We called our little group of dissenters Tutus which was Latin for safe and out of danger and we tried hard to live up to that. We just wanted to help where we could, so at least some individuals would avoid the violence we had witnessed on the streets, and the possible risk of death or internment. There were only a few houses across the city that were safe houses. Most ordinary Germans believed what they'd been told by Nazi propaganda: that the removal of the Jews was integral in winning the war and was necessary to create a country unsullied by any foreign blood.

Officials in the town didn't know about Tutus. We only ever used this name between hosts in safe houses and never shared it with our guests or anyone else. The Nazi headquarters was awash with grand schemes and complex plans, but Schmitt and his henchmen were not involved in any of this. Instead, Schmitt made it his business to impose his own justice on German citizens who broke the law. This was his project, his baby. He did discover one safe house and took away the inhabitants who included two Tutus members and two Jews in hiding, but he found no mention anywhere of other safe houses. Schmitt controlled his own small staff in a government department that handled paperwork concerned with recording relocation data and he had acquired a level of immunity and autonomy that meant he could devote time to investigate anyone he suspected of harbouring Jews. It seemed to have become an obsession with him, and he appeared to be accountable to no one, probably because he and his work was seen as unimportant in other departments.

Eventually, we had a network of people who would help disaffected Jews, but you must realise it was extremely difficult to trust anyone because we would be seen as traitors; we were, after all, working against government policy. We were a very small group. We never had Jews staying in this house. Every now and then, long after Morrie left here, Schmitt would knock on the door and rampage through the house but there was nothing for him to find. We wrote nothing down, just memorised instructions and passed them on. Schmitt seemed to have a personal vendetta against Opi. He was frustrated he could not find evidence of Opi's involvement in anti-Nazi activities, though he was convinced he was somehow involved.

Gunther was well known as the bird man. He only sold his birds to people who agreed that, as part of the deal when they bought the bird, they would train it to fly free, even if that was only in their home. This was a peculiarity of Gunther's, and he was adamant that he got a promise of this from each new owner. He bred the birds because he loved them; he loved the different varieties, the panoply of colours and markings, their fascinating behaviour and the way they interacted with one another and with him. He enjoyed caring for them, but he always knew the birds were better off in the wild. His rationale for keeping and breeding birds in captivity was so he could study them and encourage others to learn about them too. I think he assuaged his guilt for keeping them caged by believing he was educating the masses about the complex and mysterious world of birds.

Occasionally, Nazis officers would turn up and he would sell them a bird. Then, owning a bird started to become competitive, and officers began putting in orders for the most valuable or rare birds Gunther was breeding, as these were something to show off. Civilians stopped buying because they couldn't get the seed and a bird was something else to worry about when the war had already brought them great hardships and it was enough to put food on the table each day.

It was good to make friends with your enemy to avoid suspicion. Gunther charged the visiting Nazis extra too. He was crafty. He had about six Jews staying with him over a three-year period. Some stayed a few days, but one lady was there for more than a year and eventually died of a fever. She had become close to Gunther who buried her in his garden. He was never under suspicion; nobody ever saw his guests and so he continued to operate under the radar. He was known as the slightly cantankerous bird man much valued by the Nazi hierarchy. It made him smile that he had Jewish houseguests just a few feet away from Nazi officers visiting the bird house.

Opi and Gunther had organised a scheme that took them months of planning but was successful and was never detected. A river ran at the bottom of our garden and everyone who had this river frontage here had some sort of small boat or dingy. An idea came to them one day after Opi and Gunther used a dingy to rendezvous with people they were helping with the Tutus group.

Leipzig had been dubbed 'The Venice of the north' because there were so many waterways here. These provided a way to get around much of the city unnoticed. At night, at a given time, they would moor up under a bridge and wait for a stranger to walk along a riverbank or towpath and silently climb into the dingy. They would paddle to a second rendezvous where a Tutus host would be waiting and would, under cover of night, lead his new guest to his lodgings. At no time did anyone speak.

It takes time and courage, strength and determination but it was just possible, travelling by night in a small craft, to navigate the extensive waterways of Leipzig and eventually get to Hamburg via the Hamburg Canal. It was complicated, arduous and dangerous. Anyone doing this would have to be sure of a hiding place in the daytime before setting off each night. It took many days, as the canal ran right through the length of Germany and there was the constant threat of detection. If they got to Hamburg, there were ships that enabled them to get out of Germany, to Sweden, which was neutral territory, and then probably to England or Scotland. Every stage of this was a precarious journey. There were success stories. Gunther was pleased to receive an encrypted message, on a postcard from Scotland, redirected from Luxembourg that got through to him, saying 'Arrived at mother's safely.'

Some people were helped to cross to Switzerland, but we didn't have a good enough network and it was a very long way, plus the lack of accommodation, food and water as well as the risk of capture made this too frightening for most people. Many on the run opted to wait it out, stay in hiding, and not venture outside of the house for fear of discovery.

Last year, a night journey to the Hamburg canal was arranged for two Jews hiding in a house about a mile from here. Although the temperature had dropped, it was not so cold that the mission would fail. It was a night without a moon, and it was cloudy. The arrangement was that the two men would reach Gunther's via the field on his farm – on the other side of the river – then over the cattle bridge to his garden. We would pack up food for them for the journey. This had become almost impossible as food was so hard to come by, but these men had plenty of money and through the black market we were able to get sausage, cheese, pickled pork belly and crackers. Kosher meat had been banned for a long time.

Gunther and Opi would settle the men into one of the boats and they would use the other boat to guide them along the route. Staying close to the bank, staying vigilant at all times, they would gently paddle the boats in close proximity to each other until they reached the confluence of two rivers. All four men would travel down this second river which eventually fed into a lake. It was impossible to do this if there was a moon. There were sentries on bridges along the way, search-lights at certain points and patrols along the bankside to contend with, not to mention weeds and debris that was dangerous and hard to see at night. Once across the lake, Opi and Gunther would take the men to the opening of another waterway heading north before saying goodbye to them.

There would be more twist and turns before they reached the canal, and the men would now be on their own with detailed directions and suggestions about where to hide during the daylight hours. Opi and Gunther would make their return home, a journey of some three hours. They were always aware that if they were spotted that would be the end of everything.

On this particular night, 17th October 1944, everything was set. There was no moon and Opi and Gunther waited in silence in the dark. I passed the bag of food to Opi, kissed him on the cheek and left them to it. It was always a tense time for everyone, they didn't need me hovering around. The two Jewish men were due to meet in Gunther's garden at 8pm. Exactly on the given hour, I could hear movement just as I reached my garden and I suspected that the men had hidden up in the field until the appointed hour. Then there were brief introductions, and exchanges of welcome and handshakes, I imagined, as I walked onto the lawn.

No sooner had this happened then there was the sound of running feet, gunfire and the shouting of men coming across the cattle bridge from the field. Clearly, they had followed the Jewish men to Gunther's.

I don't know how much warning Opi and Gunther had, nor do I want to think about the looks on their faces.

I just heard shouts and then shots.

One, two and then another one, two and then a volley of shots rang out.

I froze.

I knew.

I did not want to see, to confirm what I already knew. But I knew I had to.

I had nearly reached the house. I turned around and began running in the dark, falling over obstacles in my haste. Running towards the bottom of the garden, almost to the river I fell, I picked myself up and started again, I ran through the copse and then I was in Gunther's garden. A bright torch shone in my eyes as I reached the yard, blinding me.

'Good evening, Frau Ostler.'

I recognised Schmitt's voice. I held my hands across my eyes and shouted at him, 'Where is my husband, what have you done?'

'Frau Ostler, it is against the law to mix with Jews. Didn't you know that? Perhaps your husband didn't know that?'

With that, the torch left my face and instead shone on the ground.

Here were the bodies of Opi, Gunther and the two men they had tried to help.

They lay where they had fallen, forming a grotesque star pattern, each with their legs bent and feet in the centre – almost like a swastika – with the wrapped food in a neat pile in the centre at their feet.

The torch went out. Schmitt shouted, 'Come!' He and his men left.

I fell to my knees and cried. I scrambled around in the dark until I found Opi's hand. It was still warm but there was no pulse. I lay across his body, shaking him in the vain hope that I could rouse him, but I knew he was dead. They had all been shot in the head.

The silence was overwhelming. I gulped it into my body, not believing what had just happened.

I held his hand and wept, silent painful tears that made my entire body ache and my breath stutter from me. I cried for Opi and I cried for me and I cried for those poor brave men we tried to help. I cried for Gunther and all those Gunthers across Germany, who had been honourable people true to themselves, and who had been lost to war.

I cried for the return of goodness and freedom.

I stayed there for some time, trying to get my thoughts together. I returned to Arkadien; it was raining now. I needed to sleep but couldn't. When I closed my eyes, I saw the four men lying in the cold mud alone in the rain, and I felt guilty that I was still alive.

At first light I realised I was still dressed in the clothes I had on last night. I went to the bottom of our garden, near the river where the wildflowers grew, and I marked out where I would bury the four men: two in our garden and two in Gunther's. Graves in graveyards were not respected these days, there were too many bodies to bury and not enough gravediggers and people were left unburied for weeks, so I didn't want to inform the authorities about this incident, at least not yet. I didn't want them asking questions about what had transpired here. I couldn't move the bodies myself, so called on my neighbours next door. Once everyone knew what had happened, they took over and buried each man with the dignity they deserved.

Gunther and one Jewish escaper, Asher Ginsberger, were buried in two graves in Gunther's garden. Opi and the other Jewish escaper, Lemuel Brath, were buried in our garden. I knew I must be strong. There were important things to do at this time and my tears could not be allowed to flow just yet.

We did not want to offend anyone. We could not deliver eulogies as we would have wanted, because we didn't know enough about the men's history or beliefs.

Opi did not believe in religion and would have been pleased to be buried in Mother Earth.

We didn't know any Jewish sacred writings to read for the Jewish men.

We did not know what Gunther believed in, save fairness and freedom.

Gustav, my ebullient neighbour from across the street and a friend of Gunther's, was an actor before the war and suggested we read something, from the German poet Goethe, to say goodbye to all of them.

Goethe wrote a poem called 'Prometheus.' In this he encouraged human beings to believe in themselves rather than in gods. Gustav read from this because it seemed appropriate.

We marked each grave with a small piece of wood with the names of each man on it,

Gunther, Asher, Lemuel and Sebastien.

My neighbours brought food and we had hot drinks. It took until the afternoon before we had finished burying the men. The women offered to stay with me, but I didn't want that. I needed nobody.

When everyone had left, I went to Gunther's house. I walked into his bird house and, one by one, I opened every door and every window.

I waved my hands and said, 'Fly away little birds, fly free.'

Gradually, they understood and tentatively left the house to fly into the sky. There was still a supply of bird food, so I knew they could stay here or return if they wanted to.

This was my tribute to Gunther, and I hoped that his spirit had hovered over the proceedings today, for long enough to witness this spectacle. I also know he would be pleased his precious birds would no longer be bought by wealthy Nazis.

Eventually, I went back home to think of Opi, who inhabited every corner of Arkadien and who would never leave me, and I let the tears flow.

Chapter 2

Friedrichstrasse

1945

HILDE

Under my bed there was still half a tray of apples picked by Opi and wrapped by Oma last October, though some might not be good enough to eat. I looked out of the little window, above my bed, at the branches smothered in bright green leaves, hitting the rusty tin roof of the kitchen. I could just spy the top of the magnificent walnut tree down near the water, though I couldn't see the river as I couldn't get my head into the window's opening.

Today we planned to do a spring clean in my bedroom though it was no longer spring, but nothing was normal anymore. Herbs that were hung here last autumn and not yet used had to be rubbed between thumb and index finger and stored in the little pottery containers with cork lids that Oma had along the shelves in the kitchen. Like Mama, she had glass jars filled with pickles too, made with the produce Opi grew in the garden: carrots and cauliflower, beetroot and onions. He was not here of course, so this year would be different, but she wanted to keep the garden growing as he would have liked; producing food for us. The tray of gladioli corms from my room had gone now, put into the garden flowerbeds, and would soon produce dozens of statuesque stems covered in hundreds of flowers.

It was not possible to buy seed anymore, so Oma relied on what Opi had in store. In Opi's workshop were seed-boxes with little packets of seeds he'd collected from his garden, or from plants that grew along the roadside or in the fields, or sometimes swapped with other gardeners. The seeds were stored in white envelopes filed one in front of the other, individually marked with the information as follows:-

1) The name of the plant in Latin.

2) The common name we knew it by.

3) Where he collected the seed from.

4) The date of collection.

 For example, there was:

1) Latin name Caltm ha palustris

2) Common name Marsh Marigold

3) Collected from the edge of Gunther's field

4) September 1944

Some of the packets were older than me, but Opi had said, 'If they were collected with care, stored with care, and planted with care they will still produce a crop even if they are old.'

We were looking for things we could grow to eat, and Oma found carrot, chard, chicory and parsnip seeds, though we were rather late in sowing. Food had become all important because we couldn't simply go and buy it. There was a building we could go to that handed out rations of bread or flour and one or two root vegetables, but it wasn't enough, we were always hungry.

At Arkadien we were lucky because we had a few things preserved from last year and fruit on the trees. We'd already gathered walnuts from the tree in our garden, picking some before they were ripe to pickle them. They turned black after a while but were delicious with cheese. The remainder we'd left to mature. We were allowed to eat a few when we cracked them open, but mainly, they were left to dry out in their shells and kept for baking cakes. Last year they were left in Opi's cellar and the mice got to them, so this year we'll store them under Oma's bed. Gunther used to fish in the river, providing Oma with fish that she dried and salted. On the other side of the river, under the trees, there were lots of wild strawberries, so Oma let me take the dingy across to collect them.

I had been drawing some of the plants in the garden. The first thing I drew was the strawberries in the basket. They were the deepest red with very tightly packed seeds on the outside, different to the strawberries we used to buy in shops. They were also very small. The basket was a pale gold with an intricate plaited handle, but some of the basketwork was broken so I think it was quite old. I ate some of the wild strawberries and couldn't believe the flavour; the most fragrant taste I had ever experienced. I was pleased that only we knew where these little gems grew. Of course, I knew I couldn't draw how delicious they were, but I wished I could capture the bright colours in paint. You couldn't tell how succulent they were drawn in graphite.

Later, I sat at the bottom of the garden by the river, close to Opi's grave, where there were many wildflowers. I examined each variety of flower and tried to draw it accurately. I learned there were many shapes of leaves, petals, sepals and stamen. When the sun was in the east, I could see the veins running through, but when the sun was in the west, at the end of the day, I could see amazing shapes, shadows and colours created by the sun. As it got dark, some of the flowers drew shut as if closing their eyes for the night. I wanted to draw each type of plant growing in this garden throughout the year for Oma, and to remember Opi, too.

I felt sad. I dreaded the thought of leaving the house. I felt safer here. Mama and I had been here for a month, but the optimism we had upon our arrival had not continued. Papa still hadn't found a job.

He'd approached many offices and employment centres but couldn't find work. He went to his old police headquarters, but they couldn't help him. He'd received a ration allowance of food but had to queue each evening to have a hot meal. I knew he didn't think he would be welcome at Arkadien and, at first, Oma didn't mention him at all. But as time went on she tried to encourage him to come to eat with us. Sadly, with Clara here, he was too ashamed and had declined. Papa, I think, felt he owed Clara a debt of duty because he didn't help her before; at the time Ben went missing. He told us he would try to find out about Morrie and Ben Silbermann as lists were updated each day in the library and civic buildings, about people who had died in camps and people who were in refugee centres. Papa promised to keep looking for Clara.

In the centre of town were dozens of notes pinned on the side of a building with descriptions and photographs of missing loved ones. Every day, more were added to this. People gathered at the noticeboard and it was a sight of much wailing and distress.

Gunther's house was empty. He had one nephew fighting in North Africa but had lost track of him years ago. The house would be the nephew's inheritance, but he might not even know Gunther had died. Oma gave Papa the key to Gunther's house, so he had somewhere to live for now.

Our home on Friedrichstrasse had gone.

The building received a direct hit from a bomb a year ago. We hadn't known about this, but Clara told us when we got here. That was the reason she was at Arkadien, she too had discovered the devastation when she returned to her home. She was distraught: all the time she was away, the thing that kept her going was the thought of returning to her old life, to her books and music and, above all, to her husband and son. The latter was getting less likely with every day that went by.

Papa had gone to our home on the day we reached Leipzig. He'd been full of hope that he could make the apartment feel like home again; with luck he would get a job and spend the next weeks painting the apartment and making it perfect for me and Mama. When he got there, he was confronted by heaps of rubble along the whole street. Amazingly, the streetlamps were still working but, otherwise, there were no landmarks, just a hand-painted sign saying Friedrichstrasse. At the end of the road, a soup kitchen had been set up. Papa stopped there and asked about the residents of our apartment block. A man knew the Müllers and informed him both the parents and the son were killed, an old man on the top floor too, but he didn't know of anyone else living there.

Mama and I decided we wanted to visit the wreckage of Friedrichstrasse once we felt up to it. We realised how lucky we were to have Oma and a home to live in. Everyone was looking for accommodation. So much had been destroyed, including many of our historical buildings in the centre of the city. Churches, schools, theatres and museums, as well as part of the University and Town Hall and famous manufacturers like the piano factory – where Clara's piano came from – had all been destroyed. Anyone who had accommodation in the city was asked to take in families with nowhere to stay.

When we finally plucked up the courage to see our old apartment block, it was just as Clara and Papa had said. Rubble everywhere. The pavements and road had been cleared but no architectural features were left. The landscape around us was a shapeless mass, mounds of broken bricks, rubble uniformly grey and brown, nothing to distinguish any building from its neighbour. The only thing standing was a skyline of chimney stacks like brick centurions refusing to surrender, guarding the now useless, fallen buildings. I knew where our block was supposed to be: as children, Morrie and I had counted the steps from the corner to our front door. It was 119 steps then but, of course, my feet were bigger, and I took bigger strides now, though it still gave us a pretty good guide. When we reached what I hoped was the right place, Mama and I stopped. I began scrambling over the bricks to get to where I thought our apartment might have been.

'Hilde, I'm not sure you should be doing that! It's not stable!' Mama said. We had witnessed soldiers pulling people off bomb sites and had heard it was now illegal to play on them.

'You act as look-out, Mama!' I called from my vantage point on top of the first mound, feeling slightly rebellious and excited by the thrill of what I might find.

The mass under me felt solid. There was the odd shift when two or three bricks fell down, but it otherwise seemed quite stable. I didn't know what I was looking for, but felt I must find something to bring back for us or for Clara, something to keep as a memento of past times. We had great memories of our time here, any little personal possession would lift our spirits. My stomach clenched. I knew I needed to do it before this site, our home, was cleared away completely.

Through the debris, I spotted the top of Herr Müller's door. It was painted the bright orange I remembered, with the coloured glass crushed and jagged. I certainly didn't want to salvage any of that. Herr Müller only gave me bad memories. I sifted through a few items of clothing, shoes and curtains, but nothing I recognised. There was little discernible colour other than brown and grey. Every item had been blackened by the explosion and coated in brick dust. In each direction, everything looked the same and I began to doubt I was even in the right place.

After around twenty minutes, I'd convinced myself I'd lost my bearings. With a heavy heart, I decided to leave and was about to join Mama who was pacing back and forth on the pavement, getting progressively impatient. Out of the corner of my eye, on the steepest part of a heap, I caught a flash of blue paint. I estimated it was no wider than a half inch deep and was protruding at an angle.

'Just a minute Mama,' I said.

'Hilde, no! Enough is enough! Come down now!'

I smiled and waved at her, but dashed away to the area I'd seen the blue flash. I had to balance across a crumbling wall to get to it. Once over that, I sat on a pile of bricks. I could just see blue paint and the top of a yellow duck. I began scraping away the debris, excitement rising in my chest.

I had found my blue chest of drawers with the yellow ducks on it. Or at least part of it. The weight of the bricks was too much to retrieve the chest. It was unlikely to be intact anyway. Only the top of a drawer was visible, a corner of it split open. I lay on my side and tried to squeeze my hand inside. I could reach two fingers in, but they weren't long enough to touch anything. Calling to Mama that I wouldn't be much longer, I hunted around and found a piece of split window frame with a nail sticking out. Holding my breath, I carefully pushed it through the gap. I didn't know if I would retrieve anything, but I had to try. Then, like a fishing rod, the nail caught on something and, gradually, I was able to pull a soft item from the drawer. I was so excited, I waved it over my head and Mama called up to me, 'What have you got, Hilde?'

I clambered over the wall, running and sliding down the bricks on my bottom until I tumbled onto the pavement.

Mama and I examined the dark grey, gritty object together. Whatever was it?

Despite the gritty texture, I recognised the feel of it.

'It's my pink cross-over ballet cardigan Oma made me,' I said incredulously.

Chapter 3

Clara returns

1945

CLARA

When I arrived at Arkadien in April, I was entirely spent. I'd been to my old home and seen the devastation all around me. I had lain on the rubble and wept.

The longed-for journey, leaving the concentration camp to return home, seemed unreal to me now. In the middle of a bleak winter, with snow flurries on and off, the Soviet troops had entered the camp. So many people were near death from starvation and disease, with skeletal bodies hanging onto life by a thread; many found it difficult to respond to this event. So many thousands had died. The majority of those had been murdered.

In the days before the soviet troops arrived, the SS started marching prisoners out of the camp towards Germany. Many were shot or died as they were leaving because they were too weak, it was bitterly cold and they were walking skeletons, dying of hunger.

I was weak and so hungry but where I worked had afforded me small privileges. I stole small valuables and could occasionally barter for food: a piece of mouldy bread or a potato I shared with my bunk mates. We didn't know what to expect of the soldiers who walked amongst us now. As prisoners, we had been scared to even look at some of the German guards, so we expected the worst. But we were not harmed or taunted by these soldiers.

I wasn't as emaciated or ill as some people but I was still very run down, with sores on my skin, a long-standing toothache, and a cough that wouldn't go away. I weighed very little. Others were much worse than me and we helped one another walk to a line of covered trucks. It had been ingrained in us, during our time here, that if we fell or were left behind we would be killed.

We were taken to another camp quite close by. Here we were processed by a mixture of soldiers and nurses. We were given hot food and slept in similar bunks to those at Auschwitz. We were warned to eat only a small amount because our bodies had grown used to surviving on so little. A bowl of thin soup each day was enough; too much food would make us ill. On the second day, I had a shower. Two of the girls I'd worked with in Kanada were in the same group. We held hands because we weren't certain if these were real showers or if we were to be gassed. Since being at Auschwitz-Birkenau I had found a resilience I didn't know I possessed. I knew the slightest vulnerability would get me killed. Yet we were treated with kindness, and it gradually sunk in: we were almost free.

I had told Morrie, 'Fill your head with as much music as you can. Whatever else is taken away from you, no-one can take away the music in your head.' I played Liszt's Liebestraum over and over in my head and convinced myself Morrie would use music to stay alive.

Maybe it was the realisation that I had left the camp, and life was again uncertainty, I don't know, but once again my mental health broke down and I was kept in the medical wing of a camp for displaced persons for several months. I was eventually put on a transport that took me to a railway station and the start of my journey back home to Leipzig.

When I reached Leipzig, I was alone and frightened. I had become used to being told what to do.

My high expectations of returning to Leipzig, built over so many years, had been dashed when I saw the ruins of Friedrichstrasse. I had visualised Morrie at the Franck's apartment, and I now prayed they were not there when it was bombed. So much had happened to me. What had happened to all of them? I feared the worse, imagining Morrie buried beneath all this rubble.

I realised I had nowhere to stay. The only possible place of safety I could think to go was Arkadien. My experiences over the past six and a half years had deprived me of any control in my life, or any form of choice, and I feared authority more than anything. I knew I would be arrested as a vagrant if I stayed in Friedrichstrasse. I had learned to trust nobody and was always looking over my shoulder.

In the camp, I feared being caught in the wrong place or drawing attention to myself and I knew that I could be one of those women who disappeared, never to return.

I knew I must try to complete this part of my journey. I remembered, approximately, where Elsa's parents' house was. I found the district, but was exhausted and struggled to walk. Relief flooded me when I stumbled upon the river running behind their garden. And then, there before me, was the house, Arkadien. I rang the bell and Elsa's mother, Inga, opened the door. I collapsed on the doorstep. I was so thin and emotionally spent I didn't know how my body had managed to get me there. I became delirious. Inga nursed me in bed for a week until I was strong enough to get up. She told me Hitler had killed himself and the war was over. I'd been told this before, but I was so institutionalised, and rumours abounded. I didn't know what to believe. We clung to each other and sobbed for so many people and so many reasons.

There had been three chickens here that provided much wanted eggs, some of which Inga exchanged for other foodstuffs, soap, or needed comestibles. She spooned chicken soup into my mouth each day. I later discovered she had sacrificed one of the hens to make sure I recovered.

I wanted to know what she knew about Morrie. She told me he'd lived with them for many months because Elsa had been in a sanatorium after a fall; that someone called Lieutenant Schmitt had been informed Morrie was here and came to remove him; that this was the same man who killed Opi; she told me Gunther, their neighbour, hid Morrie and that my son was handed over to Ernst Grauman who wanted to train him as a musician and who'd said he knew me. I hadn't known Ernst was a Nazi. I had liked him, he'd seemed friendly. He was a fine pianist. I'd always been aware he was attracted to me. I hoped and prayed this meant he would protect my boy. I didn't blame Inga for entrusting him to the care of Ernst.

Gradually, during the days of my recovery, I told her my story. It was a long story, but she listened. When I broke down, she encouraged me to keep going. Some of the terrible things I saw or experienced in the camps I left out; they were things I couldn't think about. Nor did I want to burden Inga with such images. I needed to come to terms with what I had been through, but not yet. I could verbalise nothing of the worst experiences. I hoped the world would know of this one day. Other people would tell their stories. I was just one of millions of witnesses to the atrocities.

I listened to her story too and understood that we both needed to heal. Time, I hoped, would lessen the rawness we felt. I soaked up the peace at the old house. At first, I sat in a chair, wrapped in a blanket. As my strength grew, I walked in the garden abundant with spring flowers and birdsong. I sat on the bank of the river, listening to the water gently lapping against the little rowing boat which creaked in response. The sun warmed me through the pretty cotton dress of Inga's that she'd altered to fit me. I had no shoes on my feet, not for the first time in recent years, but this time because I chose to have my feet bare. I craved the sensation of dipping my toes in the cool clear water.

Eight weeks after I arrived, Elsa and Hilde appeared. We were so delighted to see each other, we wept for joy. We hugged and could not stop touching one another, holding hands and talking incessantly, reminiscing about Friedrichstrasse and how Hilde and Morrie played and enjoyed so many experiences together.

We talked about Morrie and what might have happened to him.

Chapter 4

Leipzig

1945

ELSA

The strangeness of the house could not be ignored. The place I had always loved was no longer the same. Opi was such a big presence. He brought a sense of security, wholesomeness and completeness to our lives and the very brickwork of Arkadien. With him gone it felt like half of the energy had evaporated and we were functioning in a diluted state. Oma had become both Oma and Opi combined, but somehow it did not seem enough of either of them was left here.

I too felt diminished because my own little family was fragmented. Raoul was living at Gunther's but he couldn't sleep at night. He only fell asleep at daybreak and didn't rise until the afternoon. Some days he was full of energy but mostly he was quiet. There was a sense of dread around him.

He couldn't deny what he'd been involved in over the past eight years, but he believed he did it with integrity and in the belief it was right and for the benefit of the people of Germany. He could talk to nobody about this. It was a taboo subject. It sounded to me, from articles I read in newspapers and from the radio, that most Germans now seemed to be saying they were victims and they did nothing wrong and carried no guilt. Raoul, I knew, did carry guilt and he didn't know how to make reparation.

Tonight, Hilde and I came to Gunther's house for supper so we could see Raoul, catch up on his news and try to have some family time. It was his birthday, and this was the only celebration we could manage. I wanted to see him laugh again and talk at length, with passion about plans for our future. The loss of our home had seen him sink further into depression; setting up home again was something he couldn't do for us, and I knew he felt a failure with this too. Hilde had brought some drawings with her, including a birthday card she'd made for him. It was a self-portrait and was really very good; I would recognise her from this drawing!

I made Onion Cake for our meal as Oma had sacks full of onions, though I had no idea where she got them from. After Gunther died, his house was left empty, so she took food from his kitchen. No point in it going to waste, she said, but his cellar was the real prize and she had been able to make good use of its contents.

This was the cellar where Opi and Gunther had distilled and stored the schnapps they made. The cellar was large, dry and solid with a concrete floor. Oma had been able to exchange some schnapps for other food items such as flour. That's probably how she came to possess so many onions. As the war went on, Gunther lost his animals; they either died or he killed them for meat. He'd had four dairy cows that provided milk and cheese, but they became emaciated and died. The cockerel and all but three hens had died, now two, which still provided us with eight or nine eggs a week.

Gunther's last pig was killed more than a year ago. One side of pork had been brined and smoked. This was hung from the cellar roof and pieces sliced off when needed. The other half of the pig had provided a feast of fresh pork meat for Opi, Oma and Gunther. As always, they'd shared any glut of food that came their way. The remains of the feast were sliced and steeped in vinegar, herbs and rationed sugar to make biltong. After a week the slices were taken from this solution and hung in a long line of hooks in the cellar, where it dried tough as leather but could be rehydrated in hot water. It was very cold at all times of the year in the cellar and, because of the valuable schnapps, the door was locked and bolted, keeping out unwelcomed visitors, including rodents.

Today, there was still left hanging a small piece of smoked pork and a few strips of biltong which Oma used very sparingly.

When we opened the front door to Gunther's, Raoul embraced me and gently – too gently – almost dispassionately, kissed me and then Hilde on the cheek. I knew he was pleased to see us both but he was not himself, he was not the man who took charge of the difficult situation we found ourselves in when we had to leave the Sudetenland just a few months ago; the man who hunted in the fields for food, showed compassion towards less fortunate people walking on the road, made us a cart to get us home because I was too weak to walk all that way, and the man who made sure we were delivered safely to Arkadien. I realised that our flight had given him a spark, a purpose that he had risen to. At that time, when he was being both our protector and leader, he shone. Right now, he had no direction.

We ate the food, a delicious pastry pie filled with fried onions and topped with savoury custard which I knew was one of his favourites. Oma had made an apple cake today. She denied it was for his birthday, but I knew it was. I hoped he would feel a little more content as a result of this meal and may want to consider doing this regularly with Oma and Clara too.

'You know you can eat with us every night?' I said.

'I am fine, I know I can, but I will go to the soup kitchen, there is company there and I may find some work through speaking with other people. I don't want to take any of your food if it isn't necessary,' he said.

'But Papa, we want to share with you,' Hilde said.

'I know, leibchen,' Raoul said and squeezed her hand.

Raoul had once again been to the town hall to search the lists of people identified as refugees, survivors of concentration camps or those known to have died. He had not been successful yet but hoped to give Clara information soon on Ben and Morrie. Every day, more and more names were posted. He said sometimes there was mention of children who died but not their names or at least not their full names. This made me feel numb. How did this happen? No child should ever be exposed to this, be separated from their mother, an innocent whose life had not yet started.

Of course, Raoul had been hunting for Morrie's name, but he also had to look up Morris, Maurice and Max with a surname of Silbermann, Franck, Schwan or Grauman. We all hoped being with Ernst Grauman protected Morrie. Clara was convinced he was still alive. She had to continue to hope, otherwise she had nothing to live for.

I tried to bring up the subject of Clara with Raoul, but he never wanted to talk about her or Morrie. I couldn't help but think of her now, still a sad shadow of her former self; I had both my husband and child with me. Clara had neither.

The first night we arrived back in Leipzig I was unsettled. I hadn't had time to speak with Clara in depth. I came downstairs to find her sitting by the dying fire. She was close to tears and pulled me down on the sofa. I was so happy that we could now sit together without any restrictions.

Holding my hand tightly as if channelling my energy, she began.

'That day, Elsa, when Ben disappeared,' she said in a wavering voice. 'I cannot forgive myself. I am so sorry I left you looking after Morrie and didn't return. I wouldn't have done that if I'd known what was about to happen. Everything went terribly wrong.

'On that day in 1938, I had no time to say goodbye to anyone. I believed I would find out where Ben was, and I expected to return home after an hour or so. I had no doubt Morrie was safe with you, so this was not something to worry about.

'I left Friedrichstrasse and went to the Bruhl but it was chaotic, it was so hot, fires were still burning, police and soldiers were there in force. Bricks, wood and glass were strewn on the roads and pavements, the remnants of the events of the night before, Kristallnacht. This was now being shovelled into the backs of lorries. A damaged, unstable wall was being pulled down. It crumpled on itself, bricks skittering haphazardly onto the ground, just missing me but covering me in a cloud of dust. My sense of unease increased when I saw the road was sealed off and I couldn't get near to Ben's shop. Instead, I was redirected towards the east of the city.

'Soon, I was ushered into the park close to the Zoo. There were so many people here. I didn't think I could cope with the volume of people. I was overwhelmed. My mind couldn't accommodate it all; I just wanted to find my husband. In recent times, I'd become nervous of large crowds, and hadn't realised the extent of the disturbances. I decided to go home. It had been a bad idea to come out with all this going on. I was panicking as the crowd around me closed in and wouldn't let me through. This couldn't be happening, I thought. How had I got into this situation?

'I must go home, was all I could think. Home was safe. You were all there. At home, at the piano, I could calm myself down. Since Ben had been attacked, I'd become more aware of the anger on the street. The hatred towards us. I didn't know how to cope with it apart from to lose myself in my music. Ben had wanted me to see a doctor, but I told him I didn't need medical help. As long as I had him and Morrie, I would be fine. I had put on a confident face but frequently felt paralysed with anxiety.

'As I struggled to escape the crowd I was trapped in, I noticed there were cordons blocking our exit. Civilians had begun throwing things at us, bricks and clods of earth, and eventually we were all forced into the middle of a lake where the water got deeper. As I was thrust forward, the water rose higher until it reached my waist. I felt alone and vulnerable but was squashed up tight to people I didn't know. Where could I find the strength to overcome this?

'Inexplicably, from nowhere, a strange thought came into my head. I had read that the early Christians were stoned to death for their religion. Was this how it felt? Would I be stoned to death? I then remembered being taught at school how Christians would walk together into open water for a mass baptism. Maybe that was it? This mob was trying to convert us here. My thoughts were becoming so muddled. I wasn't sure what was real and what I was imagining. Someone shouted, 'Jews out!' and more people began chanting it, 'Jews out, Jews out!' louder and louder. My head was spinning. I began to hallucinate that the people who were screaming and attacking us were Christian warriors wielding swords and scimitars. I imagined crusaders rampaging across Europe, slaughtering Jews in their path, and I was there too, being attacked, but I had no weapon to defend myself. Part of me knew this was just in my head but I couldn't get a grip on reality.

'Shouts in my ear brought me back. People were clinging to me and swaying in the water. It was November and bitterly cold. For a brief moment, I became lucid and aware of my surroundings. I thought I would die of hypothermia. Eventually, as we were ordered out of the water, I was pushed forward, trying to keep my footing and, with everyone else, I struggled to get to dry land.

'The braying mob around us was held back. I was shuddering, stumbling and hyperventilating. A space opened up, forming a pathway, for us to walk through. Still people called us names but now they were so close they spat at us too. We walked, rather shambled, to the local homeless shelter. I was distressed. Although the shelter was just a few hundred feet away, I collapsed. When I came round, I asked a worker there to help me, but he ignored me. I knew I was losing control and I couldn't hang on to reality.

'All the men from the lake were taken somewhere else within the building. Us women left behind could hear them calling out, though we weren't sure if it was in pain, anger or both. We were given bread and cheese. I was not hungry and was too shaky to eat anyway. We'd been handed scratchy blankets and a pile of donated clothing but nothing warm, no coats. There were five of us women in a windowless room with no heating. We had camp beds to lie on. I tried to be calm and, for a while, was myself again. I lay there staring up at the ceiling, hoping for sleep so it would soon be the morning when I could request to be released. I was sure there'd been some mistake bringing me here. My demons would not sleep though, and I began pacing the small room. I felt the panic rising in me. The other women complained and told me to be quiet. I was agitated and I started banging on the door. "Let me out, let me out!" I called.

'Elsa, I remember how frightened I was. I remember, too, the room spinning and being very hot. I remember lights in my face and being held down and fighting; fighting with all my strength and then I believed Morrie was there, calling, "Mama, Mama where are you?"

'I will be with you, Morrie, I called out in my head, but nothing came out of my mouth.

'There was a high whining sound from something electric.

'There then followed a time that seemed to have no beginning, nor end. The same events were repeated hour upon hour, day upon day, month upon month. The same blankness and lack of emotion inhabited my body, the same loss of purpose. I was in a vacuum. It was a time when most of who I was had disappeared. I know there were several of us going through this in a space together. We couldn't communicate, but were aware of each other's presence.

'It was a time of noises and snatches of conversation that made no sense, and a blurring of images and interiors. I felt my body being moved, being dragged along and my feet not working, and I could never communicate. It was a time of lights and people looking at me, close to my face and other people wailing and holding my hand but not understanding what I said. This became my existence, a merry-go-round of stupor and anguish.

'Sometimes there were wires attached to my head. I was being lifted by many hands, my body jerked and juddered so violently that I sunk down, physically spent, down into deep cavern where there was a numbness that hurt more than any conventional pain and where I began breathlessly running but could never get to where I should be.

'Sometimes screams came out of my mouth but I believed some were trapped inside and could find no way to escape. I imagined they came out through my eyes. Often, I couldn't open my lids and, when I did, they burned in the light. I thought it was evil escaping from my body, so I tried to open my eyelids so I would get well. No matter how ill I was, I knew I needed to get better. Sometimes, I was aware of a sort of consciousness where I remembered and began my search in my head for Morrie, but I couldn't move my arms or legs and, although he appeared as a floating image before me, he was always outside of my reach and then faded away.

'One day, a long time later, things changed, it was announced that the asylum was being closed and we were being transferred to a camp. Those few days were all a blur at the time and still are today. I did remember I was given tablets only, no injections for the two days before we were moved. I'd hated the continuous injections in my buttocks. I was disorientated and couldn't piece together what had happened to me. I discovered I'd been having severe manic episodes which were difficult to control and needed hospitalisation and so, along with other patients, I had become an inmate. I was drugged and given electric shocks as part of my treatment. I was told by those on the ward that I was often restrained and sedated for many hours each day.

'On this day, most of the staff left, and everyone being treated in the asylum was moved out. The staff were our support and had become our friends. Some inmates were unable to leave their beds or stand and had to stay there alone to fend for themselves. For many residents whose medication was stopped abruptly, and whose only home had been here for many years, even decades, this was a bewildering and fearful time. It was 1941 when we were bundled out of the asylum and marched through the streets. I'd been there for just over two years, though I had no sense of time.'

Clara was spent and collapsed into me, overwhelmed by these memories. I took her in my arms and we both rocked back and forth for a few moments.

'My dear Clara,' I said. 'You have been through so much. But you are stronger than you give yourself credit for, because we are both here together.' I wiped the tears from her cheeks. 'You know, after my accident I was very ill, and I was in a sanatorium for nearly two years. I couldn't speak or keep my eyes open at first. I felt confused and frustrated until, one day, my mind and body started to remember who I was; it will be the same for you, Clara.'

Clara squeezed my hand and smiled back at me.

***

'Elsa! I am speaking to you; you seem miles away!' came a strident voice. Raoul's face was up close to mine. 'What are you thinking about?' he asked.

Immediately, I was thrown back into the room in Gunther's house with my husband looking quizzical, and clearly annoyed at me.

'I'm sorry Raoul, it's your birthday, I don't want to upset you, especially today,' I said, smiling at Hilde who was holding something in her outstretched hand.

Raoul was drinking schnapps and I realised he must have used the key to the cellar. If this was helping him, I supposed that it was alright, but I didn't want this taking over, blurring his life and preventing him from focusing on what he wanted. He was on new medication, Pervitin, for his depression and anxiety. He got this on the black market and said it used to be given to the bomber pilots who flew the planes over London.

'Here, Papa, I drew a picture of myself for you for your birthday,' Hilde handed over her portrait on the front of a piece of folded paper. Inside the card she had written:

To my Papa, who is the best Papa in the whole world, Hilde xxxxx

Raoul took it and looked at her drawing. He read the words inside. I think he was struggling to speak.

'Oh, Hilde, I can see it is a picture of you. It looks like you, thank you. I will keep this,' he said as his eyes reddened, and tears gathered along his lower eyelids.

Grabbing his hand to pull him to the table Hilde said, 'Look Papa, look at the drawings that I've done,' as she laid them out, one next to the other, on the table.

'They are so nicely drawn,' said Raoul. 'And accurate too. You are such a natural artist, Hilde. That is definitely wild strawberries, isn't it?'

Hilde beamed, 'Yes, Papa, it is. But I wish I could paint them, they were a deep rich red and I only have graphite pencil.'

'Come with me,' he said and left the room to go towards the back of the house. We both followed him. I had only ever been in Gunther's living room, farmyard and garden and didn't know the layout of the house. We went down some stairs, through a door as if we were going outside but then turned sharp left and up two more steps into what seemed a separate area outside of the main house. Raoul opened the door, switched on the light and led us into the room which had a small bed, a rag rug on the floor, a wicker chair, a sink and a desk.

Hilde was immediately drawn to the desk. On it were paintbrushes, tubes of paint, blocks of poster paint, charcoal, pencils, a sharp knife and dipping pens and pots for water and mixing paint. On the floor next to it was a wooden potato box full of paper. This was in a range of colours, textures and sizes. There, too, were the backs of food packages carefully cut to be painted on, as well as pieces of lino and cardboard. On a shelf above the desk was a collection of books. There was a book on Edvard Munch, one on Leonardo di Vinci, one on Van Gogh, a book showing diagrams of how to draw the human body using just circles and ovals and a book called 'The Art of Botanical Drawing' which immediately caught Hilde's eye.

I couldn't believe these were in Gunther's house. I had no idea he had interests like this. The wall opposite the desk was painted white but this colour was only visible around the edges because it was covered with pieces of art, mainly paper, many overlapping one another, all vying for importance. Some were small, exquisite oil portraits, some carefully executed pen and ink drawings of buildings, delicate watercolours, illustrations, bright confusing abstract art, still life pieces in pencil and some far more naïve pieces. I looked at them and was confused because I realised they weren't all painted by the same person. Gunther had lived alone for as long as I could remember.

As I stood and looked, I realised by the signatures that these pieces of art were the work of many people. I had only just found out about the people who had stayed here, the Jews that Gunther hid from the authorities. These paintings must all be the work of people temporarily locked in here. This was how they filled their time. It must have provided an opportunity for quiet reflection on all that had gone before, the contemplation of their future and a brief respite from immediate fear.

There was a group of maybe twelve oil portraits all by the same hand, I was sure. They had deep, almost black, backgrounds with glossy vibrant colours picked out on the clothing. The use of chiaroscuro made the subjects striking and drew you into the picture. These powerful, attractive pieces of art looked like something from the renaissance and were all signed with the name of Bina. Oma had just mentioned that name to me. This was the name of the Jewish lady who died here and who Gunther had become very fond of.

One set of watercolours were remarkable. I counted over twenty. They looked like illustrations from a book, with every line perfectly drawn and every plane blocked in with precision in sparkling clean colours, leaving the rest of the paper without so much as a smudge. These were all paintings of birds. When I looked carefully, I could see they were signed Gunther. Of course, this made sense. Gunther was always busy with his livestock when I was a child, he had little time for idle chit chat and spent most of his time, when he wasn't running the farm, alone or with his birds. He studied them in all ways but none of us knew he was an artist.

Hilde now had the paints she desperately wanted and could experiment to her heart's delight. Gunther would have been happy she had them. She turned her attention to the paintings on the wall, fascinated by all the work displayed.

'Look, Papa, here. Look, come quickly,' she pointed at a painting of a bird, one of Gunther's pieces.

'Look, Papa, it is a painting of Froh-Froh, I know it is, that's Froh-Froh!' she squealed.

Both Raoul and I looked, and we both agreed it seemed to have the exact marking of Hilde's budgerigar.

Nothing could be better than this, I thought. That little bird lives on in Gunther's painting.

But I was wrong. I was drawn to a simple, rather messy little painting done with poster paint which was slightly obscured by a bold version of Munch's, 'The Scream.'

This almost hidden little painting was a child's vision of a farmyard scene with chickens, a cow with blue horns eating orange hay, in a farmyard with a garden leading down to a river. I realised this was Gunther's garden and that it had been painted from the very window in this room that I now turned my head to look out of.

In the corner of the painting was written in orange paint, Morrie.

Chapter 5

Clara's Story

1945

CLARA

I now had something of Morrie's, a painting done by my boy. I was overjoyed.

When I went to Friedrichstrasse, I thought I would be reunited with many possessions from my past life, items touched by Ben and Morrie, clothes, books and even silly things like Morrie's baby bowl and spoon or my mother's tin opener and photographs I had not been able to part with; so many photographs of my family and Ben's family and the wonderful memories these represented. But that had all been taken away from me; none of those items existed anymore, except in my head. But now I had this wonderful little painting dreamed up and executed by Morrie. I couldn't stop looking and running my fingers over the image, but I ought to put it in a frame before it falls to pieces, already it was crumpled and soft.

Raoul Franck was still looking for the names of Ben and Morrie on various lists. There were lists of the dead, lists of survivors of concentration camps, and lists of displaced people being held in refugee camps. These were displayed at various civic buildings and on walls around the city and were updated as new information came in.

Today I went to the railway station in case either of them was on a transport because I knew trains were coming in carrying people from the camps. There had been two trains a day coming into Leipzig but, as I didn't know where Ben and Morrie had been, I had to wait in the hope they would be passengers. I didn't even know if they had been in one of the camps. This was my first excursion outside the house since I got here. Elsa thought this was too stressful for me and she was worried I might become unwell again. She had been so caring and, once again, it felt like old times. She had been my confidante and I had been hers.

Going to the train station brought back the memory of when I left the asylum and my life in the camps. I tried to comprehend what had happened to me but none of it made any sense. It flew in the face of decency, of the justice and of righteousness. Germany had stood for these values and yet, for the past ten years, seemed to have abandoned them and many of its people.

It helped that I could talk to Oma, Elsa and young Hilde. Talking let me put events into some kind of order and, in time, I hoped I would be able to separate out some of my feelings. As soon as I began to relate what happened to me, I felt a swell of anxiety, powerlessness, and horror. I couldn't help reliving what happened.

I had been in a living hell, seen mankind at his most evil and witnessed suffering beyond description.

I looked at their amiable, encouraging faces, my dear friends, and I finished telling them my story. They were so patient and kind which made the telling so much more difficult.

I didn't know the date that I left the asylum, although I knew it was early in 1941. It was not yet light. Thankfully, we only had to walk two streets away to reach the railway station. The asylum was bombed and no longer existed. Forgotten sounds and sights came back to me and surrounded me as we walked along. I felt like a baby venturing into a new phase of life – both excited and frightened. At this point, I didn't know we were at war, only that we were being transferred to another establishment. I knew my name and that I was Jewish. This was enough to know. A train was standing there. There were about two hundred people on the train, some already aboard and others waiting to get on. There were people clinging to each other and much confusion. I don't know why I did it, but in the melee, I was able to join a different group of people lined up to get on the train beside the asylum group that I was with. The group I should have been with were so distressed and disorientated I thought it would be quieter in this other carriage, and I realised I wanted to be seen as 'normal'. Some of those from the asylum were born with disabilities and cried or let out piercing screams as their only way of expressing themselves. These were some of the noises that had been part of my daily life while I had been ill, and the possibility of quiet appealed to me. I wanted to distance myself from the asylum.

We were pushed roughly into coaches about fifty people per coach. They were very high off the ground: children and the frail and elderly struggled to climb aboard. These were not passenger trains but cattle trucks with huge doors that slammed shut. Some people had possessions, bundles of clothes or a suitcase but some, like us, had nothing. There were old people with sticks and some people with bandaged limbs. Some had recent bruises and undressed cuts and grazes from incidents earlier in the day. Many were not adequately clothed. The journey lasted at least twelve hours, but we were not allowed any fresh air. The train did not stop at all for at least six hours but, even then, we were not allowed to get out. There were two young soldiers with rifles at either end of our carriage. The guards were changed when we stopped. We were given no food.

There was a bucket in the corner with drinking water which was soon empty. Another bucket was to be used as a toilet. The smell made me gag. People collapsed because they had nowhere to sit, and they couldn't stand for so long. Some used the bucket to relieved themselves but there was nothing to clean up with. The bucket soon overflowed, especially as the train lurched along. Some people urinated or messed themselves because they had no choice. I moved to a corner and slid down a wall where I relieved myself. I pushed back through the bodies and went back to where I had been standing feeling embarrassed and ashamed. I wanted to apologise to the people near the corner.

A Jewish man I stood next to told me about the war, what he knew of the camps, about the war effort, about the difficulties he and other Jews were encountering: families being split up, property confiscated and loved ones disappearing. He said we had no choices anymore: all privileges had been removed, Jews and foreigners were being gathered together and transported out of the big towns each day. I was cold, I had only a cotton jacket, no coat and was pleased we were huddled together to conserve body heat. There was so much crying and moaning. I couldn't believe we were subjected to such indignity and being treated like criminals.

At the asylum, my medication had been reduced recently, I was told I was getting better and so I was being weaned off. I had often been awake and allowed to help the orderlies on the wards during the day, but I remembered little of who I was due to the treatments and drugs I'd been given. I was still being sedated at night and given senna, a laxative, every day which was, I believed, to make life easier for the nursing staff. On this train journey, I had not been medicated for two days and, maybe triggered by anxiety, I began hallucinating and once again, as in the past, I thought all the people around me were warriors. I began to wave my arms and to hyperventilate. The man I'd been talking to put his arms around me to restrain me, putting his hand over my mouth so the guards wouldn't hear. I fainted but I was lucky I was slim and small so he was able to hold me up until I came round. 'You must be careful, if you show weakness or you are seen as a troublemaker you will be beaten or shot,' he warned. I managed to stand for the rest of the journey and would always be grateful to that man who said he was called Isaac. I hoped he had survived.

Some people were so tired they fell asleep on the effluent-wet floor. We were so packed-in that they were trampled on by many pairs of feet. The humiliation for these people was beyond belief. Although there were people from all walks of life here, most were Jews who were bourgeois, middle class professional people, well-educated, well-travelled, who ran successful businesses with employees and domestic staff in their homes and yet they were treated like rats in a sewer, except the rats would have been free to go where they pleased. One or two people who fell to the floor I believed were dead. I didn't think anyone on this train had done anything wrong; their only crimes were being mentally incapacitated like the inmates of the asylum, being Jewish or Polish, perhaps being caught committing what the Nazis believed to be misdemeanours, or being unlucky enough to be taken on the street when a round-up was happening. This was such a disgrace, but I soon realised there was no point objecting. We witnessed one person, who had complained to the guard, being hit with the end of a rifle butt.

Something Isaac said triggered a memory: he spoke of his family and asked about mine and for the first time in a long while I thought of Morrie. I had to make my brain remember, I struggled to find old memories. But once it started, bit by bit, it came back. The image of this small blond child came into my head. All the time in the asylum, doctors had tried to make me forget whatever had tipped me over the edge, Kristallnacht, or whatever made me lose my mind. So the good memories had disappeared along with the bad. Suddenly, Morrie had come back to me. I played out what I could remember. I knew I needed to find him but how I did not know. Where could he be after more than two years away from me? Was he still with Elsa and Hilde at Friedrichstrasse?

When we reached the station, we were told we were going to a camp. We were relieved to be off the train and able to breathe fresh air. It was a three mile walk to the camp and some did not make it. I was quite weak but walked now with a little added vigour. We women helped one another by linking arms.

How could I find out about Morrie? This must be my focus, from now on I must stay well. The incident on the train was humiliating and scary and I was relieved it was over. I hoped I could keep in control of my emotions, and I realised I needed to avoid crowded situations; I remembered the feeling of panic from earlier in my life. We settled into the camp which had eighteen barracks all filled with women. We came from many places, not just Germany. Over time, I made friends with women from Austria, Czechoslovakia, Poland as well as Roma travellers.

I managed to get a bunk in the far corner on my own, though months later we were all sleeping two to a bunk due to lack of space. We were set to work carrying bricks for the construction of more buildings at the camp which was heavy dirty work. In time, I got a job working inside a factory repairing uniforms. The men on the train had gone to several smaller satellite camps close by. I didn't see where my fellow inmates from the asylum went. At the camp, I was not at liberty to go anywhere. I could speak with other inmates who lived in my barracks or on work parties and sometimes we watched the new arrivals, but I couldn't look for my son. I was just as trapped as in the asylum, but now I wasn't sedated. It was a mixed blessing to be in control of the thoughts in my head: I was now aware of everything that happened to me. The conditions here were so much worse than the asylum where the staff at least tried to be caring.

I was to remain at this camp for nearly three years. It was a miserable place. We worked all day and were given little to eat. As the years went on, the food supply dropped and the quality lessened. There was a regime of bullying too, both by other inmates and by the guards who were all women and seemed sadistic. On my first day I was introduced to someone called Truda, who I later discovered was someone to be feared if she didn't like you. Truda liked me, and when I had a manic episode and couldn't work, or I was too fearful, I would stay in the barracks, and she would cover for me on the work party rota. She seemed to want to mother me. I had seen how cruel she could be to those she disliked and decided I would be docile and obeyed her wishes. I knew I must survive.

There was so much sickness. Lice were rife. We were overcrowded and consequently there were outbreaks of typhus. Thankfully, I didn't catch it, and tried to keep my few possessions as clean as I could, as well as my body, but we seldom had soap. We only had cold water to wash in and all shared the same water. I think I was just lucky. Everyone had their head shaved upon arrival as a prophylactic against infestations. My hair grew back but they were quite lax on cutting it. So as long as I had a cap on – given to me to wear while carrying building materials – I often avoided being shaved. There was no doctor or dentist at first. Some people medically trained before the war would help us where they could, but it was generally just advice as they had no tools of the trade or medication. The first toilets in the camp, used before I arrived, were made of two poles suspended over a pit that some of the camp workers had dug. People had to balance on the pole to use the toilet and they constantly fell into the pit of effluent. One or two people drowned in there. By the time I got to the camp, they had built basic toilet blocks with sinks at the end of each barracks but there was no privacy, and we were only allowed to go twice a day even though many of us suffered from dysentery.

One day, I looked across a newly staked compound with rolls of barbed wire stretched across its centre, separating the compound in two. I was watching workers constructing the men's camp, adjacent to ours. I saw a man who I thought might have been Ben. The next day, I tried to be in the same place at the same time. I was worried I would be moved on, but I wasn't. I was lucky and again I saw him. He was slightly bent over but looked just like Ben, slender long legs and sloping shoulders and seemed to have his distinctive way of walking. He smiled slightly at me. I dared not wave but instead managed a smile and small nod of my head. I do believe he nodded back. This was so dangerous, if a guard had seen either of us acknowledging each other we would have been shot instantly.

The next three days I was sent on a different work party but then I was assigned a job where I could get to that compound again. The men were still digging foundations for a building as they had been before, but the man I thought was Ben was not there. Had he just been a stranger who, like me, was desperate to find his loved one and had simply returned my smile? For the next year, I made excuses to be near that new section of the camp but never again did I see Ben – or the man I wanted to be Ben.

One day, two visiting SS men we hadn't seen before came to the camp. Us workers were called out of our barracks, or from any work we were doing, into the main compound for an extra rollcall.

'Remove all the Jews,' instructed one of the men.

Many women left. I was not removed. My name was recorded here as Clara Schwan, a petty criminal. This change of category was suggested by another Jewish woman who, like me, looked Aryan and somehow knew it may be easier to survive as a non-Jew. Neither of us had anything to identify ourselves as Jews. I had come from the asylum but had separated from the group so had no papers. When I was asked who I was, I gave my stage name. I hoped that would make life easier.

The SS men spaced us out in lines so they could walk together in front of us and then behind us. We were told if we were touched on the shoulder, we should leave the line and form a group on one side with the two female wardens waiting there. The men approached me from the front, stopped briefly, then moved on. I held my breath. But when they were behind me, I heard one of the men say something and the other reply, 'How old?' then I was touched on the shoulder. My skin crawled. They selected about twenty of us.

We were informed we had been chosen for a special role at Auschwitz, and were then transported in two trucks on a journey which took all night. We were mildly curious what this could be but lacked any real hope or interest as we had been treated with contempt up until now and were given barely enough food to keep us alive. We just hoped this selection process meant more food.

After a long journey travelling through the night, we came to a stop. We heard shouts and dogs barking. The doors at the back of the trucks opened, someone shone a torch into our faces.

'Schnell, schnell,' a loud voice said. Again, it was repeated 'Schnell, schnell.' We were prodded harshly by rifle butts as we awkwardly climbed out. The dogs were straining on their leashes, barking and competing with one another for attention. I was panicked, thinking I would be attacked by them. There were two trucks full of us women. We didn't know where we were or what sort of place this was.

It was just beginning to get light. A faint grey streak had started to grow in the sky. We detected in the faint light that we were surrounded by muddy fields as far as we could see, with trees in the distance and row upon row of low buildings with high wire fencing wherever we looked, and tall look-out towers dotted around. We could see many people behind the fences.

We were marched together in a group for about ten minutes. It was very cold. We had only dresses on, and a thin blanket given when we left the camp. We knew we must keep our eyes on the ground and not speak or look at one another or at the guards; even so, we were aware of hundreds of people walking in large groups, going in the same direction as us. I was horrified to see they were mainly women and children, as well as some people shuffling along with sticks.

We changed direction, turning off the main route and into a low red brick building.

There was a long queue of people here too, but the guards pushed them out the way and ushered us passed them to the front. In here, we tentatively looked at our surroundings.

We were told to strip. There were piles of clothes around us, and noisy autoclaves which prisoners were filling with the clothes discarded by the new arrivals. We had an audience of guards, prisoners and orderlies and I felt ashamed of my nudity. We were pushed into a large shallow bathing area and showers rained down on us. The water was unheated, and some people collapsed on the floor from exhaustion and the shock of the cold water, but we helped each other up because we knew we would be reprimanded if we looked weak. We stood there, shivering and hoping it wouldn't last too long. The shower stopped abruptly, and we were sent into an empty room to dry off. There had been no soap to wash and now no towel or cloth to dry ourselves. If we huddled together that would help us warm up, but we knew this was not a wise move: we might be beaten or shot.

We could see orderlies in the next room, cutting up the sleeves of people's clothing. A growing pile of rings, watches and necklaces found hidden in the clothes were handed to the guard who sat at a table overseeing the work. Some naked prisoners were standing on stools while their hair was cut off and their entire body shaved. Other prisoners were in a line, queuing up to have their camp number tattooed on their forearms.

Again, we chosen ones, because that was how we were beginning to see ourselves, were moved on past these processes to see the doctor. Somebody recorded our names, and we were given a number. From now on this was what we would be known as. The doctor performed an internal examination on each of us and checked our teeth while the rest of the group, still without clothes, waited their turn. When the examinations were finished, we stood an arm's length apart in two lines before him. He walked around each of us, touching our hair and skin.

We would be doing a job that came with benefits. We would have our own room and a bed and would be on the same rations as the guards so would no longer feel hungry. We would be given good clothing which we could choose from the store in the camp, and we would be given make up and silk stockings. We had to agree to a medical operation, though. This was female sterilisation, which the doctor explained would mean we would not be able to have children in the future. Only pure Aryan children could now be born in this new Germany, and we were not of the right calibre, although we had been chosen as being suitable for this particular role.

Most of the women agreed to these conditions and were happy to be sterilised. They didn't know if they would make it through this day and their only concern was getting enough food, which overrode any other consideration. If we agreed to the operation, we would be given bread immediately. No one asked what they were expected to do to be given these privileges. I was suspicious; I had seen something like this at the last camp where female guards undergoing training wanted both me and my friend Ena to sleep in their barracks. I got out of it because Truda spoke up for me, though I don't know what she said. Ena was not so lucky, but afterwards said it was not too bad, they were gentle with her, and she was fed well. Food had become currency and gave those in charge, power over us.

I believed I was the oldest of the chosen women here, though being small I looked much younger than my thirty-four years. I didn't know what would happen to me if I refused what was being offered. The thought of fresh bread was so tempting but, sick with dread, I made the decision to say 'no'. I knew I must keep in control and listen to the music in my head if I was to survive to see my family again.

Four women altogether refused the operation but, surprisingly, we did not receive any punishment. We were even allowed to keep our hair. I'd managed to keep mine hidden under my cap at the previous camp, but now my blonde tresses were on display. It had never occurred to me before, but I could see we were an attractive group of women.

We were given uniform: a thin dress, a scarf for our heads and a pair of clogs. A female guard told us four refusers to get in line and marched us through the muddy field to a barracks.

'This is where you will sleep. Rollcall is twice a day on the parade ground. You will be woken at 4am, You will have breakfast, wash and clean the barracks and be ready for work in half an hour. All the bunks are full so you will share with one or two other people. You are now in Auschwitz- Birkenau camp. You will be working at the Kanada buildings. You are lucky.'

***

None of us knew what Kanada was, but very soon we began to understand life at Auschwitz-Birkenau and realised that indeed, for the moment, we were lucky. Kanada was the land of plenty.

The women who agreed to be sterilised underwent the operation and we didn't see them again.

They became prostitutes. A brothel had been set up in Auschwitz 1 which was three kilometres from where we were. Non-Jewish male prisoners who'd completed exceptional work were rewarded with a fifteen-minute session with one of these women. We heard that German officers too would visit but this was not official. Up until now, the prostitutes had been Jewish or Roma from Auschwitz. We had been chosen as the elite. Jewish men could not visit these women no matter how hard they worked or how impressive the quotas they achieved.

We knew none of these facts at this time.

Weeks after our arrival, one of the refusers who'd become my friend told me she'd seen one of the prostitutes walking in the street when she was taken with others to do work at Auschwitz 1. She said this girl looked like a fancy-dress apparition, walking along a pathway in high heels and full make-up. She seemed a different species to us, and my friend wondered if she had made the right choice, not to be sterilized. She said she looked at this vision as the other women in the camp must have looked at us. We saw the exhausted female prisoners with shaven heads leaving the camp each day on work-parties and knew they were envious of us.

The Kanada buildings were where the property of inmates, both the living and the dead, ended up.

Later, I learned that when people went into the gas chamber to be poisoned, they believed they were about to have a shower. They were encouraged to fold their clothing carefully and tie shoelaces together so they wouldn't lose anything. This exercise kept everyone calm but, in fact, nobody returned to look for their possessions. Within an hour or so they were all dead and had been cremated. Their clothes were sent to Kanada.

We were close to the crematoria and were often showered in ash. The belongings came from the registration block, the gas chambers and the suitcases left on the railway platform when prisoners arrived. The cases, now emptied of their contents, lay unceremoniously in the mud, covered in ash. We women were worked hard and were constantly scrutinised by the guards. It was exhausting work. Everyone, including the guards, stole whatever they could get away with. As long as you weren't caught, it was the only way to survive. Occasionally, we found items of food which we were allowed to exchange for other items or could eat ourselves.

I had so little in this world, but I had grown cunning and, somehow, I was here: I'd survived the camps. I now owned a special pair of brown shoes, size nine, the same size Ben wore. Despite the risks, I had saved these for my Morrie.

Chapter 6

Leipzig

Christmas 1947

HILDE

It was soon to be Christmas. Last winter was the coldest Mama or Oma could ever remember. So many people had died. Already, we had snow here and it was so cold again. We were only allowed to use electricity in our homes three times a week. We had logs for the fire, sawn from trees on Gunther's field, but we had utilised this for several years and because many families did the same, it was a resource quickly becoming depleted. We were often so cold we wore as many clothes as we could get on.

To keep myself occupied, I read the newspapers Papa brought but nothing much in them interested me; there weren't funny stories or anything entertaining in there. Now, though, there were advertisements for the Christmas Market at Augustusplatz, which I really looked forward to, as well as many musical concerts to celebrate Christmas. I loved Christmas, the feeling of goodwill and all the old traditions. Leipzig was beautiful when all the pretty lights were lit up in the centre of town, but that was nostalgia for years ago and I wasn't sure what would happen this year.

The usual headlines in the newspapers were still about Nazi war criminals and the International War Crimes Tribunal at Nuremberg trials, which were to be extended to include soldiers and industrialists. The Soviet Union controlled the sector of Germany where we lived and they were supposed to work together with the other sectors, run by Great Britain, France and USA, that all fought to defeat the Nazis, but they seemed to disagree with each other most of the time.

I just wanted to get on with my life. I was now sixteen, as tall as Mama, and still had blond hair. I had seen posters of American films, bright colours and happy faces, and I would love to wear pretty, modern clothes like they did in these films, but I doubted that was possible anytime soon. I read there were clothing and food shortages and many people had died because they were homeless, cold and hungry. Somebody wrote in the local paper saying,

'The war is over and though there isn't fighting and bombing it seems to have left us in a state of deprivation and misery.'

This was replied to by one of our government officials saying:

'...in time we will rebuild the city and there will be a greater sharing of wealth that will benefit all citizens of Leipzig.'

We were lucky: Oma, Clara and Mama had preserved food for the winter. We caught fish in the stream, which we brined and dried, and the garden had produced food for us. But we had to be very frugal with how much we ate because it wouldn't last the winter otherwise. We made remedies to get us through the winter: rosehip syrup, from the hips I collected on the wild rose bushes in the woods, used to treat fever; apple cider vinegar (though this wasn't yet ready) to put on cloths to draw out a fever; elderberry syrup which was dark and strong and would rid any congestion on the chest. We also had honey that Oma exchanged for onions, so we were feeling ready for the cold weather. We got a bread ration most days and sometimes other food items, but what and when was anyone's guess!

I would be going to art school next year, I hoped, if the building got refurbished so it could open to students. I couldn't wait to be with girls of my age. One or two of the neighbours were teenagers, so we went to each other's houses, looked at American magazines or listened to music on the gramophone and danced around, but Mama and Papa didn't let me go out much because they said it wasn't safe on the streets.

The city was gradually being cleared, though there was still bomb damage everywhere you looked. I thought this would take years. One or two places were being rebuilt or repaired. Mama took on a job with the council. She was a rubble clearer. There were hundreds of women doing this job around the country. The idea was to clear the bricks and mortar off the ground so it was flat and, eventually, new buildings could be erected on those sites. She did it four days a week and got paid, which meant we could buy extra food, but there wasn't much available to buy. The government controlled most of the distribution but there were some unofficial vendors selling comestibles, though they asked extortionate prices. Last week, we bought Hershey Bars and the week before, canned beans and salmon.

There has been fighting in the street. Some was triggered by political disagreements, old grievances connected with the war, Nazi accusations, and a dislike of the Russians, but some has been fighting over food. My father was mostly silent. Nothing had improved for him. He was badly beaten up recently and said that he was set upon when he was out looking for work. He usually went out after dark. He was now drunk some of the time and took medication to help his mood, but it didn't work. There were many men in this town like my father, and many living on the streets.

Today, I was set up in Gunther's studio, which was what I had named the room with the painting materials and paper. Papa was sitting in the blue wicker chair in front of the window, watching me while I worked. This was when he seemed the calmest and happiest, though I didn't think he was ever truly happy these days. I thought Papa looked like a painting by Van Gogh, because he was next to the bed which had a yellow cover over it, the small square window with four panes of glass gave a vista of the countryside and a winter blue sky. Papa had dark rings beneath his eyes and there were wrinkles I hadn't noticed before. He now had a beard flecked with grey and his hair was uncombed. He had a rather sad expression on his face most of the time and, although I was painting a series of birds, I had stopped to sketch him because the dropping sun shining through the window lit up the side of his face with an orange glow. This would make a good painting using bold hues. It would be my next piece of work, I decided.

I sketched all kinds of birds in the garden, including a parrot which never left after Oma let all the birds out of Gunther's. He flies away, probably going into other people's gardens, but a few days later he returns. We left the aviary window open in Gunther's garden so he had somewhere to roost and, although we had nothing to feed him, we saw him occasionally flying in or out of the shed. Earlier today, I began painting him in all his glory. What incredible colours he was, I hoped when I finished I would do him justice.

I had recently finished a painting of 'old Holstein', the apple tree that was split in two by a bolt of lightning yet still produced apples each year. It was the most experimental I had been with paint. I composed it on the back of a piece of lino using oil paints; it stands about four foot high. I'd read about different methods of painting in one of Gunter's books. I used impasto oil paint, applying it with a pallet knife I found. It was still wet and would take weeks to dry. It was obvious what it was, I think, but I had successfully used many unexpected colours to make the bark come alive, with gold and silver apples jumping out from the branches. I was pleased at what I had achieved. Papa often sat gazing at it, saying he saw different faces in the bark each time he looked. He remembered many faces from his past. This was the only time I had seen him concentrate on anything recently. I did believe he was somewhat content when he was here with me.

Mama entered the studio. She was wearing the boiler suit she wears for work, and a pretty scarf covering her hair to keep out the brick-dust. She smiled at me and asked Papa in a firm, but not unkind, way to go into the living room of the main house with her as she wanted to speak with him. Papa followed her, but I noticed he had his head down which made me want to cry. I realised she didn't want to speak to him in front of me.

At first, I heard muted conversation, but then Mama began crying. Before long, she was shouting at my father. I couldn't hear Papa at all. I opened the studio door and climbed the stairs that led to the main hallway of the house to try to listen. Mama was talking about Papa not working.

'There is no reason you cannot get a manual job, Raoul. You are capable and have always been resilient, resourceful and strong. Please, just get out there and be the man I married. Ignore the jibes. You need to be thicker skinned! I will continue to do the work I do, but by the end of the day my weak leg aches and I'm limping. Please don't let us have to rely on me for income. I'm not sure how much more of this work I can do. We always said we were a team, you and me, but you aren't doing your share. I'm sorry if this hurts you to hear this, but you have to see how I feel, I can't do it alone!'

I couldn't hear Papa's reply.

I silently returned to the studio to continue painting the parrot, but I was too unsettled to concentrate. I would come back with fresh eyes tomorrow to finish it.

When I went down to the living room, Papa was alone and snoring loudly with his head lolling over the arm of the couch and his arm fallen to the floor, still holding a half-filled glass of clear liquid. I took the glass from his hand without waking him and put it on the table next to his newspaper.

Mama had gone to work. She was the only one of us who brought in a regular wage.

Oma ran the house and was always busy, though was far slower than she used to be, so I helped her with the heavier jobs and with cooking.

Clara was still too frightened to venture far from the house and had stopped going to the railway station. Trains no longer came in from camps; it was more than two years since the end of the war.

She still didn't know what happened to Ben and Morrie, but she never gave up hope they were alive.

There was a man, Claude, who lived on his own at the end of the street. He was blind and cared for by his sister who he'd lived with until last year when she died. We discovered he was a piano tuner, quite a common occupation for a blind person we later learned, and so we did a swap with him. The agreement was that he would tune our piano regularly and one of us would tidy his house and do some washing for him. This made him so happy. I think that he was lonely. Actually, we ended up taking him a meal once or twice a week. In return, he gave us some of his rations and he had become like an old uncle to me.

Because of Claude, Clara was able to teach piano lessons at Arkadien, on the old but now functioning piano. There weren't many customers, but every small contribution of money helped, and Clara was once again enjoying playing and felt she was being useful. When I heard Liszt's Liebestraum being played, it felt like some sort of normality was settling over us. I remembered Morrie telling me this was his Mama's happy piece of music. I could see it made Clara feel tranquil and at peace with herself.

Mama, too, seemed to have plans. She was studying. She'd gained qualifications many years ago and was now going through her old college books to refresh her memory and rekindle her love of reading. She wanted, eventually, to train to be a primary school teacher and joked she and I could go to college together. We were happy we could talk about our futures.

Finally, we were all in a routine. Even Papa had a sort of routine. Our daily lives were running quite smoothly and there seemed to be nothing on the horizon that would disrupt this.

Chapter 7

Leipzig

Sylvester 1947

ELSA

It was Sylvester, New Year's Eve, the Feast of Saint Sylvester.

We were excited for the celebration later, and that tomorrow would be the start of a New Year. The lanterns hanging in the garden from Christmas would be lit as the sun set. Oma was making cinnamon doughnuts and Hilde was preparing to decorate the front of the house with coloured paper figures she had painted for New Year. Clara was at the piano, working out a programme we hoped to sing together around the piano in the evening.

Once we'd eaten dinner, we planned to partake in Bleigiessen to see what luck we would have next year. Hilde had never done this and, although feigning nonchalance the way only teenagers can, was clearly intrigued to see what her future might bring. Bleigiessen was an old tradition connected to the church; it was the custom for German families to gather together for it each New Year's Eve.

First, you needed a little piece of lead, a candle, a spoon and a bowl of cold water. Opi had kept a tin of lead pellets in the workshop we used just for this purpose, though I didn't think he and Oma did it during the war. A pellet of lead was put on a spoon and heated over the lighted candle until it melted. The molten lead was dropped into the water and, as it cooled, it created a shape. There were set shapes to look for, the obvious being a heart meaning 'love and health', but everyone interpreted what they saw in their own way and we didn't take it too seriously. We planned to do this an hour or so before midnight to ensure we were ready to watch the fireworks display above the city.

I had made us soup for lunch and was dishing it up when there was a knock at the front door. Oma opened it and a man was standing there, holding a letter.

'Clara Silbermann?' he asked Oma.

'No.'

The man held out a letter addressed to Clara. Clara, who must have heard him, stopped playing the piano and appeared in the doorway to the hall. Oma moved aside.

'Frau Silbermann?' the man asked.

Clara nodded.

'Are you Frau Silbermann, wife of Benjamin Silbermann, formally of Friedrichstrasse?'

'Yes,' she said in a quavering voice.

The man, who I realised was wearing the uniform of a newly recruited soldier, handed her the buff-coloured envelope, saluted, then left.

Clara had gone deathly white and was motionless. I think she had a premonition about the contents of the letter.

'Clara, my dear, come sit,' said Oma, taking her hand and leading her to the sofa.

Clara walked shakily to the sofa, holding the letter in her hand as though it might explode at any moment. It was stamped with various official departmental post marks. She turned it over, noting the return address on the back. She told me later that she considered sending it back and not opening it, because then she wouldn't have to read the contents.

Clara had spent ten long years hoping her husband and son had survived the atrocities of the war, that, somehow, they had dodged the violence, the gas chambers, the dehumanising bullying and the daily grind of overwork, tiredness, hunger and disease.

Suddenly, with new resolve, she stood up, turned the letter over and tore the top away quickly, pulling out the single sheet of folded paper from inside.

Very little had been written on this, it read thus: -

Dear Frau Silbermann,

This letter is being sent to you because the original letter sent to the address we had on record in Friedrichstrasse could not be delivered. The building had been destroyed and was no longer habitable. It has taken this department some time to locate your present address.

We understand that you are the wife of Benjamin Isreal Silbermann of that address.

I am sorry to inform you of his death.

Benjamin Israel Silbermann had been moved to Theresienstadt camp in 1941. He died of dysentery in 1942 and it is believed his body was cremated there.

We have no other information.

Sincere condolences,

(Signed with an illegible signature)

The Department for information of the Deceased.

Clara's knees buckled; I caught her as she let out a howl of anguish.

'Is that it!? Is that all I get after so long? Is that all Ben was worth?' she sobbed.

We sat with her, held her hand, made sweet tea and eventually laid her on the sofa with a blanket covering her so she could sleep. I was hopeful that her anguished slumber might put a sliver of distance between the shock of this news and having to accept the reality of Ben's death. We all felt her grief. This was a finality we did not want to hear. Yet he was just one of millions. It was all too matter of fact.

Clara was still deeply traumatised by her own experiences in the camps. And, even before any of those gruelling experiences, she had suffered in life, on and off, with her mental health since the birth of her son. Ben had been her support and I knew that, until this moment, she had been hoping he was still alive and would return to her.

In my own heart-of-hearts, I didn't think he could have survived. Clara had told me of the masses of Jews she'd witnessed filing into the camps daily, and she knew most of them mysteriously disappeared. We didn't know then but, of course, we knew now that these were death camps.

This terrible news made me anxious for my friend. How would she get through this? Perhaps clinging on to her hope that Morrie was still alive would keep her going. But time had marched on and we had heard nothing of his whereabouts.

While Clara slept, we had our lunch in silence, all with our own thoughts. I took some soup to Raoul and told him the news. He listened but said nothing; just pulled his coat on and went to the door.

'Raoul, it is snowing again outside. Please eat some soup if you are going out, it'll keep you warm,' I said.

He mumbled something about 'making things right'.

But it was too late for that.

It was a sombre day, not at all as we had expected. When Clara finally awoke, she sat in a chair, unable to talk or engage in any way. As the sun set, Hilde went outside to stick the pretty painted figures on our front window, and on Gunther's too. When she returned, she told us it had stopped snowing and Papa was back because the light was on. In a futile attempt to lift the mood, she lit all the lanterns hanging from old Holstein, the lightening tree, in the back garden.

We got through the evening, but it was an ordeal. It felt so long, and we seemed to have nothing to say that hadn't been said in the past. Now the unthinkable had happened, there seemed nowhere to take the conversation. It was snowing very heavily now, but we had an extravagant log fire in celebration of New Year, piled high with logs, so, thankfully, we were all warm. Nobody really wanted dinner, though we went through the motions for Hilde's sake.

We did not do Bleigiessen. We would leave that for another year.

Clara slept again but rallied as the clock neared midnight.

Oma said with as much jollity as she could muster, 'Let's all join together to see in the New Year and hope for better fortune for dear Clara and for us all.'

We four women put our arms around each other and formed a circle, hugging each other as we wept.

At the turn of the year, bells could be heard chiming all through the city. The distant sound of fireworks popping, whizzing and exploding in the night sky marked the moment, but we didn't go outside to watch the spectacle.

We had no way of knowing if fortune would be kind to us in the New Year.

Chapter 8

Leipzig

New Year's Day 1948

ELSA

It began before dawn when it was still dark outside and everyone at Arkadien was in bed. We were exhausted, stunned by the events of yesterday and trying to come to terms with the tragic news. I didn't think any of us had slept. I was staring up at the darkness, trying to sleep, trying to stop thinking. I heard a noise. I got up and went onto the landing to see Hilde stood at the front door, which was wide open. A flurry of snow was blowing into the hall and the wind was howling. Oma joined me, both of us tying our dressing gowns as we rushed down the stairs, telling Clara to stay in bed, she was too distressed and must rest.

'Shut the door, Hilde!' Oma yelled against the sound of the weather. 'Come in now, please,' she addressed two men in the doorway.

Two uniformed policemen wearing hats and greatcoats over their uniforms stepped into the hall and stamped their snow-covered boots on the door mat. They looked embarrassed and apologised for it being so early and for making a mess. Puddles formed on the tiled floor almost immediately. They both had little piles of snow on their shoulders and hats and looked like two official snowmen. We all looked at each other, wondering what this was about. Was this more to do with Ben and what happened to him? Clara wouldn't cope with that. We were still absorbing the knowledge he was dead, surely it was impossible that more information had come to light.

'Just a moment,' said Oma.

She opened the door to the living room, and someone turned on the light. We all crowded in, Hilde clinging to my arm. Oma crossed the room to rake the fire, its red embers still twinkling from last night amidst the growing mound of grey ash. She quickly put on a large handful of kindling and a few coals; the fire sprang back to life, darting with flames. We all just stood and watched her, nobody said anything. It was as though we had to set the scene before we could listen to whatever bombshell these men were about to drop.

Clara silently joined us and took Oma's hand.

'As I was telling the young lady before,' said one policeman, 'I am here to speak to the wife of Herr Raoul Franck.'

'That's me,' I said, a little taken aback. This was not what I had expected.

We all remained standing. The policemen stood very upright, and both seemed nervous, as if trying to work out the most appropriate demeanour for this situation.

'Please take a seat, Frau Franck,' the other said.

'No! Tell me what is this about! What about Raoul? What has happened? Tell me!' I demanded. I felt dizzy and overwhelmed by fear. Whatever it was I had to know.

Speaking slowly and clearly the first officer said, 'I am sorry to tell you, but Herr Franck fell tonight and has been pronounced dead.'

We put our hands to our faces and gasped in unison. Clara fainted backwards onto the sofa and Oma sank down next to her, taking her hand. Hilde, still clinging to me, began crying. I was numb and began shaking. I found it hard to speak, my voice tremulous and small, but I managed to gasp out, 'What do you mean, he fell? How? Are you sure he is dead? Falling over wouldn't kill him. Are you sure it is Raoul? It must be someone else. How did you find me?'

There were so many questions to ask them, I realised, but instead of answering me the officer handed me a folded piece of paper. I opened it and there was Hilde's face. It was the birthday card with the self-portrait she'd made for Raoul last year. Inside was the greeting 'To the best Papa in the whole world xxxxx' and on the back she had written Hilde Franck, Arkadien, Flussgasse, Leipzig.

The policeman handed me a metal object. It was a round medal enclosed by a wreath of leaves with a crown at the top. I recognised this as the medal Raoul received in WWI. He was proud to have served his country. He said he carried it to remind himself how lucky he had been to survive, and it became his lucky charm.

He told me it had brought me to him.

His name was etched around the rim. It said *Uffz Raoul Johann Franck.**

I dropped down onto the arm of a chair, holding the card in one hand and the medal in the other. Hilde stepped back from me, tears running down her face.

'Where is he?' I said. 'Can I see him?'

'He has been taken to the hospital, there has to be a post-mortem later,' the other policemen said.

Hilde yelped at the mention of post-mortem and went to her grandmother who pulled her down next to her, wrapping her arms around her.

'Can you take me there?' I asked, realising I must be practical and try to rise above my shock. It was not yet the time to engage with my emotions or to even accept what I had been told.

The officer said, 'You can leave it a day or two if you like, I realise this is a shock.'

'No, I need to see him,' I said.

'Are you sure, Elsa?' said Oma.

---

* *Unteroffizer (Corporal)*

'Somebody has to come to the hospital to give a formal identification,' the policeman said. 'So we are happy to take you. We have a vehicle with snow tyres so it will be better if you come with us rather than trying to get through this weather yourself. We can arrange to bring you home afterwards?'

I felt like I had been taken over by some other force and was being propelled in a direction I could not stop. There seemed to be an inevitable momentum in the room that would happen even if I did not agree.

'Let me get dressed and I'll be with you,' I said.

'Can I come with you, Mama?' Hilde asked.

'Are you sure, Hilde?'

'Yes, Mama, I am old enough and I need to be there - with Papa.'

I ran up the stairs and within five minutes had washed, changed into warm day clothes, combed my hair, secured it with two combs and pulled on my fur boots. Hilde, too, got ready quickly. We located our coats, hats and gloves and met the policemen outside.

Oma stood on the step, looking worried.

'Don't worry, Oma, you look after Clara, and we will be back as soon as we can. But go inside, it is too cold for you out here and the snow is heavier still.'

***

When we returned, it was nearly evening. I had formally identified my own husband's body, which now lay cold and mangled in a mortuary. I couldn't bear to think what Hilde must be going through right now. I could barely process it myself. There were forms to fill in, many forms, but I wasn't expected to do this yet.

Yes, he did fall.

He fell from a scaffold high above the street on the new building site which was closed for the New Year. The police informed me he was not on the payroll of the building company so had no legitimate reason to be there. They didn't know how he gained entry or how he managed to get to that floor.

But they didn't know him as I did; they never knew the tenacious, resilient Raoul who could make things happen and, though I too had not seen that side of Raoul for several years, I always knew was locked in there somewhere.

Why did he do this to us? Were we not enough for him?

After making sure Oma was seeing to Hilde, I slipped back out of the house. I found myself heading to Gunther's. Raoul's desk in Gunther's house had a neat arrangement of papers and envelopes lined up in some sort of order. I recognised none of these. I didn't even know why I was here. I started leafing through the pile, imagining the last time my husband's warm fingers touched these pages. In the centre of the pile was a white envelope, and in his bold neat hand, he had written my name:

Elsa.

Shakily, I opened the envelope and read the sheets of paper within.

My dear Elsa,

You will be reading this because I will no longer be alive.

I have failed you and Hilde and cannot make things right.

I have failed myself and everyone I know and respect.

I joined the Nazi Party because I believed we would work towards a better Germany, but the ideology changed and intensified, becoming cruel and unfair. I struggled to do my job, but I have to admit that I went along with it. I became depressed, but once I was on medication it gave me a false air of confidence. My department achieved all the targets set and the level of efficiency was admired. I was moved up the pecking order, but I always made sure I avoided direct contact with families and delegated the more onerous tasks to others. I knew some of the department's working methods were questionable. Somehow, I was promoted again which meant the move to the Sudetenland.

I felt happier because this new job was about organising labour and I hoped I would not be involved with Jewish families as I had been in Leipzig. They expected me to impose a strict regime with the same bullying methods being used to control the workers there – Jews, Poles and Italians – so really, nothing was any different. I am so sorry to tell you that while I never pulled the trigger or ordered deaths, I turned a blind eye to the methods of some of the SS officers in the camp and gave them free rein to do what they wanted because I did not know how to handle the situation. I feared I would be found out and couldn't see any future for me. I worried what would become of you and Hilde.

You were both just a few hundred yards away from all that was going on at that camp. You were in the beautiful home you had made for us at the big house, which became my sanctuary. I would walk in that garden, on that soft grass, amidst the beauty of nature, smelling flowers, marvelling at the abundance of plants in the kitchen garden, while birds sang all around me. These birds that travelled great distances had a precarious existence, they survived day by day, but they were free and did not know about war. I am pleased that Hilde's budgerigar was set free. I hope she lived a better life outside of a cage.

I did not want to burden you with my troubles. I took more of the medication and was offered stronger drugs, but I felt even more trapped. You often said how calm I was and how quiet too, but that was the drugs. I had to shut off the part of my brain that had seen the deprivation and ill treatment of the prisoners and I was beginning to hate myself for being so weak.

When the camp and factory were bombed and there were casualties, I was able to take charge and be the leader I know I am capable of being. For a few months I re-established my authority. Then towards the end of 1944, when we realised that Germany was losing the war, I started to be bullied myself by the two SS officers who by now were effectively running the camp, doing the job that I couldn't do and so I struggled to remain in my post. I felt I was a laughingstock and I was pleased to leave when we did.

I am not good enough. I have never felt good enough. I always have to run away because I fail. I am a coward.

Our journey to Leipzig was gruelling but now seems, in retrospect, to have been an adventure for our little family. Since returning I have found no solace. Our home was destroyed, and I am too ashamed to live at Arkadien even if Oma had asked me. I am lonely and valueless now.

I have approached official organisations for work, but they do not want me. I was a Nazi. There is a hatred of anything to do with the Nazi Party, which I understand, though some of those now in positions of authority were Nazis too, I know. Some people I worked with have been given jobs. There is a conspiracy of silence and denial. They distance themselves from involvement with the Party and they talk about being a victim of the system. Some have changed their names and moved to new towns. If you are lucky, there seems to be a network of 'who you know' that means people have successfully gained employment within big companies, but these people are not like me.

I have always been single-minded about giving my all to my job and my family and I have never been part of any social clubs or secret brotherhoods that took me away from you. Perhaps that is where I went wrong. You and Hilde have always been the reason behind all my decisions.

I have met people recently that I knew in Leipzig, before the war who were in the police force with me, as well as army officers I knew during the war. There are certain facts I have discovered that I can no longer keep to myself and I need to tell you. It is all too much for me to deal with. I feel that I am running in circles and cannot find an escape route.

There is a price on my head, or at least some sort of warrant has been issued to apprehend me.

It seems that the department connected to The International War Crimes tribunal at Nuremberg want to interview me in connection with some events at the camp in the Sudetenland. They are looking for War Criminals to punish for their crimes. I know it will not be sufficient to say 'I didn't know' what was going on. I oversaw the camp, and it was my responsibility to run both the camp and the production in the factory. I should be able to supply a good explanation for the events that took place but, as I have already said, I will not be able to. I cannot let you experience the ignominy of my public disgrace or having to watch me go through a court case.

My name will be blackened and yours will be too, what a legacy for Hilde!

I don't think I can remain at liberty much longer. Many of the men on the streets or in hostels are desperate to move on. They want work, a home and a normal life, and turning me in may mean they are rewarded in some way. There is no love lost out there between any of the men when they have to fight for food or a dry place to sleep. Nobody knows that I live in Gunther's house, I have remained vague about where I stay and careful to avoid being followed. I cannot have any of you harmed, but one day, if things were to continue as they are now, they may discover where I live, which would leave you vulnerable.

I also need to tell you that I have done some digging and found out some facts about Morrie Silbermann. Not much, and I don't want to raise Clara's hopes or cause her any further hurt because I cannot tell her what she wants to hear. I met someone who was a guard in Auschwitz and remembers Grauman the 'musician visiting with a child prodigy'; I realised this was probably Morrie.

Ernst Grauman, it appears, had Morrie with him almost up until the time that Auschwitz was liberated. It appears that Grauman treated him like a son. They visited high-command events across Europe and went to military camps to give concerts to the upper echelons of the Party for such things as The Führer's birthday. Morrie was seen as a musical protégé and, somehow, Grauman was allowed to keep the boy with him. As far as the authorities were aware Morrie – now called Max Grauman – was an Aryan, Grauman's nephew, and he came to no harm, at least not while Ernst Grauman was alive.

The 16th December was Beethoven's birthday. The Führer identified with Beethoven, whom he thought possessed the same heroic German attitude as himself. He encouraged the playing of Beethoven's music throughout the war. On this day in 1944, many high-ranking Nazis were due to assemble for the annual Beethoven concert. Ernst and Morrie were to be the stars. It went ahead, but was not the big event expected because many officers were involved in a major military offensive launched that same day in the Ardennes.

Grauman was caught in flagrante delicto with a senior officer who had something to do with the storage of art. This was at Auschwitz, where Ernst and Morrie had put on the concert the day before. It was generally known that he was probably bisexual, but an ambush was set, orchestrated by a former lover. Grauman was found by a high-ranking SS officer who relished being able to make an example of him and his mate, who had long been an adversary of his. This man was a religious bigot who made it his business to rid the SS of such practice. It was anyway a crime that would result in severe punishment, though many officers attended parties where every sort of sexual preference was catered for. Grauman was arrested and locked up, but he got hold of a pistol and shot himself, whether this was his own choice or because he was forced, no one knows.

The trail on Morrie then goes cold.

Lieutenant Schmitt terrorised Oma and Opi and caused me difficulties when I was in Leipzig. He killed Opi and for that I cannot forgive him. He is violent and unstable. He had left Leipzig but is now back here and in hiding, avoiding the Nuremberg authorities who now want to interview him too. There were many unauthorised killings attributed to him in the war. I cannot have him return to taunt Oma and I now know where he is staying. I shall make sure he will not harm your family anymore.

My guilt cannot be apologised for. Those people buried on the hillside under the trees cannot be brought back.

My darling Elsa, you have been a good and dedicated wife and mother. Nobody could surpass you. I am sorry I did not give you the life I had promised you, was not the husband you deserved and that I will not see Hilde grow up, but you will both be better off without me. So many good people have died in this war. I am worthless and do not deserve to be here.

The present and future merge for me and my capacity to think anymore has been paralysed.

The world will soon forget I was ever here.

Thank you and I am sorry.

I love you.

Always, Raoul

*** *** ***

I sat for a long time on the wooden chair at Raoul's desk where he had sat to write this letter, only hours before. There was so much for me to understand and digest in his letter, and I realised some of it I should not share. In fact, I could think of nobody who would benefit from hearing what he'd told me. I didn't want him diminished in the eyes of others. The police didn't seem to know anything about Raoul. They'd said he was known at the soup kitchen, but nobody knew where he lived. It was assumed we were estranged and that he lived elsewhere. Nobody knew he lived in Gunther's house.

There were four identical envelopes laid out on the desk, one each for Hilde, Oma and Clara and another envelope with my name on. I picked this up, it was not sealed. He had written inside the flap of the envelope:

I will always be holding your hand - stay strong. I love you. Raoul

Inside the envelope was his wedding ring.

We had wondered, just yesterday, what fortune the New Year would bring.

I folded his letter and put it deep inside my pocket. I had to decide what to do with it. His words needed to be hidden until I could think straight. I would keep the letter for now, but I knew I had to destroy it. I didn't want Raoul being seen as a criminal of any sort. I believed he was a good man who had human frailty and did his best.

I collected the four envelopes and took a final look around the room. Before I turned off the light I said, 'Goodnight, Raoul.'

I returned to Arkadien, to my grieving family. We had suffered the news of two deaths, two husbands, in twenty-four hours.

Today was New Year's Day.

Chapter 9

Raoul's letters

1948

HILDE

Gunther's nephew was to sell the house. He hadn't come to see it and had asked Oma to organise the removal of all the furniture and effects. She and Opi were executors of Gunther's will and we discovered that Oma would inherit some money, though we didn't yet know how much it would be.

The first things we removed were Papa's things.

It's been two months since the funeral, and we all had to deal with Papa's death in our own way. I couldn't believe I would never see him again. I spent the last two weeks painting a portrait of him, mainly in yellows, orange and blue, from the sketch I did in the studio. I had to get it finished quickly while I could see him in my head still, while I could remember our conversation on that day and feel the sun shining in on us both. It would be my tribute to him.

When I closed my eyes, I thought of him, and I struggled to sleep because I knew he must have been in the pit of despair to do what he did. He had always been someone who found solutions to problems. I wished he had told me how he was feeling, but I knew I couldn't have helped any more than I did. Mama told me he believed he'd tried everything to get work and move on with his life, but he couldn't erase the memories of the war and felt he had no options left.

This was what he wrote in the note he left me. I'd read it so many times I'd memorised it.

My dear Hilde,

I shall not see you grow up, but I know you will be strong and kind and that you have so much potential to be whatever you want to be. I suspect you will be an artist or a naturalist? I hope that you will always be true to your beliefs and take care of your mother. Remember that I loved you very much and have treasured our time together. Look to the future, my dear daughter.

Papa

OMA

'Come on Hilde where are you?' I called up the stairs. 'I want you to clear Gunther's studio. Ah! There you are! All the paintings can go into this suitcase I have here. All the art materials you can store in Opi's shed. I don't mind, if you want, you can move some of the woodworking tools and set up a little bench to do your art on. What do you think?'

'That's great; I was wondering if I could keep all the art materials,' Hilde said.

'Of course you can, nobody else will want it. So, no more painting today, get on with it because I want this emptied by tomorrow when the estate agent will be looking at it,' I said. 'Once we have taken everything out, I shall hand over the keys and we won't be able to get back in here again. We've got a lot to move, but the furniture can stay, maybe the new owners will want it.'

Hilde ran upstairs with the suitcase. Oh! the energy of youth, I thought. She could now pack away all the art from the walls in the studio. I'd removed all the bedding and most of the clothes that would go to help the community. Later, we would go to the cellar and drain off the remaining schnapps and remove all the food items I stored there. We did have a very small cellar in Arkadien but it had always been full of wood for Opi's projects. I thought it was time to clear it and make that my new food store. Elsa was checking Gunther's paperwork in case there were items we needed to present to a court to do with his land and chattels, though I didn't think there were many items of value.

We'd been so embroiled with officialdom for the past two months we didn't need more people telling us what we must do! We'd had to speak with the coroner before we obtained Raoul's death certificate, which dragged on a bit, but was eventually resolved. We had several visits from the police investigating Raoul's death. The funeral directors and the local vicar came to see us. Elsa was comforted by the vicar's visits, as we all were. We told him how each of us women had lost our husbands quite recently. It was healing for us to talk together about some of our feelings around our husbands' deaths, although the circumstances for each one of us has been so different. The vicar's presence facilitated space for each of us to open up, and we were closer than ever as a result of those conversations.

There were the newspapers to deal with, of course. The journalists asked many questions and Elsa decided she would prefer to tell them about Raoul herself, rather than the reporters seeking out contacts of his who may be mischief-makers tempted to embellish, surmise or twist the truth.

As it was, she managed to be quite vague and spoke mainly about his depression and explained it was a result of the war. This was a familiar story that many people had experienced. The newspaper reported about his war service in WWI and how proud he had been to serve his country. Thankfully, it simply stated that Raoul Franck was unable to find work or settle after returning from serving in the Sudetenland and that he left a wife and a daughter.

What a terrible way to end his life. Raoul was a serious, reliable young man, a very hard worker devoted to his family. He and Opi got on well. For Opi, he was the son he never had until Raoul joined the Nazi Party. From then onwards they argued. Opi couldn't accept the new regime. I felt so very sorry for Elsa because she poured all she had into the marriage but there was nothing she could do to help him as time went on and he became isolated and without hope.

This was the note he left me.

Dear Oma,

I am so sorry to cause distress.

You and Opi have both been such supportive parents to Elsa, me and Hilde and I want you to know how grateful I am to you both. I was overcome with sadness when I learned of the manner of Opi's death; he had always been so kind to me. The perpetrator will not go unpunished.

I hope that you, Elsa and Hilde will continue to help each other. I know that you three will always be close, you have a mutual love and respect most people can only hope for. I have been lucky to be part of your family.

Thank you.

Raoul

CLARA

Elsa and I spent many evenings talking together about Raoul, Ben and Morrie. It had been a time of heartbreak and questions that had no answers. I felt it in my bones that Morrie was still alive and would return to me one day. I was his mother. I would know if the worst had happened to him. I dreaded the doorbell ringing in case it was another messenger of doom, but I told myself that he would come to me when the time was right.

I had washed all the crockery in Gunther's kitchen and was now wrapping it in newspaper and packing it into tea-chests. I was nearly finished with washing down the inside of the old corner pantry, and unpinned a few curled postcards sent to him from exotic places by old friends, in a more optimistic time. In my pocket, though, was hope. A little bit of hope I was clinging to.

It was the note left for me by Raoul. How I wished I could thank him.

Dear Clara,

I feel ashamed. I should have helped more when Ben disappeared, but I was fearful of being involved with a Jewish family. I apologise. I was a coward and I let Opi and Oma deal with the difficult situation of looking after Morrie.

I do believe Ernst Grauman was a kind man, and I thought he would look after your son better than Morrie being looked after by authorities who had no interest in his welfare.

I have discovered that Morrie was with Ernst all through the war and often performed as a pianist. On 18th December 1944 Ernst died and I do not know what happened to Morrie (who was by then called Max Grauman).

I hope he returns to you. I am sorry that I cannot help you further.

Raoul

ELSA

I was looking through Gunther's personal papers. I found photographs and a marriage in May 1895 to Anke Escher in Dresden. There was a photograph of their wedding. Everyone looked serious, probably to do with how long it took to take the picture. Gunther was handsome, wearing a black suit with a white cravat and top hat. Anke was clothed in a silk or taffeta high-necked dress in a very dark colour with a small veil and a posy of roses with ribbons hanging down. The other women's dresses were down to the ground, and the boys all wore thick, high collared double-breasted coats with woollen hats. Fashion seemed to have changed so much since then. There was also a death certificate for Anke in 1905. She had died in childbirth. I found nothing about a baby, so I guessed that the little infant, be it he or she, had not made it into this world.

There was a very happy picture taken in the Austrian Tyrol in 1901. Gunther was standing on top of a bolder wearing fall mountaineering garb, an Alpine cap with a badge, tweed jacket and plus-four trousers and climbing boots. He was carrying a stick with ropes and chains hanging from his shoulder. Anke was sitting by his feet wearing a striped hat and scarf, laughing. They looked so in love.

I didn't think he ever married again.

Gunther's nephew said to burn all the paperwork unless it related to the property or valuables; he wasn't interested in sentimental items. I planned to keep this photograph of the Tyrol, though, to remind me of Gunther, who was a good man.

I was about to start a bonfire now I'd gathered everything together.

I had another pile of papers to burn as well as Gunther's.

These were the papers that Raoul had brought with him from the Sudetenland. I wasn't sure what they related to. There were lists of prisoners with ticks and crosses next to their names. There were similar lists of officers which had been annotated in the margins. There were till receipts and stamped tickets and a pile of ration books with holes punched in them. They were all official documents and possibly of interest to someone, but I didn't want to draw any more attention to ourselves. Clearly Raoul wanted to keep them away from scrutiny, so they would be going on the fire.

I wanted to forget how Raoul died, forget the past two months, but I had to accept that my husband killed himself. I had been struggling with my conscience since reading the letter he left me. I hadn't mentioned it to anyone; they need not know the extent of Raoul's culpability. I had kept the letter hidden. As far as everyone was concerned, Raoul left me a note on the inside of an envelope with his wedding ring in it. I was pleased he'd thought of that, but then Raoul would, he always tried to look at the consequences of his actions.

Oma and I shared a secret. Neither Hilde nor Clara knew about this and maybe never would. Two weeks after Raoul had died, there was another mention of the event in the local newspaper. The coroner concluded that Raoul had taken his life while the balance of his mind was disturbed, so this was reported accordingly. We all knew he'd killed himself, but it really hurt seeing it written for all to see in the newspaper. I read this as we all did.

But it was another article that day which had caught Oma's attention. The rest of us had missed it. I was glad only she and I read it.

The body of Albert Schmitt, formally of the Leipzig NSDAP, has been formally identified today. The body was found close to Bayrische Bahnhof where the new building development is now progressing. He was found in a ditch covered by snow, but it is estimated he has been there between two and three weeks. He had been killed by a single laceration to the throat.

Please contact police headquarters if you can help in this matter. This is being treated as murder.

Oma and I just looked at the paper and couldn't speak. Raoul had said the perpetrator of Opi's death would not go unpunished. Reading this article, we knew Raoul had made sure of this.

The last time I saw Raoul alive was when he left Gunther's house on New Year's Eve. He'd muttered something about making things right.

These were the last words Raoul said to me.

Part 5

Morrie

1944-1948

Chapter 1

Wilmersdorf

1944

MORRIE

We had left home again. This time to perform in Poland.

Ernst had so many places he had to visit as the coordinator of the musical events for the Third Reich. He was happy he'd been given this job and pleased he wasn't sent to fight. He was frequently away for days, even weeks, at a time and I stayed in Wilmersdorf while he was gone. This was now my home. He left me schoolwork, poetry and novels to read, mathematics and new pieces of music to try and others that were in our repertoire to perfect. Ingrid, Ernst's sister, stayed with me, so I was not lonely.

The music Ernst organised was not performed in concert halls or in front of paying audiences but was for groups of officers, and sometimes their wives, at grand dinners or parties to celebrate German victories. These events were held in large houses or castles and, once even, at the Führer's country residence in the mountains.

Ernst and I performed separately but also did duets. Often, Marta Weiss, a mezzo soprano, would sing with us and sometimes an orchestra was brought in. These concerts were infrequent, though, because Ernst was an army officer and matters-of-state connected with the war, as well as organising the music in the camps, always came first.

Ernst's job was to ensure the 'right' music was played in labour camps situated all over Germany and Poland. There were several officers who answered to him, and they oversaw the small groups of musicians to ensure the music flowed as it should. The performers were selected to play by the SS, and they had no choice in the music. Instruments had to be found to equip them and were often recycled from the possessions brought in by the people who were transported to the camp. There were also language barriers, with so many nationalities and races living together in the camps. Sheet music was scarce and highly prized but was, of course, a universal language.

Ernst told me the camps were miserable places to go to. People were crammed together and didn't want to be there. Music was performed when the workers marched in and out of the labour camps, on work detail, or during the working day within the factories. Music was also recorded or came directly from the radio and broadcast over the loudspeakers. Those in control of the camps believed listening to music increased productivity.

It was always the same sort of rousing loud music at all the camps; none of the guards cared what the music was as long as it encouraged the workers to move quickly when they were told to. Ernst said people were told to sing, too, when they were marching or working, and these songs were usually old folk songs with simple rhythms repeated continuously, sometimes for hours. If the workers stopped singing, they might be punished. Occasionally, choirs started up, but those taking part were usually moved elsewhere. With a constant change of musicians, bands and choirs ceased to continue.

One or two camps had orchestras. They were encouraged by the commandants running these camps, as they were a matter of pride and something to brag about. They crowed that their camp was so well run there was time for the finer things in life, even an orchestra.

Playing, listening to and writing music was Ernst's life. But the camps were bleak places, and the music was never played for enjoyment. Occasionally, workers in the camps attempted to play their own traditional music but such activities got stopped and the players were often punished. Ernst was relieved whenever he came home to us. He said it was getting worse in the camps. He hated going there.

We moved here from Friedrichstrasse in 1941, so we've been here for three years. I thought about living in Leipzig sometimes, but mainly I thought of Mama, Papa, Hilde and Froh-Froh. I didn't know if anyone was still alive. I didn't say goodbye to Hilde, and I hoped she forgave me for that.

Ernst had been given this house for us to live in. As soon as it was available, we left Leipzig and came to Berlin. I wasn't happy because Ernst had promised we would always remain at the apartment in Friedrichstrasse, so Mama and Papa would have no difficulty finding me, and now I had gone away.

'They will never find me here!' I cried when we first got here.

'Max, I had no choice. If you remained in Leipzig on your own, you would have been picked up by the police who would have sent you to a camp for Jews,' he said. 'Being with me protects you and, one day, we will have time to look for your mother and father. But I must go where I am sent, and this will be a good home for us for now.'

I knew he was right, but it didn't stop me missing my old life. Memories of that life were slipping away. It was all such a long while ago. Ernst was happy in this house which was large and comfortable. The carpets and furnishings made it feel luxurious. Ernst had allowed me to bring Mama and Papa's books and paintings, which gave me some comfort. He also brought the Blüthner piano here, and so it began to feel like my home, too.

Because he had to travel so much, Ernst decided to send for his sister, Ingrid, to look after me and be my governess and companion. She was ten years younger than him, nine years older than me, and had studied at the university for just one year before the war. She wanted to be a writer and, despite having no teaching experience, she devised lessons for me. Together we studied many subjects. I wanted to go to university as well and understood I must keep studying. I was a fast learner and, though she was always ahead of me, we learned together and got along very well. She played the viola, though had not studied it seriously, and sometimes I accompanied her on the piano for fun. But Ernst expected me to be concert ready, so I had to concentrate on the recital pieces.

This summer just gone, Ernst returned from a trip and was quite subdued, though I didn't know why. The next day he asked me to sit with him on the terrace overlooking the garden. We sat in a big wicker chair padded with pretty floral cushions. The sun shone and lit up the beautiful greenery, but he looked serious.

'Max, I have something I need to tell you,' he started. 'I have been in the Leipzig area for three weeks. Much of the city has been bombed. I am sorry to tell you that all of Friedrichstrasse was destroyed. Our apartment – your apartment – has gone.'

'What about the people who lived there?' I asked. 'What about Hilde and the Francks? And did Mama and Papa get back to our apartment? Were they there when it was bombed?'

'I am sorry, Max, I couldn't find out exact details. But, apparently, everyone living there was killed.'

I was in despair and did little for the next week or so. I didn't play the piano nor do any lessons. Instead, I curled up in my bed crying, or making my mind remember all the events of the time I spent there, my parents, the Francks, Hilde and the little blue and yellow bird. And now all of them were dead. I never wanted to go to Leipzig again. There was no need for me to visit the city. Everyone I loved was dead and even the home I remembered so fondly had now gone.

Immediately after that conversation, Ernst had to visit a camp. When he returned a week later, he was annoyed I had been weepy and sentimental, and thus idle. He told me it was time I behaved in a more grown-up way. Once I was dressed, we had eaten, and had discussed a forthcoming concert, Ernst said he felt it was now time he had another conversation with me. I wasn't sure what this was about, but it turned out it was 'the' conversation that fathers were expected to have with their adolescent sons.

'Max, I am not sure what you know about the differences between women and men, females and males, girls and boys?' Ernst sounded uncomfortable.

I just blushed. I didn't actually know the facts but had seen so much in Gunther's farmyard: pigs mounting the sows, the bull mounting the cows and then the births of baby animals. I remember Hilde and me bundled out of bed in the middle of the night by Opi because he said there was something we must see. We went to one of Gunther's barns where a sow was lying, moaning, in a small straw-filled pen. Soon, hot water shot from between her rear legs, steaming in the cold night air, and a piglet slid out covered in a caul, all sticky and bloody. Mama pig licked the baby pig to clean his face and encourage him to breathe. He staggered to his feet and, half crawling, made his way to her teat and began to suckle. As soon as he was up and moving, another piglet emerged. She repeated the process many times. At one point, we waited a long time, thinking it was all over, but another two emerged. We stayed there for what seemed like hours. Eventually, the sow had given birth to ten piglets. She had ten teats, so that was perfect.

'Sometimes,' Gunther had said, 'if a sow has too many babies, we have to hand rear the last ones and rotate them on the teats if we can, so they all bond with their mother. Often the last one is the smallest, known as the runt, and we have to give him extra care to help him survive.'

When Hilde and I went swimming, I remembered looking at her when she was being undressed by her Mama and noticing she did not look the same as me. But we were so comfortable with one another that it was just how it was, and I didn't question the difference.

Ernst continued, 'When you get to your age, you may begin to notice that your body starts to change, and you may find yourself being attracted to other people. I know you haven't really been able to meet and make friends, but we can do nothing about that right now. Have you noticed liking people in a different way, or changes in your body, Max?'

I squirmed and nodded but said nothing. In fact, I really liked Ingrid. We spent so much time together and she was not so much older than me. I think I had a crush on her.

Ernst's began to stumble over his words. He said, 'You will meet all sorts of people, I mean, you will find yourself attracted to all sorts of people. Do you understand me? What I am trying to say is that you may like girls, which is good, but you may like boys too. This is also okay, but if you like boys you must be careful who knows, because it is illegal to be–err–become–erm! to show affection for someone of the same gender. Do you understand, Max?'

Once again, I nodded. Although I didn't know about this, liking boys, it did not relate to the pigs or cows in Gunther's yard, but I assumed I would find out more some other time.

'It is alright if you like both girls and boys too,' Ernst said. 'I have always liked both but that is a secret between you and me, do you understand?'

This time I nodded enthusiastically, as I felt it had got me off the hook.

Ingrid packed up a hamper for us and we set off with a driver in a staff car. We would travel to a camp in Poland called Auschwitz-Birkenau but it was a two-day journey, and we would be staying at a hunting lodge in Silesia tonight. It seemed an awfully long way to travel but it was Beethoven's birthday in two days' time and the Führer had sent a special request directly to Ernst to put on a celebratory concert. The Führer then decided it would be good for morale if it was held at Auschwitz-Birkenau, especially as the camp had an orchestra. Beethoven was much venerated in Germany and there was always a celebration to mark his birthday, the Führer made sure of that.

In the car with us was Stephan Reger who, along with many officers, had been invited to the concert. He was also stationed in Berlin and had a house close to us in Wilmersdorf. He was Ernst's friend and often stayed overnight at our house. He worked in a department that archived works of art.

German paintings, sculptures, artefacts, and sacred pieces, including valuable gold objects, were removed, saved and stored if there had been damage to churches, cathedrals and palaces or when they were thought to be at risk from enemy bombing. These items were taken to salt mines in packing cases to protect and preserve them. Many famous paintings from countries occupied by German troops had been saved too, as well as paintings taken from private houses that had been damaged and were unoccupied. Stephan said the best pieces would be displayed in Germany for the German people to see as part of the celebrations when we win the war. There was to be the Führermuseum where the art would be on display. It was to be built in the heart of Linz in Austria which would be the cultural centre of Nazi Germany.

I didn't like Stephan. He didn't talk to me, really. I always felt he was giving me a lecture. He got annoyed when Ernst and I talked. He seemed to be jealous about the ease with which Ernst and I communicated and shared ideas, particularly on music. Ernst was always kind to me, but did have very strict rules and there was a line which I knew not to cross. He and I were both enthusiastic about music making and I felt happy I was with him, but I had to remember he was not related to me and could never replace my father.

My father, Ben, was gentle and kind, he always made me laugh and, although it was a very long time ago, I remember with affection snuggling up on the sofa with him. There was a deep longing within me to see him once more but I was resigned that I might never see him nor Mama again.

I didn't know when we set off that this was to be my last concert with Ernst, and the last time I would share a car with either him or Stephan.

Chapter 2

Frieberg

1947

MORRIE

Over the past two years, I'd been living with Herr Huber. He was very kind and had done everything to make me feel at home since I arrived. Today, though, was my sixteenth birthday, and it was a day of great sadness because we buried Frau Huber in the Frieberg Municipal cemetery.

We returned to the house where the housekeeper had prepared food for those who came back here. There was a whole ham studded with cloves, black pumpernickel and white bread, preserves, both sweet and pickled, warm boiled eggs and honey cake. I knew some of the people and tried to chat to them, but many had travelled from across Germany to Frieberg and had never met me before.

I was matched with this family because of my piano playing. Herr Huber used to own a music shop in this town before the war and had a piano at home. I had been looked after by the authorities alongside dozens of displaced children who'd suffered many distressing events in their lives and were grateful to be fed. The authorities were kind to me but were unsure who ought to look after me, as I was described as 'an orphan who was playing piano in concerts'. When Herr Huber's application arrived, they jumped at it.

Coincidentally, Herr Huber and his wife had a son called Max who was a pilot in the Luftwaffe and whose plane was lost over the English Channel in 1943. When Herr Huber agreed to take me, he was unsure if using my name would be too painful for him and his wife. I said I was happy to use my real name, Morrie Silbermann, and asked if that name would be a problem.

'No, my boy,' said Herr Huber. 'It is a very Jewish name and reminds me of my Jewish friends from before the war. They were all taken away by the Nazis. I would be more than happy to have you living with us and to know that Jews can once again live freely in Germany. Beware though, my boy, many people around here still blame the Jews for the war. Most of my customers were Jewish; I miss the conversations I used to have with people who were musically curious and keen to write, perform, and explore new music as well as established classical repertoires. You, Morrie, are a breath of fresh air!'

So, after that, I travelled here to live with them. At first, Frau Huber didn't want to talk with me. She just wanted her son back. But, after a while, we became close. She never got over the loss of her Max. The neighbours said, when she'd passed away, that she died of a broken heart.

The piano waiting for me here was a solid, ebony framed upright with a lovely tone. At first, Herr Huber was reluctant to let me loose on it without supervision. Once he realised I was respectful of the instrument and could perform complex pieces without sheet music, he relaxed and began to enjoy the pieces I played. He too played the work of many composers, but Rachmaninoff was his favourite. He loved Concerto No 3 but was never happy that he'd performed it as he wanted. It was a very difficult piece to play.

'One day,' he said, 'I hope to play it perfectly. Until then, I shall keep practising!'

Frau Huber often sat beside me while I practised. Her husband had boxes of sheet music everywhere, and I spent days and weeks rifling through them. But, without the guidance of someone like Ernst, I didn't know what I wanted to tackle next. I thought I was limited in the number of composers I could play. There was Beethoven because this was what I'd learned by heart with Ernst – and what was expected by Herr Hitler – also a little Chopin, which was Ernst's favourite composer, and Franz Liszt, which I felt was the music that ran through my veins. It was the music my mother played repeatedly. I played Liszt's Liebestraum and Frau Huber declared it to be her favourite of all the pieces I played for her.

I dabbled, playing snatches of different composer's works from all the piles of music but then I decided I would learn some of Felix Mendelssohn's 'Songs without Words.' He had founded the Leipzig Conservatoire, and I knew he was important, yet during the war years his music was banned from being played because he was Jewish. I decided it was time to learn some of these pieces and, over time, grew to love them. He was my only link to Leipzig now, and to being a Jew.

On the day of Frau Huber's funeral, I gave a short performance for the mourners. At first, I played one of the 'Songs without Words' called 'Funeral' out of respect for Frau Huber, but then I played some gentle lyrical pieces and the lively 'Tarantella.' I finished with Franz Liszt's 'Liebestraum', her favourite piece as well as mine.

After everyone had left, Herr Huber and I spent time going through some of the vast array of music he had stored. The property he lived in was an old brick house, tall and narrow. The room with the piano had a window covered with lace curtains; I hadn't realised this was where he had once run his business. The room itself used to part of the shop in which he sold instruments. Herr Huber was at his happiest when he was sorting his sheet music or talking about pieces.

There was a great deal to do in the sorting process. There were boxes, some split open, some intact, and chests with many drawers; these drawers were full of piano music as well as manuscripts written for ensembles of every combination. Some of the music was more or less in order but much wasn't. Since he'd closed the shop and started living in this part of the house, the boxes had been moved several times. They'd tipped over and been piled back again in no particular order.

As the days went on, I encouraged him to catalogue everything. I tentatively suggested he reopen the shop. At first, he was not enthusiastic. He was mourning the loss of his wife and had been so very quiet of late. Yet, he'd spent much of his time caring for her and knew he had to find a way to escape the feeling of deep sadness. He didn't say it, but he was now free to do the things he liked for the first time in many years. There were so many memories of the war: the loss of his son Max, and the misery from dealing with that loss. Eventually, he came round to the idea. We discussed moving furniture to reopen the shop. He wanted me involved.

Herr Huber had a motorcar and petrol was once again available.

He said, 'We need to get you driving, Morrie. There will always be goods to be collected from the station, or delivered there, or to be taken to customers, and you can help with this. It will take us time to set up the shop. I have a few instruments packed away in my garage: some wooden recorders, an oboe and some flutes, a flugelhorn, an E flat trumpet, a glockenspiel and a few other pieces of percussion. I'll need to purchase some string instruments, plus valve oil, rosin, reeds, cleaning kits, chinrests and the like. Then we'll be ready to open the shop. But I suspect many of these items won't be easy to get.'

So I began learning to drive. It was wonderful, and I looked forward to the day I could go out on my own. Later, I admitted my dream of going to university to study music, and he agreed. I hoped I could begin in October. I knew I would have no difficulty getting accepted as my level of playing would have equalled many tutors', but there were gaps in my knowledge, and I wanted to be the best I could be. I needed to understand composition better. I needed to work with tutors who would imbue me with their wisdom.

Herr Huber gave me a present for my birthday. It was a beautiful leather music case with a brass bar across the top. It belonged to a Jewish friend of his, a composer and professor of music who was sent to a concentration camp and had never returned. He had asked Herr Huber to look after this, along with some of his compositions, until he came home.

'He will not be returning now,' said Herr Huber. 'And I know he would be pleased someone with your talent could make use of it.'

I expressed my appreciation. It was a substantial case, which held such gravitas within its fabric, but I couldn't help remembering the similar one given to me by Ernst on our first Christmas together. How grand it had seemed and how grown up I had felt. It was the first time I remembered being called a Jew – when Frau Müller told me I was a Jew and Christmas presents were not for me.

I didn't have that bag anymore. It was lost at Auschwitz-Birkenau in 1944.

Chapter 3

Auschwitz-Birkenau

December 1944

MORRIE

We arrived at the camp.

Above the entrance to Auschwitz-Birkenau it said, 'Work Makes You Free.' We were directed to an area to the right of the camp. I could see dozens of people walking along in groups, and I was curious as to what work they did here. There were men and women going in different directions. I didn't know what they were walking towards or what they had been doing. A large group of people had been coming through the gate, marching in time to loud music, and were moved aside so we could drive through. They were a work party, Ernst said. They looked very thin and dirty, with dark sunken eyes, and all of them had their heads shaven. Who were all these people? I wondered. And why did they look so ragged, sad and poor? It wasn't clear which were men or women, and I remembered what Ernst said about being attracted to people of the same gender. Maybe here, at this place, gender didn't matter.

Some people peered into the car. It was, I realised, an important looking car. They were looking at me, probably because of my hair, which was still almost white and quite long and seemed to draw comment. My mother had preferred it long and Ernst seemed to like it that way too, but he said when I was fourteen I would be getting a uniform for the Hitlerjugend and would have my hair cut in the regulation style, but for now it was allowed to hang free. I think Ernst had been criticised for not insisting it was cut, but he knew that when I played lively pieces on the piano, my hair moving around as I played up and down the keyboard added to the drama. I always stood for applause at the end of the performance and had become quite addicted to the attention I received. I wasn't allowed to interact with the audience, though. Ernst worried people would ask too many questions about my background.

We were greeted by the deputy commandant. He raised his arm in salute and everyone saluted 'Heil Hitler' back. Since a recent growth spurt, I was expected to act like an adult and salute Nazi officers too. I went through the motions, but always felt it was wrong as a Jew, so silently mouthed the words, pretending to speak. That was probably just as bad, but my refusal to voice the words was a small act of defiance on my part.

The concert would be starting at 7pm and we needed to rehearse with the orchestra. Hopefully they had practised the repertoire beforehand. From experience, we knew that as long as our piano playing was well rehearsed the concert would be a success. We had to have faith in the conductor that his orchestra could provide music to an acceptable standard; it was us the audience were coming to see. We soon found out this orchestra was not the best we had performed with: neither the brass nor the woodwind had enough players, but our short rehearsal reassured Ernst that it would be a good enough concert that evening.

The main problem, when it came to it, was the audience – or lack of it! Usually, our concerts were glittering affairs but this was so different. The hall was a large, barn type of building with a stage at one end and the smell of cooking sausages wafting in the air. We were told it was the recreation building for the soldiers in the camp. Ostensibly, there were plays, dances and boxing matches put on here and it had a busy restaurant too. There were no glamourous guests here at all, no women in attendance, none of the usual ceremony and accoutrements, no champagne in crystal glasses, no chandeliers, and just ten minutes before we were due to begin, only half the seats were occupied. At the last minute, some guards shuffled in to fill the empty chairs. Ernst and I looked out of place in our evening dress.

We played an exclusively Ludwig von Beethoven programme: two Piano Sonata and then Variations on a Waltz by Diabelli. We both played well, but it was the most lacklustre evening. I understood why Ernst disliked coming to these camps. We were applauded very politely, but not with any passion. It seemed so pointless being here when nobody was interested in us, and it had taken two days to get here. I later found out that most of the audience were engaged in a military campaign in Belgium. Ernst mumbled, 'He insisted it went ahead, but it should have been cancelled.' I wasn't sure who he meant, probably the Führer.

The few officers who did seem to appreciate the music met us after the performance. I left Ernst and Stephan having a drink with them.

I was tired and ready for bed. The driver took me to our accommodation, a ten minute drive away. I was shown to our rooms. They were on the first floor over the SS officer's quarters, and each had a washbasin and a toilet, a bed, a small wardrobe, a chair and on the wall was a poster of the Führer. Every surface was painted with grey shiny paint and the floor was oil cloth. There was a window, but it didn't have an opening. It wasn't very welcoming here and felt like an alien environment, but we were only staying one night. I knew Ernst would tell me not to complain, so I didn't.

Our luggage was brought to the rooms, so I took off my concert dress and laid it on Ernst's bed. He was particular that we always kept our performance clothes together. That way, we didn't arrive at a venue to find my shoes or bowtie was missing. I put on my pyjamas and instantly fell asleep. I recalled hearing Ernst and Stephan climbing the stairs, laughing and telling each other to be quiet, but I didn't know what time that was.

That happened two weeks ago and, since then, my life has once again dramatically changed direction.

Ernst was not in his room the day after the concert, nor was Stephan, though all their possessions were there. When I asked where the two men were I wasn't given a straight answer.

When we'd first arrived at the camp, I was assigned a young orderly called Holst. It was his job to look after me. He was less than three years older than me, and we immediately became friends. He was an orphan, like me, and because his uncle had been an officer here, he was given the job to look after the deputy commandant and any visitors staying in the guest rooms. When there were no visitors, and he'd completed the domestic chores, he helped prepare the officers' food. He told me his parents were killed when their house, close to the French border, received a direct hit from a bomb.

On that first day, he turned and said to me, 'This is an evil place, I wish I could leave but I would be shot if I tried. I have nowhere to go and am frightened what they will do to me if I complain.'

I was a little shocked, 'What about your uncle, can't you talk to him?'

'He has been sent to another camp and cannot protect me. I'm a soldier of the Third Reich, though in name only because I hate the idea of killing. I try to be unnoticeable, just do my work, but I don't know how long I can avoid being involved with what is going on here. It's too easy to be punished. I know people are murdered here all the time. There are chimneys that burn the bodies all day long and ash hangs over this place in a cloud, falling and covering the roofs of all the buildings.'

This sounded ominous and added to what Ernst had said about the camps, although he'd been deliberately vague as to their true nature.

I heard no news of Ernst and knew I should not keep asking.

Holst eventually took me to one side and told me Ernst had been taken to Block 11, the detention cells.

'But why?' I asked. It seemed strange because Ernst was always polite and pleasant, never rude, and always took pride in his work. 'Didn't they like our performance at the concert, was that it?'

That seemed very unlikely, but I couldn't think of anything else.

'I don't know. But both he and his friend were taken away in the early hours of this morning and are awaiting transport to Berlin – to be charged,' Holst said.

'Charged with what? What did he do?'

'I don't know. I asked one of the guards who works at Block 11, but he said that it has nothing to do with me.'

I decided to find out what this was all about. I asked the duty officer in the SS office downstairs if he could tell me what was going on.

'Go to the room you have been assigned to, blondie. Do not leave this building or you too will be put in the prison blocks with the Jews and gypsies! We now have to decide what we are going to do with you.'

That struck a chord. Nobody realised I was Jewish.

'I want to see my uncle, please,' I said.

'That will not be possible. You have been told go to your room and stay there, now go!' he answered.

Later that day, Holst appeared carrying a spare uniform like the one he wore: grey cotton trousers and a shirt in the same material. He also had an extra khaki apron with a swastika on the bib, like the one he wore in the kitchen.

'I was instructed to give these clothes to you while they work out where they're going to send you. You are to do the same job as me,' he said.

This new role was such a change for me. I had always been surrounded by adults, so I enjoyed spending more time with someone a similar age. We had to change beds and iron the officers' uniforms, as well as help in the kitchens and lay tables in the mess. We weren't allowed to leave the building. There were several guards patrolling the path between this SS block and the entrance to Birkenau camp; there was both a road and a railway line into the camp.

A week later, I was called in to see the commandant who'd been away at the time of the concert but had now returned. I was marched in front of him, though I didn't know how to march. He introduced himself as Commandant Hoss. He told me to stand still and listen. He said, in a straightforward, matter of fact way, 'Your uncle, Ernst Grauman is dead. He used a pistol to shoot himself. His body will be taken to Berlin. You will return there.'

Three days later, Holst and a SS guard entered my room and woke me before dawn. Both were dressed in army uniforms and hats, greatcoats and boots.

The officer barked, 'Get dressed! Get your belongings together now and report downstairs. You have five minutes. Get your hair tucked into the hat or it'll be cut off. It is cold outside and has been snowing so you'll need all of these.' He handed me a hat, greatcoat and boots.

'Where am I going? Are you taking Ernst home?' I said.

'Enough questions, you must do as I say. You have four minutes now!'

He left the room, followed by Holst who looked over his shoulder with an 'I don't know!' look.

I turned on the tap, it was icy cold. I splashed my face, gulped down a couple of handfuls of water, combed my hair. I hastily pulled on the smart clothes I'd been dressed in when I left Berlin.

Ernst's concert dress and mine had been brought here in a valet suitcase. I knew there was nothing at all in his room now – the bed was stripped and the wardrobe empty – so I had no case to put anything in. Ernst had kept my music case, along with his own, in a small trunk full of sheet music and music stands delivered here on the night of the concert. None of these items were anywhere to be seen.

I put on the greatcoat, green woollen hat, and boots which more or less fitted, and filled the pockets with the small items. I had a book of Goethe's poetry, a small notepad, two pencils, my toothbrush and comb. I left my pyjamas laid on the bed. I had no mirror, but could tell I would pass for a very young soldier.

When I reached the bottom of the stairs, Holst and the SS officer were waiting for me. A mess tin and canteen were thrust into my hand, and we left the building. It was still dark when we walked into the camp.

Already, people, mainly SS officers and guards, were busily going about their business. Suddenly, loud music blasted out of the Tannoy across the camp, followed by the roll call announcement. In the distance, through barbed wire fences, I could see hundreds of people streaming out of buildings to line up outside their huts; the same wasted, shaven-headed people I'd seen when we arrived at Auschwitz on that first day.

We continued walking until we approached the railway ramp inside the camp. A train with a single passenger carriage was waiting. On the long platform were stacks of suitcases and belongings as far as the eye could see. There were no people, so I was unsure what the belongings were doing here.

I watched as a man drove up and began picking up items – bags, cases, bundles of clothes, books and musical instruments – and throwing them into the rear of his truck. I switched my attention to watching the stoker shovelling coal as the train engine belched smoke.

The SS officer beside me spoke, 'Please get in. They are about to go.'

'Who else is this train for?' I asked.

'It is your lucky day; this train has been sent here just for you.'

Looking at Holst, the officer said, 'Private Weber will be accompanying you to Berlin.'

So that was Holst's name, I thought, Holst Weber.

'Weber, you will telephone the camp once you have handed over Master Grauman. You will then return to Auschwitz as soon as possible; do you understand your orders?' the officer said.

'Yes, Sir,' said Holst.

'You have your instructions: who you must meet, who to hand him over to, Weber?'

'Yes, Sir,' Holst said again.

The SS officer said, 'Don't get this wrong.' He stood very straight, stamped his feet and barked, 'Heil Hitler.'

Holst and I saluted, but once again my response was a barely disguised silence.

We settled in the train. The man with the truck had piled it so high the cases were swaying precariously as he drove off. The platform was still covered with an unwieldy array of property that I presumed would be transported later.

I couldn't believe this train was running just for me. But then it dawned on me they wanted to remove me from the camp because, with me being here, questions might be asked about Ernst's death. He had been an important figure, close to the Führer. I was a loose end to be tidied away. It was easier to let someone else deal with me; someone in Berlin, a long way from Auschwitz-Birkenau.

I felt strange leaving Ernst behind. He'd been the person who'd looked after me, taught me and moulded me over the past four years; he occupied a position of real affection in my life. I had never had an uncle but imagined this was how it would feel if I had. He was somewhere between uncle and father. Who would look after me now, I wondered?

The little train chugged out of the camp, through a brick archway, and was soon in the local town. Everywhere I looked, I could see soldiers surrounding groups of people, prisoners I now realised, walking in different directions.

We were on that little train for thirty-six hours. We were soon very hungry; what was in our mess tins, some sausage and pumpernickel bread, did not last long. The engine driver and his mate were friendly, giving us potatoes they'd cooked on the coals as well as hot water to drink. The train stopped and started repeatedly because of the snow which had to be cleared off the line. The men eventually decided the journey to Berlin had to be abandoned as the tracks were totally blocked by snow drifts. We had to go south. Still, we could not pick up a line to Berlin. We ended up in Westphalia when the train driver decided to make the return journey to Auschwitz.

It was Holst's job to deliver me to the authorities in Berlin, but it was impossible. He could have returned to the camp with me on the train, but the SS wouldn't be happy with that. It would be seen as a failure. He told the driver he would contact the local authorities in the nearest town to make sure I was handed over safely. The train driver wasn't interested; that was someone else's job.

Holst and I had spent so much time talking on our journey. We spoke about the war, about what Holst believed was going on in the camp, dark sadistic stories he'd heard, of torture and murder; the worrying defeats of Germany in Europe and the sinking morale of the armed forces, and we spoke about our own situations too. Holst didn't want to return to the camp. The snow drifts had given him an opportunity, and he decided he would try to make his way back to his hometown. He would be a deserter and, if he were caught – would likely be shot – but he hoped he could lie low. He believed, from conversations he'd had at the camp, that the prisoners (because that's what they were, not just workers as Ernst had said) would be moved out soon and the war would be over. He said he'd already witnessed some prisoners being marched out of the camp.

I knew far less than him and was unsure what to do. I'd always been protected and didn't know how to fend for myself. I couldn't reach Berlin, but I wondered about Ingrid and if she'd returned to Leipzig and if she knew about the death of her dear brother?

On a lonely hilltop surrounded by snow-heavy trees, I shook hands with Holst. We both said we hoped one day to meet again, though we knew it was unlikely. He went west and I went south, both of us fearful and alone.

It was New Year's Day 1945. I began to walk, though wasn't sure where to. The first night, I slept under a piece of corrugated iron sheeting in a dense copse of trees that provided some cover, but it was bitterly cold and had begun to rain.

Next day, as I walked, partly hidden by the drooping trees along the edge of the wet, deeply rutted road, I saw vehicles sliding around in the mud. I realised they had to stop before they slid dangerously into a deep, fast running ford across the road. Sheets of broken ice pushed up into pyramids, jostling for position to form a jagged causeway in the water, making the crossing hazardous. I took a chance and jumped on the back of a stationary truck carrying sand. The vehicles eventually navigated their way across the water and, once the truck had travelled into a town, I clambered down.

Here, there were many bombed-out buildings so I thought I could at least find shelter. I spoke to some boys outside a derelict church and discovered we were on the outskirts of Frankfurt. Many of the boys had learned to survive by scavenging, but I didn't have the experience or skills they had. I decided to stay here and learn from them. I soon became good at cooking over an open fire. We shared whatever we had but were always hungry. Some of the boys killed birds, rabbits and squirrels which we roasted, and we begged for scraps or went in bins where we could. After a few months, we were taken to a camp for displaced people. I had no papers and was wearing the army greatcoat and hat. I didn't know whether admitting to being Jewish was a good thing at this stage, so I said I was Max Grauman and an orphan. I didn't know what was to become of me.

Chapter 4

Leipzig

1948

MORRIE

I had said I never wanted to return to Leipzig, it held nothing but sadness for me. The good memories stayed locked in my head, and I didn't want to disturb them because they were attached to people I loved but who were all dead.

Herr Huber and I had worked so hard on the shop. After putting up shelves, cleaning walls, painting a new sign saying The Music Man where once the old one hung, and slowly stocking the store, we reopened six months ago. We still needed to buy some items for resale but so many factories were destroyed or were slow to recommence production that there were gaps in our catalogue of goods for sale.

Herr Huber was excited to receive an invitation from the Blüthner factory in Leipzig. The factory was destroyed in the war but had been painstakingly rebuilt. In two months, the first piano made since 1943 would be going on display. People in the music world in Germany were invited to come see for themselves what the company had achieved. Presumably, the company hoped for orders. Herr Huber decided this was a good opportunity for me to visit my old town, primarily for us to source some missing items for the shop and for him to consider buying a new piano.

I had absorbed myself in the work of Mendelssohn and Bach since being in Frieberg and had grown to love them. I knew how important these composers were to Leipzig and, with that in my mind, I agreed I would go. It had been years since my viewing of the factory with Ernst; I did feel that this visit would be a nostalgic connection to my childhood, though I was apprehensive. I missed Ernst and was poignantly aware that his custody of me had saved my life. Undertaking this visit would be a gesture of remembrance to him. But I feared the ghosts of my loved ones might be waiting for me; dread flooded me as it occurred to me they might be unhappy I'd not visited before. For a long time, it had been impossible for me to get back there, but for the last two years there was no excuse, save unease and my reluctance to face the reality and accept they had all gone.

***

Herr Huber was happy to be driven by me to Leipzig and slept much of the way. It was 400 miles and took us all day with a stop for lunch. We were to stay at an old Bavarian style guest house just North of the city, which had survived the bombs and bullets. We had left before sunrise and arrived at the guest house very late. The owner, a lady of about fifty, grumbled that she was about to lock up and we'd only just got here in time. We worried that she was annoyed with us, but she was actually very kind and gave us bread and cheese and made us cocoa.

We had an allotted time to visit the factory, so we arrived there promptly at 11am the following day. The piano designer I'd met before was no longer employed there, and the atmosphere was not the same as it had been years ago. There were soviet guards outside, and restrictions on what we could access. The factory ran on a regimented schedule, making it far less welcoming. We were informed that the government now had control on how the factory functioned.

The piano we were escorted to was shiny and looked perfect, just like the ones we had seen all those years ago. Herr Huber was invited to play, but he explained that I was a concert pianist and outranked him in both talent and experience and requested that I be given the opportunity to play. The assistant didn't seem too sure, presumably because I was so young, but reluctantly agreed.

I was transported back to the time Ernst had sat at the Hindenburg piano on this same site. That piano that they'd worked so hard to preserve for posterity had been destroyed in the fire of 1943. I couldn't recall what music Ernst had played on that day, but I chose to play my old favourite, Liszt's Liebestraum, because it was the piece I'd known the longest and it always seemed to meet with approval from those listening. Once I'd finished playing, the assistant exclaimed, 'Bravo, you are a beautiful pianist! We would be happy to hear you play at any time you are visiting Leipzig.'

Herr Huber came away with brochures listing the pianos he could order when he was ready, and the costs of all the extras he might want. Out of curiosity, I leafed through this information myself and was shocked at how very expensive all the pianos were. I was suddenly struck with the realisation that Herr Huber didn't possess the wealth to purchase anything, and I began to wonder if he'd taken the Blüthner invitation only as an opportunity to get me to Leipzig. He'd always been convinced that one day I would want to return, despite my reticence.

We wandered around Augustusplatz and could see where rebuilding work was underway. Most buildings in the centre of the town had been rebuilt, some civic buildings had not been damaged at all and just a few empty bombsites remained. We entered a coffee house selling steaming plates of bratwurst and sauerkraut with little bowls of potato salad with dill and pickle. Herr Huber had colleagues – in some of the establishments around the old town – whom he wanted to look up. Now that I was here, I felt a strong urge to visit old haunts. We agreed I would take the car and pick him up later in the afternoon.

I was very near the Bruhl and decided I would walk to the area where my father's shop use to be. I was aware of people sitting around on the streets, looking unkempt and thin, and was reminded that the economy was still causing hardship for much of the population. I'd been shielded from this since moving in with the Hubers in a relatively small town. People who were desperate often flocked to busy cities in search of help and were drawn to the notion of wealth and opportunity that such places might offer.

It took me just five minutes to get to the Bruhl and I was pleased I had not forgotten the way. There had been department stores and small shops here when I was a young, but I was a child and remembered more about the atmosphere, the sense of industry and the buzz of people talking and rushing around. This had been a bustling area. The businesses had predominantly been Jewish owned, with a few Polish and German (Aryan) owners dotted about. But, by the end of the war, the Jewish and foreign owned premises and businesses had been taken from them. When I came to the Bruhl as a young boy, I hadn't really understood that we were different from Germans who weren't Jewish; we all spoke the same language and were similar to look at. With my colouring, I didn't even look the way people thought Jews looked, which had made it more confusing for me.

I stepped slowly and shakily through the streets, my mind awash with memories. Above all, I remembered my father's shop. It had been a shining jewel of light, stood on a corner with wide glass windows on both sides and extravagant double doors. It had been lit with dozens of lamps – inside the cabinets and above the window displays – sending shards of light bouncing off the jewels in all directions. There had been a magnificent chandelier hanging over the carpeted area at the centre of the shop. The carpet had been royal blue and red, with a repeated swirled pattern that had fascinated me. The premises had been far more glamourous than our home. I also remembered two ladies who'd served in the shop; they'd been very smartly dressed and always happy to see me.

At the rear of the shop had been Father's workshop. This had been very different to the sales area because it was full of instruments he'd used in the production of jewellery or watchmaking. There had been wooden benches covered in a layer of metal, with lights on twisted flex hanging low over them; cases full of forceps and pliers and, on a shelf above, an impressive range of magnifying glasses and spectacles. The workshop had always smelled of turpentine, methylated spirits, pungent oils and the fumes of the Bunsen burner from melted metal in a crucible. The workshop has been a serious place, and I'd only been allowed in at the end of the day when Father was not engaged in his intricate work. I used to love sitting at the bench on one of the high stools, watching him shut up shop. My father had always been delighted to see me, showing me off with pride to any customers he was attending to. He never had a cross word to say to me, he was kind and very funny.

So, when I approached the road where the shop had been, I half expected him to come rushing toward me with his big grin and sparkling eyes to say, 'Morrie, my son, it is so good to see you! It has been such a long time.'

When I reached the corner, I was surprised to see the shop was still standing. Yet it was unrecognisable. There were no windows; brick had replaced the glass on both sides. There was no proprietor's name or business description above the unpainted wooden door, just a hand-written sign saying, 'Machinists wanted,' tacked to the door.

My father didn't belong here.

I knew I would never see him again.

***

I stumbled, nauseated, back to where we had parked the car. Somehow, I managed to start the vehicle, despite the uncontrollable trembling in my limbs. Driving jerkily, I headed for Friedrichstrasse. I recognised the junction at the end of the road; the two tall chimneys were still the same as I remembered, but our road had more or less disappeared. I abandoned the car at the junction. The streetlights were still there, and parts of the pavement. The number 119 floated into my head; it was the number of steps – baby steps – from the end of the road to the front door of our apartment. Oh how I missed Hilde.

I carefully paced out 119 steps, purposely keeping them small. There was no building, not even rubble, where once had been walls and floors, ceilings and a roof, but it had all gone, removed, presumably, ready to be built upon; there was just a layer of brick and tiles on the ground. I realised I was standing in the Müller's apartment. I walked across the floor and could just make out the footprint of the two wings of the building on either side of me, which surrounded Herr Müller's garden. The garden was now overgrown and covered with fallen masonry and human detritus. This building had been the scene of so much life, vitality and drama years ago: Hilde and me playing marbles, Froh-Froh escaping, Elsa Franck falling down the stairs, Mama and Papa, the piano and Ernst and Martin Müller, but it was all a lifetime ago.

I didn't remember getting back to the car, but I did know that I somehow drove to collect Herr Huber from our pre-arranged meeting point before heading back to the guesthouse. I had remained silent and deep in thought the whole way. I felt immense rage, and was beginning to regret I'd come back to Leipzig.

It was as I had thought; there was nothing for me here anymore.

***

After we'd eaten, Herr Huber tried to placate me by saying that this visit had drawn a line under some of the questions I'd needed to ask, as well as providing some answers. He gently reminded me that those questions I still had I might never get the answers to, and there had to be a level of acceptance. The war destroyed so much, including official records of births and deaths. Consequently, many people would never know what happened to their families.

Overhearing our conversation, the owner of the guest house revealed she had newspapers cuttings she'd collected since the summer of 1945, and if we wanted to look through them we were welcome.

'Why have you got these?' I asked.

'It started when I began looking for my brother,' she said. 'He was missing in action in 1944, so I scanned the paper for every obituary, every unidentified dead body at the mortuary, or any possible leads about people who had died alone. I then started helping a Jewish friend to look for her mother. Together, we cut out everything we could find, including the daily lists of the people coming back from the camps, as well as those lists of the dead compiled at labour camps and other concentration camps. Sadly, she never encountered any information regarding her mother, then last year she died.

'I never found out what happened to my brother either. I think he died on the Russian Front, but I never had any proof of that. If that were the case, I expected to hear from his company commander, but I think conditions were so bad, so many people died, and not every death may have been recorded. Rather, relatives are told that their loved one was missing in action. I still habitually cut out from the local paper every week. Sometimes someone gets sent to me because they are looking for someone and they have tried all other routes. I am happy to help them. We sit down to look through all the cuttings and I give them a drink and we chat. Sometimes we find some information but often we do not.'

She showed us into an office that was pitch black until she switched on the light, and we saw that the room was clad with oak panels. Above this, the walls were lined with heavy burgundy moquette fabric, the same material as the closed curtains. There were three desks, all in a dark wood, and two identical Black Forest wood carved lamps with fringed shades in red; she knelt to switch these on. Every surface in the room was covered in newspapers stacked in boxes, and piles of buff coloured files. My heart sank, we would never find anything in here.

'I keep the curtains closed,' she said, 'so that the newsprint doesn't fade.'

It looked chaotic, but we discovered that there was in fact some organisation. She had catalogued the cuttings with names in alphabetical order. The oldest cuttings were on the bottom and the most recent on top. Each letter of the alphabet had a box of its own. I started to do a quick calculation: I needed to look up S for Ben and Clara Silbermann, but also S for Clara Schwan – my mother's stage name – as well as F for Hildegard Franck. I now just wanted to know if they were not alive. If my father was dead, my mother was dead, or Hilde was dead, I would accept that, if there was proof. I hadn't wanted to come to Leipzig. This was a worse experience than I expected.

At 9 o'clock in the evening we began going through the cuttings. Herr Huber went through the Fs but found nothing. I went through the Ss but drew a blank. It was midnight when we'd finished and Herr Huber went to bed, but I didn't want to give up. I began looking through the Fs again, even though Herr Huber had already done that.

Then I saw it.

There was an article about the death of Raoul Franck. Herr Huber hadn't been looking for him and didn't even know his name. He had died nearly a year ago. Was this the Franck that I was looking for? Was this the Raoul Franck who had lived in Friedrichstrasse? The Raoul Franck who was married to Elsa and had a daughter called Hildegard?

I read further and it said, "…he leaves a wife and daughter."

I leaned back on the chair. I could hardly breathe. Could this be Elsa and Hilde?

But where were they if they were alive? I read the article and hunted through for more information but there was nothing more. There was no address.

It suddenly came to me: I realised that if Oma, Opi and Gunther were still alive they would probably know the whereabouts of Elsa and Hilde and maybe even my parents? I had briefly considered visiting them earlier in the day, but my overwhelming sense of melancholy and the fear of becoming too emotional made me put them out of my mind.

I woke Herr Huber, whom I expected to be disgruntled by being disturbed, but once I explained what I'd found, he understood my excitement, 'Let us leave it until morning Morrie, you can't go there now it is the middle of the night!'

'No, but I must,' I said. 'Don't you see? If they are alive they will want to see me, I know they will, whatever time it is. They loved me like their own.'

'Oh dear,' Herr Huber hesitated. 'I'm not sure.' However, he was a good man and he knew this was so important to me and so proceeded to get dressed, found his overcoat and keys, then said,

'You are too excited and jumpy to drive, Morrie. I shall drive you, just tell me the directions.'

He smiled at me.

At that moment I realised I'd had a very fortunate life and was so grateful to him. If I didn't find Hilde or my parents, I knew there was someone else in my life that cared for me. First Ernst had looked after me and now Herr Huber.

After several wrong directions, missed turnings and much indecision, at 2am we drove over the stone bridge and down the little road with the river running behind it. Gunther's house had a FOR SALE notice up and was in darkness, but the ivy clad house next door had a light over the front door. This was Arkadien.

I knocked at the door and waited for what seemed a very long time. Eventually a light went on inside; I heard voices and then I heard the door being unbolted.

Light flooded onto the street and there, in front of me, stood my mother and Hilde.

Afterwards 1948-1951

HILDE

Leipzig

1948-1951

On that night, I heard the word 'Mama,' come from the darkness outside. There in the half-light stood Morrie.

He looked just as I'd imagined. I thought my heart would stop beating because I couldn't draw breath. Clara let out a long low wail and threw herself at him. Without hesitation I put my arms around his back, as best I could, the only bit of his body available. Oma and Mama appeared from behind me and wrapped their arms about us. We stood half outside, on the step and pavement, clinging to one another, not daring to believe this was true.

Eventually we moved into the sitting room with Clara saying again and again, 'I knew you would come back; I knew you would come back.'

But this was mixed with crying and kissing and the stroking of his face and his hair and laughing and more crying. It was surreal, and I thought this could not be reality.

This was the last piece of the jigsaw. We had lost so much, and the hope of seeing Morrie was all that had remained. Now he was here, standing amongst us. He was tall and had retained his almost white-blond hair, which fell across his eye as it always had. He had his father's grin and build.

I moved close to him and held his hand, secretly, as I had done so often when we were small. It seemed the most natural thing in the world. It had been our response to any stressful situation.

It was only then that we realised there was a man stood waiting patiently outside the door. He was middle aged, neatly dressed and shorter than Morrie. He smiled broadly at the scene before him. Oma apologised for not speaking to him.

Morrie was still trying to take everything in, marvelling at seeing us all together. He made rather rushed introductions, saying, 'After the war, Herr Huber took me in to be part of his family. I believed I was orphaned, and they matched us up. We live in the American zone near Frieberg and Herr Huber and I run a music shop and live above it.'

We talked all night and for many days afterwards. There were years of talking to be done.

I didn't know if everything that had happened could ever be recounted, or if Morrie and I could be as close as we once were. We were now adults.

Our world changed in all ways after that night.

***

Herr Huber returned to Frieberg to open the shop and Morrie stayed with us, but he returned with Herr Huber the following weekend. There was so much to be discussed, so many stories to tell of how each of us had survived. In the case of Clara there were the past twelve years to recount. There were, too, the stories of how our loved ones had died. One by one, the sad details of each of their deaths were described; each time, the tears and heartbreak we had experienced before rose to the surface as we once again relived the details and had to accept the finality of this news. But now there was a future too, something which we had not really considered.

On the following weekend, Clara took Morrie to one side and gave him the pair of size nine men's shoes she had brought with her all the way from Auschwitz-Birkenau. Clara and Morrie had already worked out they'd both been resident in the camp at the same time for a two-week period, breathing in the same air, only a few hundred yards from each other, in December 1944.

Clara told Morrie about Kanada. A lot of what she recounted she had never told us before.

Her job there was to sort through the clothing of people who had been taken to Auschwitz-Birkenau. Once sorted, this personal property was sent to lucrative distribution centres within Germany to help fund the Third Reich. Kanada was the name given to the set of warehouses within the camp where all the looted property was stored. It was called 'Kanada' because Canada, the country, was seen as a land of plenty.

When families arrived at the camp's railway platform the families were split into two: men and older boys; and women and other children. This was called, the Selektion. First, the doctor would look each person over. He sometimes asked for age or occupation and, in a seemingly arbitrary fashion, would decide who would live and who would die. The very youngest and oldest or infirmed were sent to die. Those who were fit and healthy would be registered for work.

Those not registered for work were told to undress, sometimes outside, and informed they had to go through a disinfection process before going to their barracks. They were then crowded into very large purpose-built rooms where they were poisoned with gas. Their clothing, jewellery and gold dentures would be sent to Kanada for distribution.

Nobody thought they would lose their valuables. When they alighted from the train, all possessions were stacked up on the platforms; their owners believing they would be returned to them at a later stage. Their cases were packed with the most precious possessions, jewels and money, deeds to property and birth certificates, wedding pictures, religious books and regalia, candles and objects for Shabbat.

Realising they were targets for thieves, many Jews came up with ways of hiding valuable possessions. They would pull the lining from music cases or luggage to hide their money, carefully replacing it to look untampered with. They found many ingenious ways of hiding small items of jewellery, stitching it into the seams of clothing.

Corruption was rife within Kanada. The female prisoners working there were very privileged compared to others in the camp. The women were allowed to grow their hair. It was common practice for these women to steal some of the personal items they came across to barter for food, alcohol and cigarettes. Many guards turned a blind eye or expected favours in return. Jewellery or gold, though, was different. The Nazi Party did not care about murdering thousands of people, but prisoners and guards who were found to have stolen jewels and gold were severely punished. The workers were encouraged to look for jewels to supply the Third Reich, and all valuables had to be logged and processed through official routes. Despite the risks, Clara knew most guards stole a portion of the valuable items that were found.

There were huge, separated mounds of clothing, shoes, emptied suitcases, hairbrushes, baskets, toys and other items which were continuously topped up with every new trainload of people. The workers – prisoners – would never finish the task; it was relentless. With so much to get through, Clara became adept at running her hand along hemlines as she sorted the women's and men's clothing into separate bins. With so many goods piled together, it was easy for Clara and her friends to stash away items to retrieve later. But they had to be careful. They risked their lives to do it.

Cleverly, Clara told a guard that her husband had been a jeweller and diamond merchant and she said she knew a little about the 'three C's' – colour, carat and cut – and soon an eyepiece was obtained so she could check the stones officially for the SS. This meant she could also confirm the value of the stones she had managed to hide.

Clara found a pair of shoes that once belonged to a prisoner and had been custom-made to hide jewels. She had seen a similar shoe before that another worker had found. That one had a heel that twisted on the outside to reveal a small cavity where a ruby had been stashed.

The shoes Clara found were size nine brown lace-up shoes. They had been tied together and were exquisite: soft leather, hand stitched, highly polished and looked brand new with hardly any marks on the soles. Whoever had owned these shoes, thought Clara, had money. Ben had worn size nine shoes and she thought perhaps Morrie did too by now, so she smuggled the pair of expensive shoes out of Kanada and hid them in a hole under some bricks beneath her bunk. She thought these could be a gift for Morrie when she was finally reunited with him. It was another way of keeping his memory alive. Later, when there was no one around, she retrieved the shoes from the hole and carefully examined them.

The heel didn't swivel and, at first, she thought what she had was just a very nice pair of handmade shoes with no other monetary value. She then noticed that one of the inner soles was slightly curled; she tugged at the edge with her fingernail and found a little silk tab above a circular indentation in the leather on the floor of the shoe. She carefully pulled the tab and the circle came away, revealing a small receptacle in which she found a piece of fine woven cotton fabric containing three diamonds, two that she thought were about one carat and one that was nearer two. The heel was quite built up, deeper than usual, and there was room for more stones in the cavity. The cloth the stones were wrapped in stopped any jangling noise when walking, and the smooth surface on the insole against the foot meant the shoe was not uncomfortable. The circular piece of leather had been made precisely and clicked back into position with ease. She replaced the inner sole. Clara spent the next year constantly worrying about the shoes and moving them from one hiding place to the next. On more than one occasion, she thought she had lost them.

During that year, diamonds, rubies, emeralds and sapphires were found as well as rings, necklaces, pins, earrings and broaches. Most were logged and handed in; maybe 10% were syphoned off by the guards. Every now and then, Clara's eyepiece was used to find an exquisite stone which she put in a small pocket she'd sewn in the hem of her overall. When she could, she added these to Morrie's shoe and to what was to become his little inheritance. There was only room for seven stones, so each time she found something better, she would replace the least valuable one until the seven she had – five diamonds, one emerald and one sapphire – were rare cuts and the very best quality: worth a small fortune.

When Clara first handed Morrie the shoes, he tried them on and – like Cinderella – they fitted him perfectly, which made everyone laugh. Clara, who'd been through so much to give the shoes to her son, was both laughing and crying at the same time. We all gathered around the table to see the big reveal when Morrie lifted the insole to reveal the circular indentation. He pulled the tab and carefully took out the grubby cloth inside to reveal the stones. Seven tiny sparkling stones tumbled out and lay glistening under the light hanging above Oma's kitchen table.

'This will secure your future,' said Clara.

How could these little stones be so valuable, I wondered?

None of us knew anything about precious stones but we didn't doubt Clara's judgement. We were amazed at her tenacity, that she had been so determined to give these to Morrie, and that the shoes had been here all this time yet she had remained silent about the existence of the gems because, until Morrie came back, which she knew he would, she would hold onto that secret.

'Mama, I can't believe you have done this for me; risked danger, even death. Thank you. I will not squander them; I will make sure your sacrifice was worth it and I'll put them to good use,' Morrie said.

Clara said, 'I had thought, is this right, taking the property of other Jews for our personal benefit? Then I thought, the Nazis stole all the jewellery from Papa's shop and if I take these jewels, I will not be depriving Jews but stopping the Nazi's having any more Jewish valuables. I would like you to sell one stone straight away, Morrie, so you have money available now for anything you need. And I do think you must buy a car, so Herr Huber doesn't need to worry about ferrying you around anymore.'

Things moved fast from then.

Morrie went back with Herr Huber, and Clara went too, to see where Morrie had been living. Morrie bought a car and divided his time between Frieberg in the West of Germany, and Leipzig in the

East. Clara went back and forth and, as time went on, she helped Herr Huber more and more in the shop.

Morrie and I spent all our time together when he was in Leipzig, when I wasn't painting and he wasn't playing the piano, that is. We were still each other's best friend, only now it had developed into more than that. We were both nervous of committing to one another in case what we felt was nothing more than sentimentality or nostalgia or – even worse – out of a sense of duty, a duty to the past and to our mothers. But it was far more than that. I had hated being apart from him and he too had felt the same. Nobody could ever replace Morrie, in my eyes. We had never experienced being with any other partner and didn't think we ever would.

Morrie went in search of Ernst Grauman's family and discovered that Ingrid, his sister, had come back to Leipzig, and that a headstone to Ernst had been erected in a local cemetery. Morrie arranged to meet her and took me with him because he wanted Ingrid to meet the girl he always spoke about. We all stood around the grave and talked about Ernst the man, the proxy uncle and father to Morrie, his teacher, protector and mentor. Ingrid said that he had surrounded her with so much love and wisdom. Morrie said that Ernst was a wonderful human being whose understanding and passion for music had made Morrie the performer he was today.

Morrie would not have survived the war if it weren't for Ernst. Yes, he was a Nazi, but he didn't deserve to die as he had. I thought of my father then. He too was a Nazi and he'd made mistakes, but he was a good man and didn't deserve to die as he had, either.

This was the pity of war, no one individual was to blame yet we all carried some burden of guilt. I felt guilt today for being my father's daughter, and I felt guilt for my privilege which had rendered me insensitive. As a German child, I didn't notice or empathise with what was happening to Jews all around me. Perhaps I was protected from the truth, or it had been trivialised, or maybe I was seeking to excuse myself.

***

We were together again. I could not say all together of course, but this was a time to celebrate. In the summer of 1949, we planned a summer party in the garden. Mama and Oma baked and stirred and strained dishes and presented cakes, pies and mousses. Neighbours and friends joined us, and we were able to celebrate all the birthdays, Christmases and Hanukkahs we had missed for so many years. We gave each other small gifts and played games. I made all the women a chain of wildflowers for their hair, and Morrie and I collected a big basket of wild strawberries from the other side of the river. When everyone went home, we laid on the grass until it was dark and we could track the stars in the sky.

***

Leipzig had changed. The clearing of bombed building sites was an ongoing project. Up until now, Mama had been part of that workforce, but now she was not strong enough for manual labour and found the job exhausting. Instead, she was studying and making good progress. New buildings were underway. Construction sites were concentrating on building much needed apartment blocks for the workforce.

Walking the streets was a little unnerving because restrictions came in daily. We were often stopped and asked where we were going and why. East Germany was now ruled by the Soviet government and had been renamed the German Democratic Republic. We were told we were a socialist workers' state and were promised greater prosperity for all once the ravages of war had been overcome. West Germany was called the Federal Republic of Germany. This was the American, British and French zones joined up and, rumour had it, was a land of greater freedoms and prosperity.

One day, Morrie and I went out in the car on the long road towards the Sudetenland, to see if we could find the old building my parents and I had sheltered in on the way home to Leipzig, and where Mama had collapsed; where we put Hermes out to graze; where the Soviet soldiers fired their guns and where Papa left our suitcases with the hospital orderly, in his locked workshop.

Nobody stopped us, so we had an enormous sense of freedom. It took us three hours to get there, but we immediately realised it had been a futile exercise. The building had no roof and only part of the walls remained; a mechanised wrecking ball was standing in the yard. The workshop at the rear was no longer there and so the hopes of finding our suitcases evaporated. I had yearned to reunite Mama with some of her pretty dresses but knew they had long gone.

We drove into the nearest town and found a place offering hot food. We were a little deflated. To raise our spirits, we walked round the town and discovered several shops selling second hand furniture. Morrie wanted a small desk to sit at when he was composing his music, so we went inside a large, dimly lit emporium offering an eclectic mix of used household goods. There was some impressive grand furniture as well as a hodgepodge of utilitarian items. We had to lift tables off cupboards and cupboards off wardrobes to see what was underneath. Legs of chairs poked out at right angles and several light fittings were balanced precariously on piles of mattresses. Rows of ceramic Rumtoft jars lined the floor. I pulled out the biggest of these jars; it was highly glazed and a good eighteen inches tall, deep red with raised motifs of pears and plums. Oma would love this, and would fill it with fruit and alcohol ready for next Christmas. I decided to buy it.

As I lifted the jar, what looked like a filigree fire guard caught my attention. I quickly realised it was a birdcage. As I brought it into the light, it felt so familiar. I could see a small ornate rose on top with a hook to hang the cage from, and detected the remains of blue and yellow paint on the wire strands.

'Morrie, quickly come here! I have found Froh-Froh's cage,' I shouted so loudly that I made the shop owner turn to stare at me.

Morrie clambered over furniture and stood looking at the cage.

This was remarkable.

'How long has this been here?' I asked the shop owner.

'I don't know,' the owner said. 'It was here when I took over the shop at the end of 'forty-five. It's not sold because it lost its door and hasn't got much paint left on it either. If you want it, you can have it for five marks, I can't say fairer than that.'

'Thank you, sir, we'll take it,' said Morrie with a broad grin. He looked at me and tears filled my eyes. I couldn't speak. I pushed the Rumtoft jar into his arms and he said, 'And this Rumtoft too.'

We drove back to Leipzig with the cage on my lap, a smile on both our faces, and a large Rumtoft for Oma lying wrapped in newspaper on the back seat.

***

Each time we crossed into the American zone, questions were asked of us, and we realised that soon we may have difficulty going there. The Soviet guards did not like us taking valuables out of the sector and always checked our luggage. The Americans were concerned about our identity, looking for escaping Nazis or Soviet spies. Sometimes they checked our vehicle underneath. We knew that life in the American zone was less tense and people had more freedom. We made the decision that if we wanted to be together, and we did, we must resettle in Frieberg, but it needed to be soon, and we needed to plan for this. Oma put her house on the market. She was unsure if the new Soviet authorities would allow her to sell it, but she was successful, and the sale went through. She had also received a legacy from Gunther's estate and so now felt financially secure.

Clara was the first to move. She went to live with Herr Huber and began giving piano lessons. Clara and Herr Huber clearly filled a void in each other's lives. They talked music endlessly and the pain they felt after losing their partners was something they could cope with now they found contentment in each other. Although Clara was happier than I had ever seen her, I'm sure she still played Franz Liszt's Leibestraum most days. She was slowly healing. She needed to remind herself of who she was and that included thinking about her time in the asylum and all the people who had played a part in her life at the camps. She would never forget the horrors she had witnessed. Herr Huber still practised Rachmaninoff No 3, determined to master the piece though he was never satisfied with his performance.

Because the Soviet government did not want its people moving out of East Germany, fearing a lack of manpower, we moved our possessions and money bit by bit, so as not to be questioned unduly or draw attention to ourselves. Each time we crossed over we took clothing or small items of furniture; we didn't need to take everything we owned; we could buy most things in Frieberg and the surrounding area. If questioned, we said we were carrying gifts or returning possessions to people who now lived in the West.

The final time we crossed over into the American zone, Morrie wore his brown lace-up shoes. We didn't know that, within a year, barriers would be built, and more border guards employed, further increasing the difficulty of relocating from East to West. We were very lucky.

Mama asked to be alone in the garden at Arkadien on the day we moved. She lit a small bonfire and burnt some papers of Papa's that she said she'd been hanging on to but were no longer needed. I watched from a respectful distance as she went up to old Holstein. I did not hear what she said, but she put her arms around the trunk and kissed it; I think she was saying goodbye to Opi and to her childhood.

Oma used the proceeds from the sale of Arkadien and Gunther's property to purchase a rambling old house close to The Music Man shop where Herr Huber and Clara lived in Frieberg. Clara once again played music just for the joy of it, which could often be heard when you walked past the shop. Oma's house occupied a prominent corner position and also included a shop facing the main street. It was tall and narrow with a turret on the roof but went back many yards and was divided into two maisonettes.

Oma and Mama moved into one of these maisonettes. Mama had gained her teaching qualifications and taught privately after school at home and occasionally at the junior school when they needed her. She had to use a stick to walk now.

Morrie and I were both nineteen years old. With everyone's approval, we married last autumn and moved into the other maisonette. I began collating my work and hoped to have an exhibition of my paintings featuring natural history studies very soon. I didn't go to university because it still hadn't been set up properly after the war, but I joined a collective of young artists, connected to the university, who shared ideas and resources.

Morrie could not attend university either but, through contacts of Herr Huber, he began working with a Professor of Composition who inspired him to pursue his own ideas. On Saturdays, Morrie performed in The Music Man shop and always drew a crowd. He was quite a celebrity. He had even been booked for a concert tour of Germany and Great Britain next year. Morrie had no piano of his own but had put in an order for a new Blüthner piano, paid for with another of Clara's gems. Sadly, Oma's old piano had stayed at Arkadien because we felt that too many questions would be asked if we tried to take it with us.

To the side of our new house in Frieberg, there was a triangle of grassland. On it was a huge walnut tree, which reminded us of Arkadien. We put three small gravestones, remembering Opi, Ben and my Papa, so they were always with us under the shade of this tree. The back part of this land Oma made into a vegetable garden. She had already begun making jars of preserves for winter and soon there would be newly pickled carrots, onions and cauliflower.

This week, we opened a café in the corner shop of Oma's property. In Frieberg, food was more readily available than Leipzig, as most rationing had stopped in the West. The café was run by Oma and Mama, who once again spent their time cooking delicious food. Oma displayed jars of brightly coloured preserves she had brought with her from Leipzig, as well as her dark red Rumtoft jar full of pears and cherries in Kirsch ready for a celebration. The café was painted blue and yellow with blue and white gingham tablecloths. Outside, dotted about on the grass, were dainty wire tables and chairs where visitors could sit to eat and drink on warm days.

We called the café '*The Budgerigar*'.

On the walnut tree hung the birdcage with seed and a sprig of millet to feed the local birds. Morrie had repainted the cage in its original colours. There was still no door on it because, as Gunther taught us, birds should be free.

> *To Morrie,*
>
> *Human beings, like birds, should be able to go wherever they choose.*
>
> *One day, I hope you can go wherever you choose without fear.*
>
> *May peace go with you.*
>
> *Gunther*

Thank you, Gunther.

Author's Note

This story is based in truth and was passed on to me by someone who grew up in Germany during the Second World War. She was the daughter of a Nazi officer, though she was unaware of this fact when she was a child. I took elements of what she had told me and built upon it to create the story of The Budgerigar. I knew when I spoke to her that I would write this book. I told her that she had something unique to say and asked for her permission to use what she had told me. She said that there was more to tell, but she became evasive, and I learned no more from her. She died leaving no family. I then began researching the time and place.

During my own childhood, 'The War' loomed large. All the adults I knew, including the women, had been in the services and their interest in all aspects of those years was fed by countless films, documentaries, and literature. It is a subject that I was exposed to and, as I grew up, became an interest of mine too. The war, and its aftermath, was woven into the fabric of my life. My father wore his heavy leather flying (RAF) jacket to ride his motorbike, and when collecting me from school I would bury my head in his back as we rode home (no helmet!). My parents told endless stories about daily life when they were serving. My father spoke of the desert in North Africa; of befriending small hungry children and giving them rations; and of eating with Italian families near Naples. My mother, who served in the WAAF, seemed to do a lot of fraternising with American servicemen in Norfolk, who offered nylon stockings and chocolates in return for a little innocent companionship because they were homesick. I was born after the war and so the war and its traumas were what people spoke about endlessly.

We didn't get a TV until 1955 and there wasn't much to watch but documentaries about the war were always being made. There was a lot of emphasis on the fact that we had won the war; a lot of chest-banging! There was still rationing, though, and queues for all commodities. There were bomb sites in every city until the late sixties and my grandmother related tales of The Blitz and sheltering under a table, in the underground where neighbours and strangers squashed in together and sang popular songs or in flooded out Anderson shelters in the garden; so we were constantly reminded of the events of 1939 to 1945.

I, and every one of my generation, were subsumed by this huge cloud that hung over our parents, of loss and detachment, starting again, hoping it was all worth it and wondering if life would ever get better.

Until I wrote The Budgerigar I had not thought about what it must have been like for a child during WW2 in Germany. In Britain there was so much primary evidence available. After the war there was a reticence in Germany to speak of events that had transpired in

Nazi Germany. There was a tendency to deny some incidents and people were afraid to be seen as culpable for anything that could be seen as crimes against humanity. They wanted to get on with their lives and forget the past few years. Furthermore, most of the population was starving. There was still a great deal of anti-Jewish feeling; it did not suddenly disappear and life was very hard. Trying to piece together what life was like in Leipzig during the period of the book was difficult. I do not speak German. I found some short translations of children's memories of the time and relied on historical text and maps to describe how it was for the Silbermanns and Francks families in Leipzig.

In October 2022 I was invited to go to a seminar with journalists at the Auschwitz – Birkenau Memorial and Museum in Poland. This is the largest of the Nazi death camps and where both Morrie and Clara were in 1944.

Despite three years of research to write this book, nothing could prepare me for the size of the camp, the appalling conditions human beings lived in or the seemingly limitless stories of horror and evil that were perpetrated there; to touch the cold walls of cells or the poorly constructed rough walls of Birkenau barracks or to see the blue staining of Zyklon B gas in a building or to stand before the Death Wall where many people were shot or to touch a cattle truck used to transport human beings to the camp assaulted my senses and

I shall never forget them. This was a site of torture starvation and the murder of more than one million people mostly Jews. The camp was set up specifically to deal with 'The Jewish Question' once and for all; an extermination camp where women, children and the frail or elderly were immediately gassed and then cremated. We were taken to places that are not generally open to the public. This museum seeks to conserve the site and its artefacts and to educate its visitors in the hope that such atrocities do not happen again.

I will never forget the personal testaments that I have read or heard, of people who survived the concentration camps and who witnessed atrocities. These events were real this was no story, only they can convey what they went through at the time. Their experiences and those of others who did not survive is a catalogue of cruelty, injustice, and profound sadness.

I have aimed for authenticity wherever possible but of course I was not born until after the events written took place, but I hope you can look past this and enjoy my novel as a work of fiction that has borrowed many true events from that time and woven them into a story. The utter desperation of the war, the lack of freedom and the physical difficulties of getting back to your hometown or finding enough to eat even when the war was over, is heart-breaking and exhausting. I hope in this work of fiction I have been able to bring to life characters that lived through this era. I hope I have not offended anyone.

I wanted this story to be about the resilience of the human spirit against all the odds. The Budgerigar of the title is a fragile but brave little bird who symbolises the hope of the characters in the book.